Praise for *Unholy Land*

"Lavie Tidhar does it again. A jewelled little box of miracles. Magnificent."
—Warren Ellis, author of *Gun Machine*

"★ World Fantasy Award winner Tidhar (*Central Station*) will leave readers' heads spinning with this disorienting and gripping alternate history. Author Lior Tirosh, grieving a personal tragedy, travels home after years abroad and immediately has a series of strange encounters that pull him into a complex plot to destroy the border between worlds. He arrives in Palestina, the land that the Jews were offered on the Ugandan border in 1904, which both closely resembles and is profoundly different from the Israel of our world, and is followed by two government agents who are trying to stop the destruction of 'borders,' though it's unclear whose side they are really on. Tirosh discovers a niece he had forgotten, is accused of murder, narrowly dodges threats to his life, and takes on the role of a detective from one of his own novels as he tries to understand what is endangered and by whom. 'No matter what we do, human history always attempts to repeat itself,' Tidhar writes, even as he explores the substantial differences in history that might arise from single but significant choices. Readers of all kinds, and particularly fans of detective stories and puzzles, will enjoy grappling with the numerous questions raised by this stellar work."
—*Publishers Weekly*, starred review

"Extraordinary, confronting, intriguing. *Unholy Land* is a dream of a home that's never existed, but is no less real for that: a dream that smells like blood and gunpowder. It's precisely what we've come to expect of Tidhar, a writer who just keeps getting better."
—Angela Slatter, author of the World Fantasy Award-winner *The Bitterwood Bible*

"There are SFF writers. There are good SFF writers. And there is Lavie Tidhar. *Unholy Land* is a twisted piece of alt-history/geography that refuses to go where lesser writers would drive it. Bold and witty and smoky, it plays games and coquetries, makes dark dalliances, and will leave you dazzled and delighted."
—Ian McDonald, author of *Time Was*

"Lavie Tidhar's daring *Unholy Land* brilliantly showcases one of the foremost science fiction authors of our generation."
—Silvia Moreno-Garcia, World Fantasy Award-winning editor and author of *Certain Dark Things*

"Lavie Tidhar takes us through a haunting, mesmerizing Judea, across multiple timelines into the promised night shelter in British East Africa. Here is an expedition at once proposed and taken, an alternate reality in which the holocaust is averted but the mechanics of displacement remain the same, where people are oppressed and oppressor at the same time. A genius, dreamlike fantasy for those who slip across might-have-been worlds."
—Saad Z. Hossain, author of *Escape from Baghdad!*

"Lavie Tidhar has given us a mystically charged, morally complex vision of Theodor Herzl's famous Jewish state that might have been."
—James Morrow, author of *The Last Witchfinder* and *Shambling Towards Hiroshima*

"*Unholy Land* is a stunning achievement. It is packed to the brim with engaging ideas and features a captivating story . . . beautiful and thought-provoking."
—*The Speculative Shelf*

"*Unholy Land* is probably *better* than Michael Chabon's *Yiddish Policemen's Union.*"
—Bradley Horner, author of the *Darkside Earther* series

Praise for *Central Station*

2018 Neukom Literary Arts Award Winner
2017 John W. Campbell Award Winner
2017 Arthur C. Clarke Award Finalist
2016 British Science Fiction Award Longlist
NPR Best Books of 2016
Amazon Featured Monthly Best Sci-Fi & Fantasy Books
Barnes and Noble Best Science Fiction and Fantasy of 2016
2016 Locus Recommended Reading List

"Beautiful, original, a shimmering tapestry of connections and images—I can't think of another SF novel quite like it."
—Alastair Reynolds, author of the Revelation Space series

"A dazzling tale of complicated politics and even more complicated souls. Beautiful."
—Ken Liu, author of *The Paper Menagerie* and *The Grace of Kings*

"★ World Fantasy Award–winner Tidhar (*A Man Lies Dreaming*) magnificently blends literary and speculative elements in this streetwise mosaic novel set under the towering titular spaceport . . . Readers of all persuasions will be entranced."
—*Publishers Weekly*, starred review

"★ A fascinating future glimpsed through the lens of a tight-knit community."
—*Library Journal*, starred review

"If Nalo Hopkinson and William Gibson held a séance to channel the spirit of Ray Bradbury, they might be inspired to produce a work as grimy, as gorgeous, and as downright sensual as *Central Station*."
—Peter Watts, author of *Blindsight* and *The Freeze-Frame Revolution*

"A unique marriage of Philip K. Dick, William Gibson, C. L. Moore, China Miéville, and Larry Niven with 50 degrees of compassion and the bizarre added. An irresistible cocktail."
—Maxim Jakubowski, author of the *Sunday Times* bestselling Vina Jackson novels

"A mosaic of mind-blowing ideas and a dazzling look at a richly-imagined, textured future."
—Aliette de Bodard, author of *The House of Shattered Wings*

Other Books by Lavie Tidhar

The Bookman (2010)

Camera Obscura (2011)

Osama (2011)

The Great Game (2012)

The Violent Century (2013)

A Man Lies Dreaming (2014)

Central Station (2016)

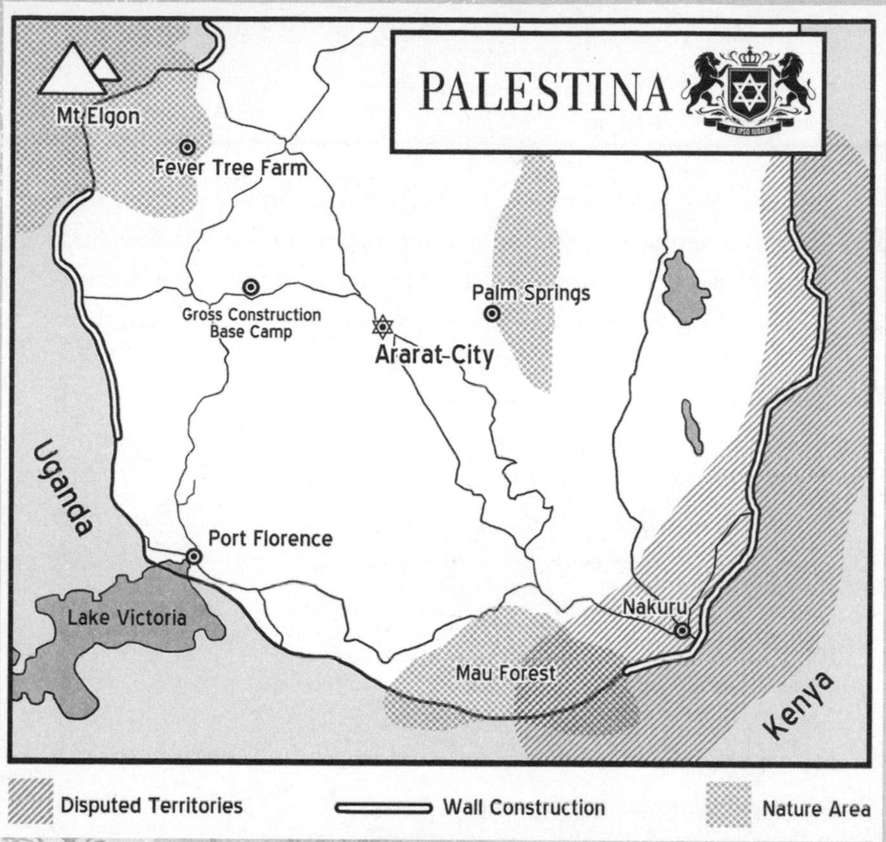

PALESTINA
AB IPSO IUDAEO
Mt Elgon
Fever Tree Farm
Gross Construction
Base Camp
Palm Springs
Ararat-City
Uganda
Port Florence
Lake Victoria
Nakuru
Mau Forest
Kenya
Disputed Territories
Wall Construction
Nature Area

UGANDA
THE CONGO
SOMALIA
Mogadishu
PALESTINA
Kampala
KENYA
Lake
Victoria
RWANDA
BURUNDI
Mombasa
Indian
Ocean
TANZANIA
EAST AFRICA
Dar es Salaam

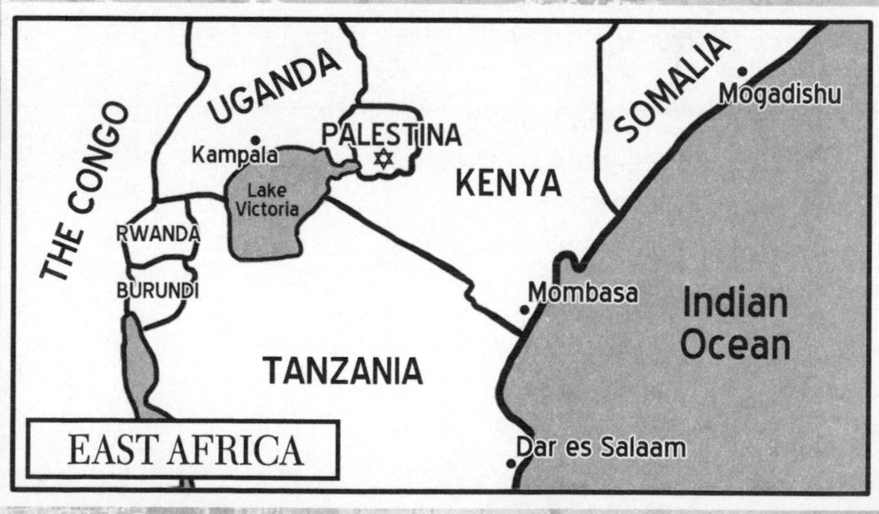

Unholy Land

Interior design by Elizabeth Story
Map design by Elizabeth Story

Tachyon Publications LLC
1459 18th Street #139
San Francisco, CA 94107
415.285.5615
www.tachyonpublications.com
tachyon@tachyonpublications.com

Series Editor: Jacob Weisman
Editor: Jill Roberts

Print ISBN: 978-1-61696-304-0
Digital ISBN: 978-1-61696-305-7

Printed in the United States by Worzalla

First Edition: 2018
9 8 7 6 5 4 3 2 1

To Eliot

UNHOLY LAND

LAVIE TIDHAR

TACHYON | SAN FRANCISCO

Years ago, prompted by the vague recollection of a childhood story, I visited the Wiener Library in London. There, stored on microfilm, I found the 1904 report of an ill-fated expedition to the Uasin Gishu region, in what was then British East Africa. The expedition was sent by Theodor Herzl, the ailing leader of the Zionist movement, due to an extraordinary offer extended to him by Joseph Chamberlain, the British colonial secretary at the time.

The offer: a piece of land on the border of Uganda that would be set aside as a Jewish homeland.

In the midst of a vigorous debate in the Zionist Congress—between the "Territorialists" who favoured any available land and the "Holy Landers" who were determined on settlement in then-Ottoman Palestine—Herzl saw fit to nevertheless commission a small expedition to the territory.

In 1904, a young Russian Jew named Nahum Wilbusch

departed Trieste on board the S.S. *Africa*, bound for the port of Mombasa. There he was joined by two unlikely companions: Major Alfred St. Hill Gibbons, a noted British explorer and old "Africa hand," and Alfred Kaiser, a Swiss naturalist.

The three men arrived in Nakuru, on the border of the proposed settlement, on the 18th of January. There they were delayed waiting for their luggage and while Gibbons attempted to round up porters for the expedition. It kept raining. By the 28th they had made camp in the territory.

The expedition did not fare well. In their two months traversing the Uasin Gishu plateau, Wilbusch became lost and separated from the others, while a hostile force of Nandi attacked the men toward the end of the journey.

Their reports are striking in difference: where Gibbons sees a pleasant, fertile land, Wilbusch sees no sign of water or pasture. Both reported the settlement of native tribes in the area.

From Mombasa, Wilbusch travelled to Palestine. He returned an overwhelmingly negative report on the possibility of Jewish settlement in British East Africa, an offer seen, by its proponents, as a *Nachtasyl*, or "night shelter," for the beleaguered Jews of Europe.

By the time the members of the expedition returned their reports, Theodor Herzl was dead, and the "Holy Landers"—to whom Wilbusch, it seemed, had belonged all along—had won sway over the Zionist Congress. The plan for Jewish settlement in Africa was abandoned, and today remains merely a curious footnote to history. A perhaps apocryphal story tells of an aging Wilbusch flying over the territory many years later, ruefully reflecting that the Holocaust might never have happened had the plan gone ahead. But this is the nature of what-ifs: that they are merely flights of fancy, and not to be taken too seriously.

A decade after I'd first read the Expedition's report I was living back in Israel for a time. There we inhabited a small, cramped apartment a stone's throw away from the old city of Jaffa. Set in the ruins of an old Arab cinema, it was joined together with the other flats by a small stone courtyard in which grew a solitary orange tree, planted there by the original owner many years before.

We lived next door to the old Alhambra Theatre, a giant art deco building where Umm Kulthum and Farid al-Atrash both once performed. It stood abandoned for years and was now undergoing construction work. Twice we were woken up to the sound of gunfire. The first time someone had attempted to set the place on fire. The second, they tried to ram a truck full of explosives into the building. No one was entirely certain why this was happening.

I walked through the Jaffa flea market nearly every day, stopping at a café on the corner by the old Ottoman clock tower, from where I could hear and smell the sea. Traffic moved sluggishly across the road in the heat. Once I arrived to find the waiter crying soundlessly, all the while carrying out his duties. I never did find out why.

The flea market itself was vast, and filled with hard-lived people selling every manner of abandoned and unwanted things. It lay in the shadow of the old town and its ancient

Egyptian fort on the hill. There was too much history all mangled together in that place.

It was here that I picked up treasures of dubious provenance. Old Hebrew erotica and westerns, a Zionist romance pamphlet and an early adventure of *David Tidhar: The First Hebrew Detective*, from 1938 or so, with an advert at the back for the Landwer Café in Tel Aviv, for which the great draw was a new, electric radio.

One night, it might have been spring, I dreamed of Palestina. It was a nation in a world that's never been, a Jewish state founded in East Africa. I saw for myself the white buildings of Ararat City, the refugee camps across the newly-built separation wall in Nakuru, and the mercenaries fighting under the shadow of Mount Elgon as a herd of elephants silently trespassed under a full moon. The dream lingered in my mind.

A few months later, I left Israel once again. By then they'd just arrested the man behind the attempted attacks on the Alhambra next door. He turned out to be a Jewish lawyer from north Tel Aviv, who'd hired a group of Arab bombers to carry out the job simply so that he could claim the extra money on the insurance. In the event, he wasn't even convicted. Some things, I'm afraid, you just can't make up.

But by then I was living elsewhere.

"The goal of our present endeavours must not be the 'Holy Land' but a land of our own. We need nothing but a large piece of land for our poor brothers; a piece of land which shall remain our property from which no foreign master can expel us."

—Leo Pinsker, *Auto-Emancipation*, 1882

PART ONE
ARRIVALS

1.

The flight from Berlin was delayed. Tirosh dawdled by the gate. He was wrapped in a light coat. The airport's lines were cold and clean. The parquet floor gleamed. The glass walls let in a grey, diffuse light. Tirosh watched people go past.

People in airports were travellers taken out of time. Their clothes did not match their geography, their tan or lack of it did not correspond to the sunlight or the season. Their languages came from nowhere and went elsewhere, bringing with them always the scent of other, more real places, of brine and hot rain, seared fat, crushed flowers. The airport by contrast had the comforting artificiality of a well-constructed null-point, a sort of reassuring void. Earlier, going through security, Tirosh was lulled by the by-now familiar rhythm of checks and scans. He stood in the line gladly, shuffled forward slowly with the others, removed his shoes with a sort of glad compliance, took off his belt, emptied his pockets, turned off and on his phone.

The metal detector did not beep as he trod through it in his socks. Standing awkwardly by the conveyor belt, Tirosh reassembled those parts of himself that had been detached and scanned, put on his shoes, refilled his pockets, tied on his belt. For a time he wandered through the duty-free stores, amidst shelves filled with luxuries he had no interest in. In the bookshop he hesitated by the shelves densely packed with thrillers in which improbable men did improbable things. He did not find his own books there.

At the checkout counter he paused by the newspaper rack. The first page of several of the leading papers carried the latest atrocity from back home, but the pictures of the dead were all the same after a while, and he had grown immune to them. A few months earlier, reluctantly, he had participated in a topical news show on Arte where the interviewer began, straightaway, by accusing him of writing fantasy, and wasn't that an escape, to which he'd responded, somewhat defensively, that on the contrary, fantasy was the only way that allowed one to examine alternate realities, and wasn't that an important thing to do, politically, under the circumstances—but really he supposed it wasn't much of an argument. Mostly, Tirosh wrote a series of moderately successful detective novels, the sort that featured buxom girls and men in hats on the covers, the sort that used to sell in kiosks and petrol stations and pharmacies. He was not perhaps a hack, exactly: but after a promising start, he had abandoned his youthful ideals for the promise of a steady paycheque, and the writing of books which were delivered promptly and published cheaply and on time.

Purchasing nothing, he checked the departure board with a sudden sense of impatience (Isaac on his hands and knees crawling with a sort of dumbfounded delight as fast he could go; Isaac with his finger tracing circles on an empty phone socket, again and again) but saw that the flight was delayed. The people coming and going between flights seemed to him like revenants or ghosts, haunting the terminal corridors with the same sort of cancerous, restless energy he himself felt right then. He thought about Isaac. There was not a day gone past when he had not thought about his son.

He decided to keep moving, it was better that way. He found a café and ordered an overpriced orange juice and sat down to drink it. His telephone rang: his agent, calling from London.

"Where are you?" his agent demanded.

Tirosh said, "I'm still in Berlin. The flight keeps getting delayed."

"It will do you good to get away," his agent said. Her name was Elsa, and besides Tirosh she represented several more or less successful footballers and glamour models turned novelists; a former circus performer whose sex-filled, tell-all memoir stayed for ten straight weeks at the top of the best-seller lists; and a gaggle of desperate-looking crime and fantasy writers: their only fantasy was that they were successful, and their only crimes were committed against literature, as Elsa sometimes, uncharitably, told him. Sometimes Tirosh wondered what she said about him when he wasn't there.

"I don't know," he said. "I keep feeling it's a mistake, that I shouldn't go back. The place has probably changed beyond recognition by now."

"Nonsense," Elsa said. "You'll love it when you get there.

All that sun and . . ." She cast about for something else to offer him. "I hear the street food is nice. Anyway it will do you good. How are you feeling?"

"I'm fine," he said, feeling irritated. "Why does everyone feel the need to mollycoddle me?"

He knew why, of course. He just didn't want to think it, and by thinking it to make it real.

He heard her silence on the line, then her breathing as she decided to change tack.

"Maybe you could do some articles while you're there," Elsa said. "I can speak to *Der Spiegel*, they're always looking for good coverage of the political situation there."

"I saw," he said, tiredly. "I'm not interested."

"Money's good," Elsa said. She always tried to get him to earn more. "Write a love story," she said one year. "Write something funny," she said a year later. "Everyone loves a comedy." Finally Tirosh, a little drunk, said, "Why don't I write a book about, I don't know, Adolf Hitler as a private detective or something, is that the sort of thing you mean?" and Elsa took a sip of her wine, frostily, and said, "Well if you're going to be like *that*, then forget it."

"It's the sort of place everyone has an opinion about," he said now, trying to justify himself and not really sure why. "But no one really cares."

"Do you still think of it as home?" Elsa said, perhaps a little sharply. Tirosh tried to formulate his thoughts. He glanced at the board. It said the flight was now, finally, preparing to board.

"I don't know. I mean it's me, it's a part of me, but I left, didn't I. It's in my language, it's in the way I think and see the world, but it's not to say I'm comfortable with it."

"You could do with a rest," Elsa said. "See some old friends, relax in the sunshine. Get drunk. Forget everything."

"Yes," he said. "Yes, that sounds like a good idea."

"Good, good," Elsa said. She sounded strangely relieved. Tirosh said, "I'd better go. I think the flight's finally boarding."

"Safe travels, then," Elsa said.

"I'll talk to you soon." He hung up and stood to leave with a sense of relief. People were congregating by the gate now, lining up in two rows. There weren't that many passengers. He noticed a woman, queuing in the line he hadn't chosen. It was only a glimpse, for him. He saw a woman with brown hair and pinned back delicate ears, which reminded him of his ex-wife, but with a sense of solidity about her, as though she were somehow more real than the artifice of the airport all about her. Perhaps she somehow sensed him watching, because she turned her head and frowned.

The passengers boarded the plane without incident. Tirosh settled back in his seat with a sigh of relief, or weariness. Images of his son kept flashing through his mind, and he blinked, rapidly, staring out of the window though it was fogged; it must have been raining. The woman with the brown hair sat nearer the front. He saw just the top of her head. The flight attendants went through the safety routine. The inside of the plane smelled of warm plastic, stale breath. There was a piece of gum stuck to the underside of the food tray. The engines thrummed alive. Tirosh watched small grey figures through the window, moving with a clear but unguessed-at purpose. He watched the runway move past, and tensed as the plane began to accelerate, then took to the air with a bump. The airport grew wider before growing smaller. For some moments there was the flash of fields, the density of a city, the silver snail trail of cars on a highway. Then they entered the clouds and the world turned white and grey, and fine strands of fog drifted past outside the window. Tirosh put his head back and closed his eyes.

"Hush, Isaac," he murmured. "Daddy is trying to sleep."

He thought he felt the touch of tiny hands, pulling on his hair; warm clear breath on his ear, and a delighted giggle, but it was nothing, just noise in the engines.

After a time he slept.

2.

When Tirosh woke up, his mind felt clearer than it had for a long time. He did not know how long they'd been flying. He felt curiously refreshed, renewed. He realised there were very few passengers on the flight, far fewer than he'd initially thought. His mind must have been playing games on him, earlier, but he had been tired, troubled by some vague memories he could no longer recall. He stretched and saw that the woman with the brown hair was there, sitting alone at the window next to two empty seats. When he peered out of the window, he saw the green slopes of the Cherangani Hills, growing blue towards the distance, with low-rising clouds settling over the higher peaks. Small villages sat amidst seas of green, and Tirosh saw the smoke of cooking fires undulate gently into the air.

"We will soon begin our descent into Ararat City," the pilot said. "Please fasten your seat belts."

A wash of memories came upon Tirosh then. How could he have ever forgotten Palestina? One does not forget one's homeland, no matter how long he may go away, how long he may dwell elsewhere, under a different sky, speaking a different tongue. The worries and the doubts of the past days fell away from him. Already the air in the cabin felt different, warmer and more humid. As the plane began to descend, Tirosh saw the hills peel away, and over a vast distance the Great Rift Valley opening and beyond it, like a smudge of pale blue, the sea.

Then, too, as the plane drew lower and lower still, Tirosh could see a fault in the land. A white towering wall cut through the sloping hills and fertile farmland. It snaked its way through fields and forests, separating settlements and villages, rising and falling with the land like an annotated series of discordant notes. Its whiteness stood glaring against the rich earth and its tones, startling against a sky already thickening with rain.

He looked and kept looking but could see no end to the wall in either direction, though it went round and out of his sight, continuing elsewhere. He began to discern new features on the ground, straight roads, slow peaceful cars like beetles, modern buildings gathering first in clumps and then in larger convocations until they became, at long last, one continuous wave as Ararat City rose in the view ahead.

He felt a pang of loss and a pang of joy at the sight. He wished Isaac were with him then, sitting in his lap, chattering nonsense words at the window, eyes round as he saw everything new. Ararat towered into the sky, with new, modern skyscrapers jutting out of the ground like grasping fingers. Glass and metal set off a contradiction against the dusty green beyond, and the white houses were like bold strokes of a painter's brush against concrete and asphalt and paved stone.

"Prepare for landing," the pilot said, tersely. He spoke Judean, and Tirosh realised he had missed the sound of his mother tongue. He searched for familiar landmarks, but the city had grown and changed in his absence, nothing he could have pointed out to Isaac were he sitting there, but then Isaac was away, back in Europe with his mother; he must have been; and he would see him again, soon.

The landing strip came up abruptly. The plane banked hard, then coasted, and the few passengers clapped. It was a strange custom, as though the landing were some remarkable achievement, a performance to be applauded, like the conclusion to a symphony performed by a full orchestra. But it was home; it was the done thing.

They disembarked shortly after. Ahead of Tirosh was the woman with brown hair; between them, carrying heavy luggage, was an elderly Orthodox man in the black garb and the felt hat of an Unterlander, accompanied by a wife and two children. The Unterlander turned and caught Tirosh's eye. He unexpectedly smiled, and gave Tirosh a wink. "*A bi gezunt!*" he said; which meant, "Don't worry so much, at least you still have your health."

Tirosh shrugged; and the man dismissed him with a "Psssht!" and a flick of the hand and turned back to his family.

As Tirosh stepped out of the plane, the humidity and heat engulfed him as though he had stepped from one world to the next. With them came the smell of Palestina: a mixture of tropical rain and car exhaust fumes, frangipani and jasmine and foods fried in oil. Tirosh took a deep breath, and when he expelled, it was the old breath of Europe he was expelling, and when he breathed again he felt renewed, much more himself. He was a Palestinian.

On the hot tarmac a bus idled impatiently, the driver smoking a cigarette by the doors. Tirosh climbed on board with the other passengers. He saw other planes parked out in the airfield, two British BOAC planes, a Uganda Aviation Twin Otter and an old Palestinian air force Spitfire, as well as a private jet, outside which a welcoming committee of sorts had formed, with suited dignitaries standing stiffly, only now and then turning their heads up to glance at the clouds. It was going to rain. The driver finished his cigarette and took the wheel. "Everyone here?" he shouted over his shoulder and, not waiting for a reply, drove them away at some speed. Tirosh watched the jet as the stairs lowered, and a line of Maasai men in ceremonial robes of animal hides emerged gravely, to be welcomed by the waiting dignitaries.

Then they were lost from sight as the bus came to the terminal building of the Nahum Wilbusch International Airport. Tirosh followed the others into the building and queued with his passport already held in his hand. It depicted the twin stylized lions of the old British Judea, holding between them a Star of David.

As a child, Tirosh still remembered hearing the lions in the distance, at dusk, on his father's farm. Sitting on the porch, watching the red sun set over the distant peaks of Mount Elgon, he'd hear them, calling with a sort of lonely pride across the distance.

It was then, with the cooling of the day, that the animals of the veld would come out to the watering holes, and a fragile sort of peace reigned, for a time, in the animal kingdom: lions would drink within sight of elephants and gazelles, intermingled with brazen birds, snakes, and crocodiles. Now, he thought, they must be all but hunted to extinction: farmers shot them, as the lions often attacked and killed the cattle.

"Tirosh?"

The border control officer was young and her hair was tied back severely. She wore the baobab-grey uniform of the Palestinian Defence Force.

"Yes?"

He tried not to look nervous. Even that simple word, *y'a*, came out haltingly, as though he had forgotten his own tongue and how to speak. He always felt awkward crossing borders, which were strange animate things to Tirosh, nebulous worm-like creatures which shifted between two states of existence, and also he feared officials. His grandfather, who had settled here as a young man fleeing Europe, had instilled in him a fear of officialdom which he had never quite lost.

The girl looked at his face, then at the passport, and she frowned. "You live outside?" she said.

There was something strange about the way she said it, as though it meant something more than he realised. He said, "Yes, in Berlin—" feeling like he was making excuses for himself, trying to justify a whole lot of things he couldn't say.

"What is the purpose of your visit?"

"My father," he said. "He is ill."

"Where does he live?"

She had the metallic delivery of an automaton, he thought.

"Fever Tree Farm," Tirosh said, feeling self-conscious. "In Elgon District."

The girl's eyes opened very slightly larger and she said, "*That* Tirosh?"

Tirosh shrugged. The girl looked at him again, doubt in her eyes, then handed him back his passport.

"Welcome to Palestina," she said.

He hurried away towards the barrier where more soldiers were standing. He saw the Maasai delegation enter the hall, accompanied by slightly wet-looking men in suits, who carried dark umbrellas.

A man in civilian clothing stood by the barrier. His receding hair was cut short and he had soft, sad eyes, or so an ex-girlfriend once told me.

There was no reason for Tirosh to know who I was; not then.

"Passport," I said. He looked at me, that sort of half-glance that doesn't really register: seeing a function, not the man.

"Tirosh?"

"Yes," he said, tiredly. Perhaps he didn't like his own name. There had been a fashion in the 1970s for modern, Hebrew-sounding names. His old name would have been something like Heisikovits.

"Is this your luggage?" I said. The soldiers brought it over, put it down on the examination table. They were good kids, not too bright, but eager. I gestured for them to put on the gloves and open the bag. Tirosh travelled light.

"Yes?"

"Could you empty your pockets, please?"

He complied, a man used to the indignities of travel.

"What is this about?" he said.

"Routine check," I said. "You understand."

"I'm not sure that I do."

I shrugged, apologetically. "Quarantine," I said. "We have to take extra precaution with people coming in from the outside. We can't afford any contamination."

"Do you mean biological?" he said. "I'm not bringing in any seeds or plants."

"It could be anything," I said. "Anything from the outside. Do you have a phone?"

"A phone?" he said. "What would I plug it into?"

I glanced at his eyes. They were clear and a little tired.

"Check everything," I said.

I watched his eyes as items were brought out, one by one. An analog watch, a toiletries bag, two folded shirts, a box of matches. I held the matchbox between thumb and forefinger, rattling it. I watched his eyes.

"Do you smoke?"

"No." A flash of confusion in his eyes. I nodded to the soldiers.

"Bag it."

"But what is this about?" he said.

"You have been outside for a long time?"

"I've been away, yes?"

I shrugged. "Sometimes you pick things up without even knowing it. Traces. It's best to be thorough. You understand."

He looked like he wanted to argue, but he didn't. I wanted

to tell him about mimicry, about how organisms can disguise themselves visually in a foreign environment: like weeds pretending to be useful crops so as to avoid destruction.

I didn't, of course. To him I was just a petty official, then.

"Stop."

The soldier was little more than a boy, and no more aware of the procedure than Tirosh was. He hesitated with the case in his hand. "Sir?"

"My glasses case," Tirosh said.

I looked at him sharply. "You use glasses?"

"For reading," he said; unwillingly, I thought. I couldn't read his eyes.

"Are you sure you had them with you, when you boarded?"

"Excuse me? I don't understand your question."

I should have confiscated them. I don't know why I didn't. I don't think it really made a difference, in the end.

We confiscated a few items. A ring, a pack of cards. They could have been nothing. Tirosh was an unknown quantity. He'd been away a long time. He bore watching.

"You're free to go," I said, at last.

"Thanks," he said. "That's nice to know."

"Just doing my job, Mr. Tirosh."

"Curious sort of job," he said.

"You know Palestina," I said, and he almost smiled. "It's a curious sort of place."

I watched him walk away. He didn't look disoriented. He had this sort of gait that looked like he was always somewhat in a hurry but was making himself slow down. A sort of active nervousness. I hoped he wouldn't turn out to be trouble but, of course, he did.

3.

Tirosh left the terminal building behind and stepped into the hot air outside. A row of stunted baobabs lined the road, their severity softened by the blooming jasmine shrubs that pressed against the airport fence. The rain had come and gone swiftly; mosquitoes buzzed drowsily in the air. A row of cars, all local make—Susita, Kaiser-Frazer, Sabra—were queued up in the taxi rank, the drivers leaning against the fibreglass chassis of their individual vehicles, all smoking. He saw the woman ahead, talking animatedly to one of the drivers—arguing the price, he thought—who finally shrugged, tossed his cigarette to the ground carelessly, and gestured at the car. She nodded, and a moment later the car took off. Tirosh raised his head, following the Susita as it drove down the tree-lined road. Wilbusch Airport was located some distance from the city. Ararat rose against the horizon in the distance, and he marvelled at how much it had grown. When he had left, it was a quiet, dusty town, filled with low buildings, wide avenues, small stores which shut, promptly, with the heat of the afternoon and only reopened before sundown, and public parks where old men sat cross-legged on the grass playing bao, and mothers pushed babies around in prams imported from Europe. It was a town filled with little hidey-holes and strange, dusty alcoves where tradesmen worked much as they had back in Europe: carpenters, watchmakers, shoemakers, goldsmiths, tailors, and book binders, leather workers, and their like. On Tuesdays the tea and coffee market sprang to life around Wissotzky Square as farmers brought in their produce from all over the countryside, and along Herzl Avenue the latest fashions from Paris and Rome were displayed in the shop windows. On Fridays the whole town quietened, the synagogues shone with light, and a hush descended with the coming of the Shabbat. Tirosh remembered serious-faced, black-clad avreichim following, spellbound, as their rabbi walked ahead, explaining that week's parashah with a raised finger that rose and dipped like a conductor's baton.

It was a city, too, where one could still come, unexpectedly, across a wild animal walking about through the thin traffic, reminding one abruptly of where they were: once he saw a giraffe stop at a red light; at another time, he was pulled forcefully away by an adult as a lioness, far from home, sat hypnotised outside a butcher's window, licking her lips.

Now the city had sprouted new towers of metal and glass, office buildings reaching out to the sky like the tower of Babel once had, and it had spread over the plateau in all directions, white house neighbourhoods growing on the outskirts like weeds, erasing the forest and the veld with their merciless encroachment. He did not know this city, he realised. He had been gone too long, and the world he'd thought he knew was no longer there, had been replaced with something mysterious and foreign.

He was not aware of me watching him.

He approached the taxi stand. The driver's chequered shirt was taut over his bulging belly. He had a farmer's tan and a smoker's cough. He said, "Where to, friend?"

"Ararat."

"Got a place in mind?"

Tirosh considered. His visit had been hastily arranged. No one expected him but his father. In a way, it had been less a decision to come than a push away from where he was, an escape from things he didn't clearly remember anymore.

"Know any good hotels?" he said. "Not too expensive?"

"The Queen of Sheba is all right," the driver said. Tirosh shrugged. He followed the driver into the car. It was hot and stuffy, and he rolled down the window and stuck his hand out. They followed the fence and the line of baobabs along the dark asphalt road. When they came to the airport gates, they were stopped by more young soldiers, standing there with rifles slung over their shoulders. They checked Tirosh's papers cursorily and waved him through. The airport fell behind them, and Tirosh now saw well-remembered vistas, the plateau opening on both sides of the fenced road with cultivated fields of wheat, replaced by grasslands farther away. He saw a herd of giraffes in the distance, silhouetted against the peaks of Mount Sergoit, and felt a sense of relief he couldn't quite explain. Some of the old Palestina, at least, was still there.

My men were following at a distance.

"I saw the wall from the airplane," Tirosh said, searching for a topic of conversation. "It looks almost completed."

"Don't be fooled," the driver said. "It looks impressive around the city, but it's not even reached as far as Eldoret yet, and the local tribesmen are refusing to work anywhere near Mount Elgon, and it doesn't seem to matter how much money you offer them."

"Why?" Tirosh said, a little uneasily. They were coming to the outskirts of the city, Tirosh saw. The fields ended and neighbourhoods began, and he saw children playing next to a running water tap by the side of the road.

The driver shrugged. "They say it's haunted. But then they always say that, don't they?"

The file I had on Tirosh was incomplete, troubling. He had grown up near the mountain, an extinct volcano on Palestina's border. It was and remained a strangely inhospitable land, where nature was left much as it had been when Wilbusch first came here, on that long ago expedition in 1904. Lions still prowled on the slopes and the farmers went armed, less for the wildlife than against incursions from Ugandan raiders, since the border was drawn through that region. The boy, Tirosh, grew up there, on his father's farm, and when his mother moved to Ararat City and took him and his brother with her, he still continued to visit regularly.

There were gaps in the collective knowledge, absences. It was the same way with the maps. Some parts of the plateau had never been accurately charted. Cattle disappeared in the Mau Escarpment, without a trace. Loggers going into the Nandi

Forest reported strange sightings, of ice age carnivores the locals had named *Ngoloko* or *Kerit*, and which are otherwise called the Nandi bears. Exploring the cave system of the Elgon volcano, one came across strange objects sometimes, things that had no earthly reason to exist.

Tirosh must have known some of this.

He had been outside.

As they came into the city, the world changed again, the neighbourhoods dropping off like leaves. Buildings began to have two and three stories, and Tirosh began to see shop fronts, and pedestrians walking past. Traffic grew heavier and the noise level higher. The sun beat down through a now-clear sky. They passed an open bakery, and the smell came wafting through the open car's window, of rye bread and rugelach, followed, as they continued onwards along the Alfred Kaiser Highway, with the smell of chickens roasting on open grills, of beef fat spitting and pots of rice and maize sending fragrant wafts of steam into the air, mixing with the car fumes and the smell of the women's long thin cigarettes and the men's stubby cigars. Soon they were stuck in traffic, going slow, radios blaring outside: kwasa-kwasa music from the Congo, kwaito from Johannesburg, and Malawi reggae, intermixed with klezmer, orchestral music, and the latest Europop hit. Tirosh took it all in. He was home again, and it felt good. Already details of his life in Berlin were slipping away. He wished Isaac was with him, that he could show him his roots, where he came from. He never spoke Judean to Isaac. The boy heard only his mother's tongue. Now Tirosh heard it all about him, and the familiar cadences, the mix of Ben-Yehuda's Hebrew with Yiddish and Swahili lending a sing-song lilt and dance to even the coarsest shout, as different from German as it was possible to be.

"Here we are," the taxi driver said. Tirosh had been day-dreaming. He shook himself awake with some surprise, and saw the entrance to the Queen of Sheba hotel rise outside the window. He paid the driver, who insisted on walking him inside, no doubt to collect his cut from the reception. Cold air hit him as soon as he crossed the threshold, as though he were leaving one climate for another, foreign one.

At the reception desk, he paid for a room and collected his key. One of my men followed him in a few minutes later and confirmed where Tirosh was staying. We were not aware of anyone else taking an interest. In that we were wrong.

Tirosh showered and changed. He felt energised. He left the hotel after half an hour and stepped out into the pedestrian traffic. My man followed him but lost him in the throng. For that he was later reprimanded.

At that time, too, there was a terrorist attack in Ben Yehuda. Tirosh returned to the hotel sometime at night. Unbeknownst to me and my men, a visitor was waiting for him in his room. Words were exchanged. The first I knew of it was the next morning, when Sergeant Katz called me and woke me from a fitful sleep to tell me they'd arrested Tirosh for the murder of a man.

4.

My path had crossed with Tirosh's own that night, though I did not know it at the time. He had left the hotel as described. At a roadside stall he ordered ugali with beef stew, then perched, uncomfortably, on a low plastic table, painted a chipped blue, as he ate.

It was perhaps the first time in years that Tirosh had had this kind of food. He watched the foot traffic.

Black-clad chasidim and children in shorts ran and weaved their way through the traffic laughing, just the way he himself had when he was a kid. He saw a group of Nandi workmen walk past, and he was witness to a road construction site nearby, which caused delays in the traffic. A taxi driver leaned out of his car's window and screamed abuse at the supervisor, who shrugged resignedly.

Tirosh paid and strolled away with a glass of cool sugarcane juice. The taste of the juice took him back years, to another Palestina, another life. He was not a man much given to confrontation, had notions of justice and fairness quite at odds with the running of a country. He was most comfortable in his books, his little *what if* fantasies. The sugarcane, raw and cold with the ice, sweet and yet with that pungent, aromatic aftertaste, revived him. He tried to think of his son but the thoughts slid away like water. The air was cooling down slowly as the sun began to set. It cast long shadows from the aerials on the rooftops, which looked like the masts on a ship, and the nightjars and swifts that stood on their tips cried like lookouts spotting new continents. Somewhere nearby a small neat Yemenite performed the three-card monte on an upturned box in the street, and a small crowd had gathered to watch and to bet. Tirosh had always admired the skill involved in this confidence game, and stopped to watch for a while, though he declined, wisely, to play.

I myself was on my way back into the city. The Maasai delegation had arrived safely from Mombasa, the latest group to appear for the summit which was about to start. Their security was not my main concern. Borders are more than mere walls; they take other, more insidious forms.

Night had fallen and the street lights along Zangwill Road came alive, and the air was warm, jasmine-scented, full of promise. Dusk was the time when Ararat City woke to life. Everyone was out on the street. Old men sitting outside the tea stalls played bao with great intensity, the wooden boards between them, the only sound the rhythmic song of the hard seeds constantly lifted and placed into holes across the board, and lifted again and scattered, on and on in an endless sowing. Tirosh's father had been a bao master in his day, a *Bingwa*, and when he took Tirosh with him on his trips across the country, his father would sit down anywhere, with an old farmer or a market seller, a child or a grandmother, and play, and take delight in the game. Tirosh had forgotten bao, in Berlin. Now it came back to him and with it an aching understanding that his past was gone, erased, that those moments he remembered existed now only in his memory and would be gone with him. Something niggled at him, another memory, about another kind of loss, but he pushed it away. It was easy to do, now.

He saw the bus come to a stop directly ahead. It was a red, unremarkable Sharona Co-Op bus, of the sort that ran everywhere across the plateau and beyond. It was just a city bus, and it stopped with a rattling of the brakes, and the pneumatic doors opened to let passengers out. Only a handful of passengers were waiting at the bus stop. As they began to climb into the bus, Tirosh noticed the figure of a chasidic man approach from across the road. The man was heavily clad in a long black wool coat that was wrapped tightly around him, and his head was covered in a *shtreimel*, a fur hat, which was pulled down low and hid his face from sight. As Tirosh watched, the man stumbled across the road as though drunk. The last of the passengers got on the bus as he came to the bus stop and made to follow them. As he did, however, his coat flapped open and Tirosh saw, with mute incomprehension, the explosives strapped to the man's chest and back. The driver began to shout and the man leaped onto the bus as the door was beginning to close. The driver pushed from his seat, neither young nor fit, and attacked the man, whose shtreimel fell down, exposing his frightened but determined face.

Tirosh heard screams from on board the bus. He saw a terrified passenger look out of the window. Then an explosion ripped through the night air and all the windows on the bus blew out. Metal groaned and tore with a hideous scream, and Tirosh smelled gunpowder and blood. The heat of the explosion seared his face. All around him people were running, screaming, and he saw soldiers with guns running to the scene, past him, and sirens came alive in the distance, screaming mindlessly.

The bus was on fire and people tried to crawl out of the windows, and all Tirosh could hear was the cries of the dying inside, a sort of broken murmuring punctuated sharply with screams. He ran towards the bus, trying to reach one of the windows, to pull someone to safety, and his hands caught on the broken glass and his blood joined that of the dying. He searched desperately for the face he'd seen. He'd seen it so quickly, and it was just the eyes, the helpless, terrified look in the person's eyes just before the explosion. He was not aware of his cuts or burns. Someone grabbed him hard and pulled him away and he fought them, but then there were more than one and they were dragging him away, cursing and sobbing, as there was a second boom and the bus shelter and the back end of the bus exploded and sent shards of molten metal and glass everywhere.

5.

I was not aware of Tirosh's presence at the time. I was still in the car when the call came, and I turned it around instantly and headed to the scene of the attack. Tirosh was taken to a first aid station and given a mild sedative. His hands were bandaged. His burns were minor. The medics had more important cases to deal with just then.

The police had secured the scene by the time I arrived. The fire had been put out and the area swept for further explosives.

The bomber's accomplices would be on the run now, trying to hide.

They were just beginning to bring out the bodies when I'd parked the car. This was not strictly speaking in my purview, but I stayed. There were several survivors, and the police had cut into the skeleton of the bus and brought them out to the waiting ambulances. Tirosh meanwhile had wandered away, and no one thought to detain him for questioning. Once again he'd slipped through the cracks.

There were plenty of witnesses. Journalists were also on the scene, and television cameras with reporters speaking in that high urgent tone they use for such occasions.

"This is why we need the wall!" someone said, and another said, "It was one of them Africans, I saw the whole thing, only he was dressed like a yeshiva boy."

It was happening more and more frequently. The wall was needed to stop the bleed, the echoes. But the speakers didn't know that; they were just angry and frightened, and tonight innocent labourers and naturalised tribespeople would be locking their doors and praying to see the morning undamaged. It was not uncommon for the people seek retaliation, and at such times innocence or guilt counted little but for the colour of one's skin. I remained on the scene until the last of the survivors and the last of the dead were carried away and the onlookers and the media pushed back. This would delay and perhaps even scupper the talks entirely, and the Congress was assembling tomorrow for the first time in full.

Tirosh meanwhile had stumbled away until thought cohered again in his mind. He remembered other violences, other atrocities. He'd done his military service in the Disputed

Territories and then served during the Second Ugandan War. Something cold and hard returned to him now. He went into a bar and ordered two shots of Waragi and downed them one after the other and then he felt calm. He had not been himself, he thought, until he returned here. He had been playing the part of somebody else.

Do not misunderstand me. I think he was badly shaken, a man out of place in more ways than one. He did not really realise what was happening. He went back to the hotel, where my men finally spotted him. They saw him go up to his room. They did not realise someone was already waiting there for him.

By the time I got to my office the next morning, Tirosh was sporting a black eye in addition to his injured hands. One of my men may have gotten carried away earlier. It was not uncommon for suspects to accidentally stumble down stairs or walk into doors. One does not run a security apparatus by being squeamish. Tirosh was pacing the length of my office.

"What is the meaning of this?" he demanded when I came in.

"Why don't I ask the questions, Mr. Tirosh?" I suggested.

"I didn't do anything!" He only then seemed to register my face. "You're that man from the airport," he said, confused.

"I am Special Investigator Bloom," I said. "I apologise for not introducing myself, before. But then, I had not expected that we'd meet again so soon, Mr. Tirosh."

"But listen, you have to believe me!" he said. "I didn't kill him."

I looked at him. I did not dislike him. What information

we could obtain from the outside about our visitor was that he'd suffered a loss, was divorced, and wrote novels of little worth, and which likewise received an equal amount of attention. How he'd managed the return, I didn't know. He had slipped once before. It was my job to prevent slippages or, failing that, to contain them. The borders between the worlds are porous.

Yet Tirosh, I thought, could be useful to me.

"Why not tell me what happened?" I suggested. There was a knock on the door and Katz came in with the tea. I liked it prepared the Tanzanian way, with the leaves soaked in hot milk rather than water. Katz placed the tray on my desk and departed, silently. He was a good, reliable man.

"I didn't do anything," Tirosh said, sullenly.

I stirred my tea. Gestured for him to sit down. He stared at me, hard. I waited. The air left him like a deflating balloon, and he sat down.

"He was waiting for me in my room," he said.

"Menhaim?"

He looked at me dully.

"Yes," he said. "We were friends at school."

Tirosh had returned to the hotel. He had gone up to his room. The carpeted hallway swallowed the sound of his feet. The hum of unseen air conditioners behind the walls provided a sort of static vibration, cancelling noise. When he got to his room, the door was very slightly ajar. Tirosh pushed the door open. There was a man sitting quite comfortably on the edge of the bed, holding a bottle from the hotel minibar. The top was open and the man had just lowered it from his lips when Tirosh walked in. The man had once been athletic but was now going to fat. His potbelly pressed against his chequered shirt. He had tanned, hairy arms and soft sad eyes that brightened when he saw Tirosh.

"Lior," he said. "It's been a while."

Tirosh stood there watching him. He recognised him immediately, though the years had taken their toll on the man. Meeting old friends for the first time in years is always bittersweet: one's recall instantly coagulates and is transformed as the young turn old in an instant. Tirosh found himself scrutinizing wrinkles, a heaviness to the face that hadn't been there before, the strands of white woven into the man's thinning yet once luxurious hair. He said, "Menhaim. What are you doing here?"

"So you remember."

In truth he had not been so much Tirosh's friend but Gideon's, his brother. A few years older than Tirosh, he was often at their house, a tall, tanned boy, back then full of mischief. He had given Tirosh his first cigarette, and that sense of illicit complicity had made Tirosh feel all grown up, if but for a moment. They were under the eucalyptus trees, in the shade behind the small synagogue. Tirosh had taken in a mouthful of smoke and then begun to cough, horribly, as Menhaim laughed with delight. Later, Menhaim had been an officer in Tirosh's platoon. They had been on the Ugandan border for long, wearing days of patrols and ambushes. It was Menhaim who came to tell Tirosh about Gideon's fall in the failed assault on Entebbe.

He had not seen the man since Gideon's funeral, all that

time ago. It seemed another lifetime to Tirosh. In the intervening years he'd heard that Menhaim had gradually dropped out, had married a Ugandan woman, became a journalist working for small, left-leaning magazines. The war had wounded the boy he'd once been. His joy had diminished. Once he'd been radiant, the sort of boy you'd follow anywhere, and inevitably into trouble.

Now, sitting heavily on Tirosh's neatly made hotel bed, he looked beat-up and weary, a middle-aged man who had never become what his boyhood promised. The wedding ring was missing from his ring finger, but a light band of skin against his tan showed that it had been there until recently. The bottle in his hand was three quarters empty, and he made a futile little gesture and suddenly smiled; for a moment Tirosh saw the Menhaim he remembered.

"How did you get in?" he said.

Menhaim shrugged. "These doors," he said. "There's not much to them."

"I don't mean to say I'm not glad to see you," Tirosh said, "but what the hell are you doing in my room, Menhaim? How did you even know I was here?"

"Famous author returns to his homeland, that's not big news?" Menhaim said.

Tirosh, exasperated, said, "I'm not even *published* here!"

"Truly, there is no prophet in his own land," Menhaim said. Tirosh realised the man was not going anywhere. He went to the sink and poured himself a glass of water and downed it. He pulled over one of the two chairs and sat down, facing Menhaim.

"I've just seen a suicide bombing," Tirosh said.

"They're more frequent now. They say they'll stop after the wall is finished." He gave a short, bitter laugh. "It's a travesty, that wall. We were supposed to have a homeland, somewhere safe from oppression. Not to become the oppressors ourselves. By keeping them out we're merely keeping ourselves in, building a modern-day ghetto. I'd hoped those days were long in the past."

Tirosh looked at him curiously. "You were never political," he said.

"No, Lior, *you* were never political," Menhaim said; there was a savage tone to his voice. His hostility startled Tirosh. "You left, so you wouldn't have to deal with reality on the ground. You ran. You like to think you believe in fairness, in justice, but you're not willing to *do* anything about it. Anything but writing your little fantasies like you can change the world with empty words."

"Writing is a weapon," Tirosh said. "Words have power."

Menhaim snorted. "I saw what we did in Uganda," he said. "What we're doing in Nakuru now. There were people living here before us. We pretend they didn't; or that they were recent arrivals, so it doesn't matter if they left; we say they ran, so it's their fault; we say all kinds of things so we can sleep at night, Lior. But some of us don't trust words anymore. Some of us believe in action."

"So, what, you'll be a terrorist?" Tirosh said. He was tired; he could still hear the screams of the dying; he didn't think that Menhaim had the right to break into his room, force his acquaintance on him after so many years and, worse, be so *dull* about it. Tirosh found revolutionaries tiring, their wild-eyed idealism as implausible as one of the plots of his novels. He did not agree with what was happening in his country, perhaps, but it was a long way from that to, well, this kind of talk. "What do you *want*, Menhaim? I've had a long day."

"I'm sorry," Menhaim said. He shook his head. Where once the gesture would have been like a young lion shaking his mane, this was more the act of an old rhino bull. "How are you, Lior, anyway? I heard you got married."

"I did. It didn't last."

"I'm sorry. Any children?"

"No," Tirosh said. Then, catching himself—why had he said that?—"I mean, yes, a boy. Isaac."

"You must be very happy," Menhaim said.

"Yes," Tirosh said. "Happy."

They sat and looked at each other, two men, neither young, neither as successful or as joyous as they had perhaps once thought they would be. Gideon's death lay between them, the shared Gehenna valley between their respective hills. Menhaim, as though gathering his courage, emptied the last of the remaining small minibar bottles into his mouth and corked it with a practiced turn.

"You might be wondering why I'm here," Menhaim began, awkwardly.

"You still haven't told me how you found me," Tirosh said.

Menhaim shrugged. "We keep an eye on recent arrivals," he said.

"We?"

"A loose alliance," Menhaim said. "People who care."

Tirosh sighed. "So what do you want, Menhaim?" he said. "That I should join your little revolution?"

"Would you?"

"No."

"I didn't think so, Tirosh. You're just a tourist. The rest of us have to live here."

Tirosh let it go. He waited. Menhaim looked at his hands, in his lap, considering. Finally he raised his head and looked at Tirosh. "It's about Gideon's daughter. Deborah."

"What?"

Tirosh was taken aback. He remembered a serious-faced little girl with black curly hair. She stood holding tight to her mother's hand, at the funeral. She didn't cry, not even when the body was lowered into the ground and the earth piled on top, one spadeful at a time. He'd gone over and spoken to the mother, Miri. She had been Gideon's girlfriend. The pregnancy had surprised everyone. Last he'd heard they had left Ararat, lived somewhere near Port Florence.

"Deborah?" he said. "But she's just a little girl."

Menhaim snorted. "She's a grown woman, Tirosh."

"Has it really been that long?"

Menhaim looked at him curiously. "You've been outside . . ." he said, softly.

"What does that mean?"

"Nothing. I heard . . ." But what he'd heard he seemed reluctant to say.

"Well, what about Deborah?" Tirosh said. He'd had vague ideas of visiting Miri and the child, though the awkwardness of meeting relatives was one he'd have preferred to avoid.

"She's missing," Menhaim said.

"Missing?" Tirosh said. The word seemed to have no meaning he could discern. Missing from what? From where? He had all but forgotten his brother even had a child. It had seemed so unlike him. Missing from Tirosh's life? She would be Isaac's cousin, he thought with a pang of regret. Palestinians were big on family, but he had always quietly preferred his isolated life in Berlin.

"Yes, Lior. Missing. Pay attention. It's important."

"She was working with you?" The thought made him angry. He did not want Menhaim dragging his niece into his sordid business. People got hurt that way.

"She is politically conscious, if that's what you mean," Menhaim said, with his own flash of anger. "She was studying at the Nordau Institute. Very bright. A doctoral candidate. Do you know anything about this wall we're building, Lior?"

"I know it's long," Tirosh said.

"Do you know how expensive it is?" Menhaim said. "We're talking billions here, Lior. Billions. The maintenance contract alone is going to make someone rich beyond their dreams."

"What are you trying to say?"

"Deborah was looking into the wall's construction, Lior. She was poking her nose into dangerous places. And now she's gone." He made a magician's gesture with his fingers, like releasing a puff of smoke.

"You think she's dead?"

"I don't know what to think."

Money. That was something that made sense to Tirosh. Politics was a mesh of shifting alliances, compromises, deals. But money was always just money. You either had it or you didn't, and if you didn't have it, you tried to get it. People died for the sake of ideology, sure; but a lot more died for the sake of a Palestinian pound.

"What do you want me to do about it?"

Menhaim shrugged; another helpless little gesture. "I don't know," he said. "I thought you should know."

"Was she involved in anything else?" Tirosh felt spooked. He went to the door and locked it.

Menhaim watched him in amusement. "You think those people care about locks?" he said.

"I don't know," Tirosh said. He didn't know what to think. He felt responsible for Deborah. Maybe that was Menhaim's whole point. He was going to dump this on Tirosh. Make it his responsibility. Ignoring Menhaim, Tirosh went into the bathroom and shut the door. He ran the tap and splashed cold water on his face. When he stared in the mirror, he barely recognised the man who was looking back at him. Who are you, Lior Tirosh? he asked himself. What is your place in the great scheme of things?

He didn't know. Fleetingly he thought of Isaac's podgy little face in the morning, rising over him, fat little fingers poking his face with delight. "Dahdahdahdad." Like the verse to a modernist poem. Tirosh blinking back sleep, holding out his arms, marvelling—where did something so small get so much energy?

He dried his hands and his face. Stepped back into the room.

"Menhaim?" he said.

Nothing had been disturbed. The door remained locked and the windows were shut and dark. Menhaim was on the floor, on his side, one arm splayed against the carpet. There were traces of a white, chalky foam on his lips. His eyes stared at the pattern on the carpet. His hair was matted with sweat.

Tirosh knelt down beside him and took his arm gently and

felt for a pulse, but there wasn't one.

Menhaim was dead.

6.

"But I didn't kill him, Bloom. Why would I?" Tirosh said. I sipped my tea and regarded him thoughtfully. The sunlight streamed in through the window. Outside, Ararat City gleamed anew after a bout of rain, and low, wispy clouds embraced the top floors of the skyscrapers. It looked solid and durable, yet I knew how quickly things can change. I would not let that happen. I turned my attention back to Tirosh.

"Then who did?" I said.

"How should I know? He shows up with a half-baked story for me, acting paranoid, and ends up dead. Maybe he had a heart attack."

"It's a mystery, isn't it?" I said. "After all, the room was locked from the inside, and you were the only other person in the room."

"I didn't dislike him enough to kill him," Tirosh said, and gave a sudden, surprised laugh. "He was just someone I used to know."

"And this niece of yours? This Deborah?"

He gave a helpless shrug. "I don't know."

"The mother's name was Glassner?"

"Miriam Glassner, yes."

"We don't have a record of a Deborah Glassner studying at the Nordau Institute," I said.

He looked relieved. "Well, that's that then," he said.

"However there is a record for a Deborah Glass."

"Yes," he said. "I see."

"No one has reported her missing," I told him.

He didn't like that. I could see it in his face. He didn't like that at all. He had a coiled sort of quality about him. He kept a lot of who he was deep inside. People like that could unravel, I knew. But they could also be used.

"I called the Institute," I said. "They haven't seen her in a few days. But that's hardly unusual."

"You've been thorough," he said. He regarded me with some suspicion. I nodded.

"As for your murdered man," I said. "There isn't much of a mystery, really. He was poisoned."

"Poisoned?" Tirosh looked past me. I couldn't read his eyes. "How?"

"The drink," I said. "From the hotel minibar. It was laced with oleander extract. Frankly, he must have had the constitution of a rhino. He should have been dead before he ever spoke to you."

"He drank the whole bottle," Tirosh said.

"He must have had the seizure when you were out of the room," I said. "Nasty stuff, oleander, but pretty flowers. They grow everywhere. It's the sort of homemade stuff they used to use on war arrows. But anyone could have prepared it, really."

"But why would anyone want to kill Menhaim?" he said. I could see he still didn't get it. "And why in such an elaborate fashion?"

I waited him out. I could see his mind working, almost the exact moment he realised the truth and the air left him. "Oh."

"It would have been a ridiculous way to assassinate Menhaim," I said, gently. "But a perfectly reasonable one if Menhaim wasn't the intended target. If the intended target was, in fact, you."

"Yes," he said, dully.

"Menhaim talked a good talk," I said. "But he was no threat. I was aware of his activities. You may not credit it, Tirosh, but I usually keep a good lid on things."

"I believe you," he said.

"Someone must have come in when you were out and put the poison in the bottles," I said. "Not all the bottles, maybe half. Perhaps they were interrupted. Any idea why anyone would go to so much trouble, Tirosh? Or maybe they just didn't like your novels."

"Everyone's a critic," he said. I laughed. I had to hand it to him, he was handling it well. Perhaps it was his return. It changes you, slipping. He was becoming someone else again.

"So I can go?" he said. "You're not going to hold me?"

"You're free to go," I said. "Can I give you a bit of advice, though?"

He was already pushing the chair back to rise. He looked at me. I could see he didn't trust me. I said, "Tread carefully, Tirosh. In this land you can be one thing or the other, but not both. Sooner or later, you have to pick a side."

"Is that it?" He stood up. I could see he had already dismissed me. It was his mistake. I watched him walk to the door. I wondered what he'd do next.

I had some ideas. He would bear watching.

"Yes," I said. "That's it."

"Thanks," he said. "I'll be sure to keep that in mind."

I watched him go. Katz came in a moment later and I

nodded. He withdrew without words. Unlike Tirosh, I remembered more of the outside. I remembered my own home world. I remembered Altneuland.

Long yellow beaches and grey gulls crying high, and the white buildings rising against the startling blue of the sky. I remembered the silent airships floating, serenely, above the newly built Temple on the Mount. Remembered the serenity of the old new lands, of Judea, Samara and Gaza; hills of cyclamen and poppies in dazzling pinks and reds, as far as the eye could see, and new cities, dazzling with electric light, along the shores of the Mediterranean. My Altneuland. Sometimes it seemed a dream to me, only a dream. It was hard to be sure if it had ever been real.

PART TWO

INVESTIGATIONS

7.

Tirosh returned to the hotel. He was given a different room. He showered and changed. His hands felt raw and his eye hurt where one of my men had hit him, but he was otherwise fine. He left the hotel and headed west along Herzl Avenue. He paused outside a hatter's shop, then went inside and purchased himself a fedora. The hatter was an elderly chasid, and the shop, already at that hour, was busy with the chatter of chasidim young and old who mixed Yiddish freely with modern Judean. It was hot and stuffy inside the shop, and smelled of new leather, warm ironed cloth and sweat. Adorned with the new fedora, an affectation for Tirosh yet common headwear in this land against the sun, he stepped out of doors again and continued on his way. Usually he only wore a hat when he wrote.

As he passed a bus stop he saw a red bus pull to a stop and involuntarily took a step back. He watched passengers disembark. Amongst them he spotted a figure strangely familiar to him, but it took him a moment to place her: it was the woman from the plane, whom he had last seen at the airport. He had lost sight of her after that.

She wore dark shades in the hot sun and long, practical clothes. A scarf covered her face, an expensive one, from Paris. She blended into the crowd. She could have been anyone.

She wasn't.

I had been busy elsewhere. The bomber of the previous night had not acted alone. There were many workers from the Disputed Territories in Palestine. Someone had to clean our streets, wash the dirty dishes, look after our elderly and frail. Someone to do the menial jobs on the cheap.

The security services had rounded up the usual suspects. One of them held my interest and so I had requested to conduct the interview. That is where I was heading at the time.

Palm Springs had once sat on the site of a pleasant confluence of small brooks where Nahum Wilbusch bathed on his first expedition into the territory. Since then the palms had disappeared and the brooks dried or turned into underground sewers, and concrete slabs of buildings had been erected in their place. Initially this had been a customs station for the British East Africa Police Service Battalion, and was turned into a temporary holding facility for prisoners during that long, regrettable conflict between the British and German empires which ended, in an uneasy truce, on the assassination of Adolf Hitler in 1948. Following the War, Palm Springs was left unused for some time, but on Palestina gaining, at last, independence from its colonial overlords, it was converted into a permanent prison, with new structures erected and the old ones updated and reinforced. After all, did not the poet Natfali Herz Imber once say that until Palestina had its own Jewish thieves, its own Jewish prostitutes, it would not be a nation as all other nations? And he should have known, drunk philanderer that he was.

The prison lay outside the bounds of Ararat City, on a high elevation on the outskirts of the Nandi Hills. It was quite isolated, yet a road cut clear through the greenery that led into the city, and it was on this road that I travelled with Katz that morning, on our way to interview the suspect. Katz never spoke much, which suited me fine. He drove. The windows were closed and the air conditioning was on. We were inside a world within a world, small and self-contained, with its own climate, its own rules. I stared out of the closed window at the lush, tropical vegetation outside. I loved this country; I felt an immigrant's devotion to it that might have shocked or amused a native-born Palestinian. The attack, I was sure, had been part of a pattern. A lock picker would use picks to carefully feel and then press a series of pins inside the lock, all the while applying pressure with a torsion wrench. If the correct pressure was applied at the correct points, the wrench would abruptly spring the mechanism free.

I could not explain any of this to Katz, but I didn't need to. My department was a specialist one, and I had made it my own. I hummed to myself as we drove, a klezmer tune without words. Before long the facility came into view. We were stopped at the electric gate. I presented my authorization and we were let in, the gate shutting behind us. Katz accompanied me inside, and I was led to the interrogation chamber.

The prisoner sat in a low, uncomfortable chair. His hands were cuffed to the arms of the chair and he had been stripped: he sat there only in his underwear. His hair was cut short, his arms lean and muscled for all that he was not a young man. His name was Joseph. He looked up at me with bloodshot eyes when I came in, yet he smiled when he saw me. I made a gesture and the door was shut behind us, locking me in with him. There was another chair behind the interrogator's desk—a comfortable one. I sat down and regarded him in silence.

He said nothing. His breath was laboured and it was loud in the room. The room was underground. The walls were strong. It was hot in the room and muggy, and I could smell his sweat. They'd worked him for some time before I got there. There were thin strips of opened skin all along his chest and arms. Bamboo is very versatile.

"Tell me about the attack on the bus," I said.

His nostrils flared. He said nothing.

"Whatever you say will stay in this room," I said, and he laughed, deeply and suddenly.

"I know," he said.

I smiled back at him.

"We don't have to make this hard," I said.

He was still a man; he was still afraid. I knew how much pain he must be in. He had been chained to that chair for hours.

"Is that my choice?" he said.

"I could end this right now. The door is there," I said.

"There are other doors," he said, and that infuriated me.

"The only way you will leave this room is on a bloody stretcher on your way to a hole in the ground," I said. In fact there would be no burial. His corpse would be dumped into the old rivers and washed away in the sewers. By the time he emerged into sunlight his bones would be bleached clean of his flesh.

"Death? Your only threat to me is death?"

He spoke a good if accented Judean.

"Death is a given," I said. "And after all, what is so very wrong in death? Everybody dies. All that remains is to pick the time and the place, and to do it with dignity, Joseph. The place has already been decreed. It is this room. But the time is your decision. We could end this quickly. Or we could . . . postpone. I do not recommend postponement."

He tried to smile at me again, but he cried out at the pressure on his back. "Pain is a great motivator," he said.

"Tell me about the bombing!"

"It was not my doing."

"That doesn't matter, though, does it?"

"No," he agreed, sadly. "That does not matter."

"You work at the Queen of Sheba Hotel? As a cook?"

"A chef," he said, with some pride.

"You send money home?"

"I have mouths to feed."

"Yet who would feed them now that you are gone?"

I could see his hatred then. Only for a moment, and then it was gone. They keep it buried deep, but it is there all the same.

"Perhaps your daughters could whore themselves to survive,"

I suggested. "Perhaps your wife could find another husband to provide for her and share her bed. Perhaps your sons could find work as houseboys in the settlements, cleaning the dog's shit from the master's floor."

"Perhaps," he said. His eyes saw me, and I felt a flash of fear.

"Perhaps, perhaps," he said again, mocking me. I thought of Tirosh then. "You would know about ifs and perhapses, outsider. But this is our land. We will survive. We will endure. The people go, the land remains. What do you care what happens to me?"

"I don't."

He laughed. It came out as a weak gurgle. There was blood on his lips. How long had he been here without water or sleep? How long had they beaten him? He had soiled himself, I saw. But he sat there like he was sitting on a throne.

"There are other ways out," he said. "Other doors. You should know this, more than any."

"Is that what you are trying to do? Open a gate? The wall—"

"The wall will not hold us!" He was angry now, too. We were both angry.

"How does it work?" I said. "What is the pattern?" I was shouting. "What is the pattern!"

He laughed in my face. I pulled out a gun. I walked around the desk and came to him and put it to his head. There was no sound in the room then, but for the laboured breathing, his and mine. I watched a trail of sweat along his forehead. "Tell me," I said. Whispered. "And this could all go away."

"Do what you must, outsider," he said, and I said, "Don't call me that!"

His eyes were soft and sad. "You have seen it, though," he said.

"I don't know what you mean."

"'Two vast and trunkless legs of stone stand in the desert,'" he said. "'Where the lone and level sands stretch far away . . .'" He was quoting that awful poem by Shelley.

I flinched and he saw it. My finger stuttered. That was all it took. The sound of the gunshot was enormous in the small room, where so many had died before. Thunder, underground. I didn't mean to kill him. It was just that he knew too much. It rained. Blood spattered the walls. I breathed in the humid air, microscopic bits of brain and skull.

He'd escaped me.

But there would be others.

I took another deep breath, re-holstered my gun and straightened my clothes. When I stepped out of the room, I told them to clean up the mess inside.

8.

Tirosh, meanwhile, had seen the woman get off the bus. There was nothing about this crossing to arouse suspicion. She did not appear to see him, and after a moment, she walked off, at a brisk pace, down a side street, Der Nister. Tirosh looked after her, vaguely troubled, then looked away, his mind elsewhere. He set off again down Herzl, where he saw young soldiers patrolling the street.

They were so young, he thought. In London or Berlin those same kids would be in college, drinking in bars, working jobs to save for a round-the-world trip, or just hanging out, flirting, falling in love, playing or listening to music—not carrying guns along a hot street in the African sun, watching for invisible threats. He thought of his own son, though the thoughts were like water and kept trying to wash away, like a tide. He had never wanted Isaac to grow up to be a soldier.

"Long march of about sixteen miles along the Elgeyo boundary," Wilbusch had reported in his long-ago journal of the first expedition. "The rear of the caravan was attacked by a Nandi tribe, and as the porters had no good guns, the loads were stolen and the head man was wounded. Gibbons, I and some porters pursued the Nandi about five miles, but could not find them in the wood."

Could it have all been different? Tirosh wondered. The Zionist Congress knew the land wasn't truly empty, no more so than Palestine, in the distant Middle East, had been. There had been people living on the land then and now. Their attacks now were merely replications of attacks then, fractals of a larger whole, history repeating. And yet what was the answer? If the Jews had remained in Europe, it would have surely meant a death sentence.

It was hot but Tirosh walked. He did not want to ride the bus. At last he came to the main campus of the Nordau Institute. It was a large, sprawling, colonial-era building, surrounded by pleasant grounds, with an assortment of newer outer buildings around it in a ring. Trees provided ample shade and students lay on the grass, talking, laughing, passing time. Some even studied their textbooks. Tirosh was stopped at the gate by a bored security guard and given a pass. He made his way to the stone steps and entered the building. Inside it was blessedly cool, and he went up to the second floor, for his appointment.

He found the door without undue difficulty. The metal sign, affixed to the door with four neat, small metal screws, attested that here resided Professor Falk, of the Anthropology Department. Tirosh had been taken aback by this choice, on his initial query. He had called the Institute, one of the finest universities in Palestina, and inquired as to his niece, assuming—based only on Menhaim's vague proclamations—that his niece was studying business, or economics: something solid and sound, at any rate, even if it had led her down avenues of dubious politics.

Instead, he had found that she studied anthropology and folklore, with a concentration on the old legends of settlement and of the Displaced. He had spoken to the departmental secretary, who had agreed to schedule him an appointment with Deborah's thesis adviser—on whose door Tirosh was now knocking.

"Come in," a voice said. Tirosh pushed the door open. Beyond lay a small office crammed with floor-to-ceiling bookshelves, framed old maps of the settlement and curious wooden sculptures of ferocious creatures with high front shoulders and a sloping back, like a mixture of hyena and bear. Behind the large, untidy desk sat a stooped old woman with long white hair and fever-bright eyes. She straightened as Tirosh came in and gave him a sharp glance.

"Tirosh, Tirosh," she said, as though trying out the name and finding it wanting, "I read one of your books."

"What did you think?"

"Eh."

She looked at him in amusement. "Please, sit down."

Tirosh cleared a stack of books from a chair and sat facing her. "I was told you're Deborah's thesis adviser?"

"That's correct."

"Have you seen her recently?"

Professor Falk shrugged. "A doctorate takes three years to complete, Mr. Tirosh, at a minimum. Deborah only comes in when she needs to talk something over, or consult one of the books in the library. Sometimes I don't see her for weeks at a time. Here at the Nordau Institute we encourage our students to conduct their research in the field. Forgive me if I'm blunt, but one doesn't get to know a culture by sitting on one's ass reading novels."

Tirosh let it go. It occurred to him, too, that Professor Falk hadn't really answered his question. He said, "So you haven't seen here recently?"

"Didn't I just say?"

"Not really."

She gave him another sharp glance. He got the sense she didn't like him. She said, "I haven't seen her since the last time she came in to see me."

"Which was when?"

"Last *month*, maybe?"

"And you don't find this a cause for concern?"

"Why, do you?"

Tirosh shrugged. "She's my niece," he said.

"Who you haven't seen for years. Why the sudden concern, Mr. Tirosh?"

Because a man died to deliver a warning, Tirosh wanted to say, but didn't. Was Deborah really at risk? He had only

Menhaim's word for that, and Menheim had seemed unstable, almost delirious, like an old Biblical prophet ranting about the nation's sins.

"I feel responsible," he said. "My brother—"

"Your brother the hero, who died in the war, yes, yes," she said. "In our nation's heroic and never ceasing war against its neighbours. Like I said, I don't see why the sudden interest."

"And I don't see the need for obfuscation," Tirosh said, stiffly. "I get the impression you disapprove of my family, Professor Falk."

Falk stared at him, then sighed and massaged the bridge of her nose. "I'm sorry," she said, after a moment. "I didn't mean—"

"I am not my father," Tirosh said.

"General Tirosh," she said, and he knew the look in her eyes, had seen it so often before, when people realised who his father was. That fascination. "What is he *like*?"

Tirosh shrugged, feeling weary. "I've not seen him in years," he said.

"Was it difficult, growing up with such a father?"

"I don't have anyone to compare with," Tirosh said. "Anyway, we lived with my mother after a while."

"You are not close, you and your father?"

He had sworn when Isaac was born that he'd be different than his father. That he'd love him wholeheartedly, that he'd be there every moment of the day for his son. When Isaac woke up crying in the night, Tirosh was there to pick him up and comfort him, and when he held his son's tiny form in his arms, pressing the little crying creature into his chest, he would put his face to the top of the baby's head and inhale his scent, and he thought of his father, wondering if the man had ever done the same when Tirosh himself was a boy. His father was a distant, towering figure, a powerful man moving with economic grace, always busy, surrounded by acolytes, his lieutenants and adjutants, with visiting politicians trying to press his father into service, with newspapermen and photographers looking for a story, or fundraisers looking for endorsement. Even the foreign press came calling, and in his father's study were cut images from interviews in *Le Monde* or *Der Spiegel* or *Time*, of his father in uniform, later in civilian clothes, tall, tanned, smiling, posing with a rifle against the shores of Lake Victoria or with Mount Elgon in the background. As a boy Tirosh had loved and admired his father from afar; the way one only looks at a volcano.

"No," he said. "We are not close. Professor Falk, about my niece—"

"Yes, I'm sorry. Do you really think there is cause for concern?"

"I don't know. Can you tell me what she is working on? I was only told it was to do with the wall."

"The wall?" Professor Falk sounded genuinely surprised. "What on Earth makes you say that?"

"What?" Tirosh said. Ever since he'd come into this office he felt they had been at cross purposes, he and this Falk. Menhaim had been quite clear, had he not? Had he been lying?

"Deborah is working on a study of certain legends of settlement," Professor Falk said.

"Legends?"

"Yes, Mr. Tirosh. This *is* the Anthropology department."

"How is that connected to the wall?"

"It isn't! The wall, the wall. There was no wall here before settlement, Mr. Tirosh."

"But what has that got to do with—"

"You know about the first expedition, of course," Professor Falk said.

"Yes?"

"The newly formed Zionist Congress, at the time, was bitterly torn between two factions. The majority supported settlement in Palestine, a return to the Holy Land as the only acceptable option for the Jewish people. Others, who called themselves the Territorialists, wanted to seek any available land for Jewish settlement. Theodor Herzl, the Congress's founder and its president, supported the latter. When the so-called Uganda Offer was made, Herzl supported it, but most of the Congress was opposed to the plan, and the eventual expedition reflected that. Wilbusch himself, though they don't teach this in the history books, was a Holy Lander. He was opposed to the Uganda Plan."

"Wilbusch? Wilbusch was opposed to the plan?"

Professor Falk smiled grimly. "Wilbusch was the Holy Landers' secret weapon: their man in Africa. He was guaranteed to deliver a negative verdict. In many ways, the Uganda Plan was effectively over before it had even begun."

"Wilbusch was a saboteur?" Tirosh said, bemused.

Professor Falk smiled. "He was," she said. "But, of course, he changed his mind in the end. Or we wouldn't be here now, would we?"

"What changed his mind?" Tirosh said.

"You know how the story goes," Professor Falk said. "The

men arrived at the territory. Wilbusch got lost. A hostile tribe attacked them. This is all part of the historical record."

"Yes."

"In his journal, Wilbusch makes a strange reference. He was lost, alone, on the plateau. He was out of food, perhaps delirious. He saw no living being. You have to understand he had never been to Africa before, to him this place was as remote as the mountains of the moon. On the sixth day Wilbusch found himself in the shadow of an acacia tree. The tree was decorated with dozens of bleached human skulls, hanging from the branches. It marked the presence of a holy place. Years later, in an unguarded moment, he called it a crosshatch."

Tirosh stirred uneasily. The chair felt uncomfortable, constricting. "What's a crosshatch?" he said.

"A crossing point. A place where worlds meet."

Tirosh stared out of the window. It had begun to rain, and the students on the grass ran back inside, textbooks over bare heads, laughing. He forgot Deborah, forgot Menhaim lying dead on the hotel room floor. Professor Falk's voice had assumed a hypnotic quality. It was the only sound in the room. Tirosh wet his lips. They were dry.

"Did Wilbusch say where this place was?" he said.

"He did not. He makes no further reference to it in his report. The legend, however, tells that Wilbusch found something in that place. A mirror. And he was granted a vision, of sorts."

He could barely hear her. There was a place where a tree grew, in secret, in the dark, and its fruit were skulls. Wilbusch, dehydrated, lost, had stumbled into an in-between place. He followed the shadowed path into the dark. He came to a place, where a black mirror lay.

"Wilbusch looked into the black mirror," Professor Falk said. Her voice was soft and sad. She may have been talking for some time. He wasn't sure.

"What did he see?" Tirosh said.

Shadows crawled along the walls of Professor Falk's study. They were skeletal humans marching across a great frozen wasteland where a fire burned, day and night. Black ash rose from the fire that was contained in great big ovens, and the people marched, near naked and hollow eyed, towards its warmth.

"It showed him the future," Professor Falk said. "One future."

Pain built behind Tirosh's eyes and he closed them. The images came unbidden, from somewhere he did not know: from outside. Trains travelling across the frozen plains, spilling out human cargo onto the ice, great gates, barbed wire walls, watchtowers, soldiers. Jews with yellow stars of David on their arms. A great fire, burning, a fire that never stopped.

"Wilbusch returned a positive report, of course," Professor Falk said. "The Congress authorised the plan. European Jewry, widely persecuted, were the first to emigrate en masse to the new land. It was said the ships never stopped coming; that if one stood on the rooftops of Mombasa, all one could see were ships like a flying carpet on the ocean, and they were all filled with Jews."

The pain behind his eyes ceased. When he blinked, it was the world as it's always been, will always be. Outside the rain had stopped, and the sky was clear. Droplets of water shone brightly on the big green leaves of all the trees outside. He imagined the refugees arriving, lifting their faces to the sun and feeling the light on their faces. What must it have felt like, to be the first to arrive? A new world, a new future.

"Like I said, it's just a legend," Professor Falk said.

"A legend Deborah was studying? Is studying?"

A note of genuine concern entered Professor Falk's voice for the first time. "You really think she's missing? I wouldn't even know how to track her down. She is always off to some remote region or another. I mean, she's a grown woman, after all. Her life is her own. No, I am sure she is fine. She'll be in touch, sooner or later. There is no cause for alarm."

"I hope so," Tirosh said.

"I should have offered you a cup of tea. How rude of me. Would you like some tea, Mr. Tirosh? You look terrible, you know."

"I know," he said. "And no, thank you. That's kind of you, though."

He stood to leave. "Do you know where she last went? Did she give any indication?"

"Kisumu, I think," Professor Falk said. "She said something about a relic from the first expedition."

"Kisumu? She went to the lake?"

"As far as I recall."

"Can you remember what exactly she was looking for?"

"No, I'm sorry. She didn't go into detail."

"Thank you, Professor Falk."

The professor stood. She extended her hand for a shake. Her skin was dry and her grip strong. "Good luck, Mr. Tirosh," she said. "I hope you find what it is you're looking for."

Tirosh nodded. A tree of skulls bloomed in his mind. He thought of Isaac, looking up at him with bright feverish eyes, saying, "Dadad, Dadad!" A bottomless pool of despair, a black mirror in which he could see no reflection, the touch of cold water, the sound of suppressed crying coming from another room. He did not want to confront his memories. He was just a man, neither good nor bad. He hoped Falk was wrong, and that he would not find it: not again.

9.

My men watched Tirosh exit the main university building. He was not so much tall as long-legged, with the hesitant gait of a man who never quite felt comfortable in his own skin. He wore faded jeans and a T-shirt advertising a long-disbanded, German rock band. There was on his face a pinched sort of expression, one that I had sometimes seen in my own reflection in the mirror. It is a sort of existential anguish, a tearing of the mind between two incompatible recollections. Imagine that you are one thing and, at the same time, something other entirely, both trying to coexist at once. That is the condition of being a Jew, I sometimes think—to always be one thing and another, to never quite fit. We are the grains of sand that irritate the oyster shell of the world.

Or perhaps I am, in my quiet moments, merely being fanciful. Tirosh remembered that which wasn't real. This did not make him insane, for human memory is a highly fallible one, and strongly coloured by the imagination. Indeed, I myself, for a long time, was unsure as to the reality of my own situation. For a time I even believed myself delusional, and yet I could remember Altneuland with an aching clarity of mind: the peal of bells ringing, clearly and swiftly, across the white cities of the coastal plane, the flight of a dove over the David Tower in Jerusalem, the view from on high over the Jordan River snaking through fertile fields, the lazy hum of bees in the clear, pure air. My home had been a paradise, its breadth after the Liberation stretching from Beirut to Baghdad: a land of freed Jews, an old, new land.

There, I had been a *Shomer*, or watchman, a member of that illustrious organisation of guards. Here, in my new land, I quickly ascended through the ranks of my chosen profession, until I had carved for myself a high role in the security services. And yet my memory of that other place was vague, and it was easy, too easy perhaps, to slip into a solitary set of recollections, to believe none of the other *sephirot* real. It was against such slippages that I guarded, against intruders that I remained vigilant. I believed in Palestina. I would not see her hurt.

As Tirosh departed through the doors, a man came running after him: young, podgy, in shorts—a graduate student, as sure as rain is hot or sky is blue. He was panting as he ran, calling out, "Mr Tirosh! Mr Tirosh?" with the mechanical precision of a rooster at sundown.Tirosh halted. He turned with that bemused expression of a man hearing his name called when he does not expect it—the sense that a mistake, surely, had been made, and one or the other was certain to shortly realise it.

"Yes?" he said, puzzled.

The man stopped and wheezed as he caught his breath. The expression he presented to Tirosh was one of a delighted smile. "Mr. Tirosh? Lior Tirosh? The *author*?"

"I . . . yes?" Tirosh said. He remained bewildered. He was not, truth be told, a well-known author. He wrote entertainments, cheap escapes. When he was forced to declare his occupation, well-meaning officials always produced sceptical but encouraging words, such as "Well, I hope you get something published one day," or "Maybe when you become famous I could say I met you."

He had not succeeded in becoming famous, but the truth was that fame did not appeal to Tirosh. His father, the general, was famous in Palestina, if by fame we mean a mixture of admiration and fear, even awe. As a boy, his father seemed to him like Mount Elgon: distant and terrible, a landmark seen and known by all on sight, yet never known at all.

"Do I know you?" he said.

"Mr. Tirosh, I am Leonid Rozman?"

"Yes?"

"From the *reading group*?"

"Yes?" Tirosh said. He had no idea what this Leonid was talking about.

"I'm so sorry," Leonid said, at last catching the bemused look on Tirosh's face. His own turned to a cringe of embarrassment. "We arranged . . . but were you not informed . . . I thought you were here because of the lecture."

"The lecture?" A vague memory stirred in Tirosh's mind.

"You *are* Lior Tirosh? Author of *Death Stalks the Graveyard* and *The Corpse Had No Face*?"

"Yes," Tirosh said. "You've read them?"

He felt that mixture of pride and terror that only came on him in those rare moments when he was confronted unexpectedly with someone who had actually read one of his books.

"I *loved* them!" Leonid said, with undisguised enthusiasm. "We were hoping you could perhaps give a talk? We have a reading group, you see, here at the Institute. Where do you get your ideas from?"

"I don't know," Tirosh said. He stared at Leonid. He seemed harmless, not much more than a boy. Yet like Tirosh himself at his age, he would have done his military service by now, out there in the Disputed Territories or on the Ugandan border, stopping civilians with the power of the gun, worrying about suicide bombers or an ambush in a side street of some nameless village, of a smiling child running up to you with a grenade hidden in her hand. Tirosh could not clearly remember his life outside Palestina. He knew he lived in Berlin, remembered Isaac, remembered a battered typewriter and a window through which sunlight came spilling in. He remembered sitting at that window typing, the words just forming out of nowhere, a black art of some sort he could never understand or explain, the letters punched with force into the pliable white page, the sound of the keys like the belching pops coming out of a gun.

In his work he sought to escape himself, the words came unbidden: murder was stylized on the page, brutality as entertainment, an order imposed over life's random violence. The people who read his books did not seek truth, some nebulous epiphany. Their lives were hard enough, made up of little indignities, personal tragedies, lingering, senseless deaths of relatives and friends, not in battle, yet dead all the same. In Tirosh's books they sought nothing more than a sort of shelter, a few hours away from their troubles, from the small dingy flat, the crying kids, the drunk husband or the wife one had fallen out of love with, quietly: the way people lived together for years and woke up one morning and were strangers to each other.

He said, "Sure, I suppose I could. Tell me, Leonid, do you know Deborah Glass?"

"Deborah?" Leonid said. His frown creased neatly, like pressed trousers. "Sure, why?"

"She's my niece," Tirosh said. "Look, do you know anything about what she's been doing recently? Any friends I could talk to? Hobbies she had?"

"Hobbies?" Leonid's smile was lopsided. "If you call going on demonstrations is a hobby."

"What do you mean?"

"She was always marching for something. Anything. For the rights of the Displaced. Against the building of the wall. For peace with the Ugandans. For giving back land to the Nandi. You'd think she was one of them, she loves them so much. If you ask me, such people are traitors, Mr. Tirosh, I mean no offense. But this is our land, given to us in covenant by the British. It is our *Nachtasyl*, our night shelter. No one will take it from us, no one!"

"You know her well?"

Tirosh's guess hit home. The boy blushed. "Not as well as I'd like to," he mumbled, sullenly. Tirosh smiled. Here at least was a motivation he could understand.

"You like her?"

"I told you, she is so *wrong*!" Leonid said. "About everything."

"That's not what I asked."

"Sure, I like her," Leonid said, and tried to grin. "What's not to like?"

Tirosh laughed. They were just two boys talking together about a girl. "Any idea where she went?"

"She's always gone someplace," Leonid said. "You'll probably find her in some Kalenjin village, learning to sew cow hides."

Tirosh's opinion of Leonid had been plummeting like mercury in a thermometer on a Berlin winter. Yet the truth was that statements such as these were not uncommon; you would hear them at the barber's or in the supermarket checkout line, over dinner with relatives or friends. They were just something to say, fillers in between more meaningful words. *You know what they're like*, or *What do you expect from, you know*, and then maybe someone would make a joke about cannibals.

"Is that a thing she would do?" Tirosh said, and Leonid, perhaps sensing the warning tone under Tirosh's voice, quickly backtracked. "No, of course not, I mean, she is just always so interested in the, you know, native cultures and . . ."

"You know her quite well, then?"

"No, I mean, I know her to say hi to, you know, it's not like we ever—"

"What I want to know, Leonid, is where I can find her, you see?"

"Yes, I understand, I just don't—"

"So she was against the building of the separation wall?"

"Deborah?"

"Yes."

"Sure. She was against it. She said it was a travesty, how we lock people into—she called them *ghettos*, Mr. Tirosh. Ghettos! How she can compare the plight of our forefathers in Europe and elsewhere to the . . . conditions of the natives I just don't know. They have a good life there. We wouldn't even need the wall if it weren't for the attacks. Suicide bombings, Mr. Tirosh! Who but a savage would do such a thing?"

"Someone desperate," Tirosh said. "Someone with nothing left to lose."

He turned away from Leonid. The boy could tell him nothing. Something nagged at him. He had asked Professor Falk about the wall, yet she denied that Deborah had any interest in it. Leonid was still talking. He just wouldn't shut up. Tirosh just nodded to agree, only belatedly realising he'd just confirmed giving a lecture at the university later that night.

"Tell me, Leonid, where can I find some of Deborah's friends? You know, her demonstrator friends."

Leonid shrugged. "Try the Hare & Coconut, on Chamberlain Road."

"The Hare & Coconut?"

"It's a pub in the old town. The sort where the beer is warm and you can get two-week-old copies of the *Guardian*."

"Have you ever been to London?" Tirosh said.

"I've been to Zimbabwe twice, to see the Victoria Falls," Leonid said. "And to Zanzibar once, for a youth conference."

When he at last left him, Tirosh was struck by how much he envied Leonid, in a strange way. To have convictions; to believe so fully in one set of values, in one point of view—to have no *doubt*, Tirosh thought, must be a wonderful thing. He wasn't, couldn't, be this way. Tirosh doubted constantly. He agonised over every choice; where others were certain, he was always left doubtful, unsure of the right way: unsure, even, if there was one.

Outside the campus, he caught a bus. He hesitated before he boarded it, but eventually he did. Unbeknown to him, my men were following him still. Unbeknown to *us*, we were not his only shadows.

10.

The bus ambled along without hurrying. It had the patient rhythm of an old beast of burden, a donkey or a mule long years in service, resigned to its lot, as familiar with its route as though it were pushing the same old-fashioned pump wheel round and round, like in old photos of the early settlement. Its passengers were the city's blood: old women returning from market with their bamboo baskets laden with shopping; a chicken bound, its head bobbing up and down in wounded dignity; students from the Institute, forming one distinct group, their talk and laughter louder than anyone else's around them; a man sweating inside a dark business suit; a pair of lovers on the back seat, entwined in each other's arms as the Orthodox man sitting away from the window and the sun's heat tutted disapprovingly. Tirosh remembered other buses, other days: riding with his mother to the old quarter of the city, where the second-hand bookshops proliferated and he could lose himself among their shelves, the musty smell, the murmur of little old ladies purchasing that day's quota of romance, while his mother spent her time outside, looking in the shops of almost-new clothes and obscure European knickknacks brought over God only knew why or when.

Shops of curios, too, proliferated here, amongst the numerous ugali stands and old-world tea rooms, where patient women and men sat all day, some behind stalls, some on the ground, with mats on the floor, offering carvings of game animals, masks and human figurines. Everyone in Ararat had an African curio or two in the home—a mask on the wall, a carved giraffe in a corner—and Shabbat candles on the windowsill.

And mezuzahs on all the doors, of course. The anonymous carvers in their villages had soon spotted a trend: for a time every second mezuzah was hand-carved out of ebony or soapstone, even ivory, which he had seen once. The parchments inside were made individually, by Jewish men of learning, the Sofrei Stam, whose job it was to inscribe holy texts. As a boy, Tirosh often wondered what was written on these mysterious hides, rolled carefully inside the mezuzot, what secret words, what awful names they contained within.

The bus stopped and started in fits; at each stop passengers came and went like raindrops. Beyond the window the city calmed, traffic eased, and cresting a hill, Tirosh could see far away, beyond the city, where the white buildings stopped and greenery began, startling against the deep blue of the sky. Then the bus descended, passing anonymous neighbourhoods where, in the fifties, the Congress had built cheap housing for the influx of immigrants departing the Reichsland in faraway Europe.

Then the city changed again. They were coming to its oldest part, the old town where the original settlers first came. Here Wilbusch had first made camp, which he had named Promised Land. Once it had been a green, pleasant encampment, near flowing water, with good views of the distant Mount Sergoit. Then came the immigrants, by rail from Mombasa to Nakuru and from there on the long march, over the plateau, men, women and children, who had never seen such wilderness, never felt such sun.

The mosquitoes savaged them. That first year many succumbed to malaria, and in the coming years, until the eucalyptus trees were planted, the swamps dried out; though still one could encounter the disease, and in the long wet season, beyond the city, one might wake up cold and hot at once, shivering uncontrollably. Tirosh had been sick of it once, on his father's farm, and he remembered it well: for three days he threw up uncontrollably, could eat nothing, drank only the water from coconuts, which is heavy in salts. But he got better. His dreams had been bad all through the nights, and he saw Mount Elgon as it must have once been, volcanic fire erupting from its peak, the flames illuminating the dark sky, blotting out the stars. His mother told him he'd been mumbling all night, in his half sleep, speaking of impossible things: planes crashing into tall buildings, children thrown into ovens, a helmeted man walking on the moon. She held him close when he woke up: the fever had broken and the sun rose outside, and the fever trees glistened with new rain.

"Don't you ever *do* that again!" his mother said.

But that was long in the past. The past was a place Tirosh did not like, these days, to visit. There were things there better left undisturbed. The past no longer existed, just as the future was not yet formed. All that there was was a single point of reference, an eternal present, and he was borne aloft on it: it was safer that way.

He looked out of the window, as the buildings became chipped white stone and the roads narrow: they twisted and merged here, built long ago, piecemeal, without design. Back then the settlers had used horse and wagon if they used anything at all, and these roads barely allowed a car to pass. In the eighties, the city council had undertaken an ambitious regeneration programme for the area, and now Tirosh saw that trendy tea rooms had replaced the old ugali stands, and art galleries stood where the curio sellers used to be. Many of the buildings had been restored, and the clock tower, built there on the occasion of the coronation of the Queen, dominated the old square, looking as good as new.

Something rang, inside his pocket.

Tirosh ignored the strange noise. The noise kept coming. He noticed with acute discomfort how the other passengers glanced his way and then looked elsewhere, troubled. He didn't know what it was, what could be making such a sound. He reached into his pocket and fished out his phone, which, for just a moment, had seemed to him merely a case for holding reading glasses.

"Hello?"

"Tirosh, where the hell are you?"

The voice on the other side of the line had a crackly quality, as though it were coming from somewhere impossibly distant.

"Elsa?" Tirosh said. "Elsa, is that you?"

"Who did you think it was? Really, I'll never understand you. Where *are* you?"

"I'm here," he said, confused. "You knew I was going home."

"How is it over there?" she said. "From here, you know, all we ever see is the bombings and the rockets, dead people in the streets."

"It's not like that," he said, "it's not like that at all."

People were giving him strange looks. It occurred to him that there was something strange about what he was doing: no one else on the bus was speaking on a mobile phone. It was as though they'd never seen one at all.

The bus came to a halt at last and Tirosh climbed off. He listened to the noise on the line. It had a strange crackling quality, seemingly random, and yet he felt he could discern shapes in the sound, a pattern he once knew.

"Hello?" he said. "Elsa? Are you still there?"

"I'm here, but I don't understand where you are, Tirosh. You've not been answering your phone and the university people say they've not even heard from you?"

"The university, Elsa?"

"The talk!" Elsa said. "I arranged a talk for you, you were supposed to deliver a lecture, about alternate realities or the death of the novel, anyway something riveting like that."

"But I did talk to them," Tirosh said, feeling reassured. "I most definitely did, just now. The lecture, of course. It's all taken care of, I promise you."

There was that noise-filled silence again.

"Well, if you say so," Elsa said at last. She did not sound convinced. "I'll speak to them again. Is everything OK otherwise?"

"It's all going fine."

"Visited your father yet?"

"Not yet. I got distracted . . . some family business to attend to first."

"Really, Tirosh, you sound very strange."

"I'm perfectly fine, Elsa. I'm seeing everything a lot clearer now."

He didn't hear her sigh, but he knew it was there.

"Speaking of," she said. "Ada called me the other day."

"Ada?"

"Your ex-wife, Tirosh?"

"Yes, I know. I mean, what did she want?"

Elsa hesitated. People were looking at him, passersby on the street. A kid, pulled by his mother's hand, pointed at Tirosh, and the mother dragged him away, giving Tirosh a wide berth. Did they think he was crazy? Unreasonable anger made him grip the phone. Have they never seen—

"She asked if you had Isaac's yellow duck. She said to ask you. She's better, really, you know. I think she was at work when she called me."

"I'm glad. Work is good."

"She says it was the first one you bought him. Together. Do you know what she's asking for?"

"Of course I do. We bought it for him when he was so small. He didn't know what to do with it. We used to wash him in this red plastic tub that had a sort of slip he could sit on. The duck would just bob there. Then when he got a little bigger he'd play with it for hours. It was just a yellow duck, Elsa. Can't you tell her that? It was just a fucking yellow duck!"

"You're shouting. Maybe I should call another time."

"Tell her that, Elsa!"

"Lior, you have to take it easy. Please."

"I'm fine. I have a case, Elsa."

"A case, Tirosh?"

"A missing girl case."

"You're not a detective, Lior."

"What? I can't hear you. You're breaking up."

"I said, you're not a fucking det—"

The noise, like the humming of the air before a rainstorm, ceased abruptly. Tirosh stared at the case of glasses in his hand. After a moment he put it back in his pocket. He felt much better, much more awake.

He found himself on Chamberlain Road. Back then, in the time of settlement, this had been British Judea, a faraway province of a great empire, and the streets had been named for those long-gone benefactors: Chamberlain Road, Edward VII Avenue, Balfour Boulevard. British-style pubs and tea rooms littered the streets, and Tirosh saw even a fish and chips shop, though the fish must have been flown in from Dar es Salaam or Mombasa. Farther along on Chamberlain, he saw the Hare & Coconut.

Inside, it was cool dark wood, a long bar with taps for local Bar Kokhba beer and imported ales, and the air smelled of cigar and pipe smoke: yet for all that, the pub was near empty at this hour but for a group of students in a booth by the window, talking in intense yet low voices, and a small, hunched figure on a bar stool, of a man wearing a jazzy little trilby hat, with a feather in its band. Tirosh slid onto a nearby stool with a well-practiced motion. He knew bars the way other men knew stocks, or gardening.

The bartender was young, a student himself, Tirosh thought. He wore a faded T-shirt and jeans.

"What can I get you?" he said.

"Waragi," Tirosh said.

"We don't serve African drinks," the bartender said, apologetically.

"Gut-rot," the man perched on the next stool said. He turned, and the wan light caught his face: aged, with unshaved bristles on his cheeks, and bright piercing eyes. "Don't serve Africans drink," he said, and sniggered. "Quite right, quite right."

"But I can do you one on the house," the bartender said, fishing out an unlabeled bottle of clear liquid from under the counter. He grinned at Tirosh and poured him a measure.

"Made just across the border," he said, confidentially.

The old man beside Tirosh glared, but Tirosh knocked back the drink and felt the alcohol hit him: it was like being punched in the face by a drunk.

"Another one?"

"Just a beer. Thanks."

"No worries."

The bartender poured Tirosh a glass. Tirosh looked around. He wondered if any of the students by the window were Deborah's friends. The old man beside him said, "So what brings you here?" He was drinking a gin and tonic, with a pickled chilli in the bottom of the glass in place of lemon: it was an old twist, favoured by the sort of people who referred to themselves as old Africa hands.

"What's it to you?" Tirosh said, and the old man grinned, revealing long, leonine teeth.

"Got to keep an eye on things, haven't we?" the old man said.

"He's a snoop for Internal Intelligence," the bartender said. He laughed at Tirosh's surprised look, then shrugged. "He came sniffing around about six months ago, asking questions. We get a lot of students here. Quiet now, but it picks up in the evening."

"You a student, too?"

"Sure. Got to work."

"Not saving up to go travelling?" Tirosh said, setting aside for the moment the curious case of the old man.

"Where to? Europe? Palestine—the old Palestine, I mean? What's there, right? Rocks and camels."

"Jerusalem," the old man said. "I've been to Jerusalem, once. We went on a Holy Land Tour. Sea of Galilee, Safed, Acre where the Crusaders were. The Dead Sea. You could float on your back and look up and see nothing but skies. The air smelled funny. I remember that."

"Potassium bromide," Tirosh said, and they both looked at him, with a surprised look, and he said, "It's supposed to have a calming influence."

"Anyway we went to Jerusalem," the old man said, with a finality. "Old stones and nothing but mosques and churches, and half the girls had their faces covered. Me, I prefer them wearing less."

"You prefer them wearing nothing," the bartender said,

and the old man grinned again, and took a noisy sip of his drink. The ice cubes had almost melted in the glass.

Tirosh looked between the two of them. Their relationship seemed friendly, unforced, born of long familiarity. He said, "You're with Internal Intelligence?" to the old man, who puffed his chest in reply.

"Was," he said. "Retired, now. Still helping out. Amos Barashi, ex-sergeant."

"He came sniffing around, like I said," the bartender said. "Asking questions. Listening. He thinks we're all conspiring against the Congress. That we're, what, some sort of internal terrorists?" But he said it without malice.

"Can't be trusted," the old man said. "I know, I hear things."

"So now there's a, what do you call it," the bartender said, "détente? He keeps tabs on us, and at least we know who it is who's spying. I'm Nir, by the way."

"Tirosh."

"I know you," the old man said, pointing a stubby finger accusingly. "You're the old general's son. I knew him, you know. Served under him against the Mau Mau. Your brother, he was the hero of Entebbe."

The bartender looked at Tirosh with renewed interest. "*That* Tirosh?" he said.

Feeling conspicuous, Tirosh shook his head mutely. There was something surreal in sitting here, in this fake British pub in the middle of the African mainland, where once British officers might have sat much as they did now, perched at the dark wood bar, speaking of the faraway places they'd seen. Jerusalem. Did it even exist? Was it in any way real?

The old man, this Barashi, said, "You've not been here in a long time, have you, Tirosh? You've been outside."

"Outside, outside," the bartender, Nir, said. "He always talks about the outside."

"I was with the old general in the Mau Forest," Barashi said. "I know what I saw. You think you know everything, you young people. You want to bring down the wall, for what? The Nandi? They have no claim to this land. It's ours. Granted and paid for in full."

"Paid in blood," Nir said.

"Paid in blood!" the old man said, thundering, and the students by the window turned and watched, with amused expressions. They must have been used to Barashi's outbursts. "Paid in blood, our blood. I saw men die in the mud. Friends. Brothers. I saw Lake Nakuru run red with their blood and the flamingos shot and killed and roasted on a fire. This is *our* land. This will always be our land." He turned small, mean, glittering eyes on Tirosh, and Tirosh realised how drunk the old man must already be, even at this hour. "*He* is showing *interest* in you," he said. His voice was a sort of reptilian hiss. Tirosh drew back, only half-aware, his hand trailing down to his side, but of course, he no longer wore a gun there.

"Who?" he said, uneasily. A name came into his mind and he spoke it, without thinking. "Bloom?"

"Bloom!" Barashi said. The very act of speaking the name seemed to sober him up. "I watch. I listen. I once killed four men in an ambush. It was in the forest, during the Mau Mau rebellion. They had come out of the trees, like ghosts. Four of them. I didn't know if they were men or spirits. One minute there was no one there and the next they appeared, out of nowhere. I killed them." He was breathing heavily. "I fired, in all directions. The bullets tore them in half. They were real enough then. They came out of nowhere. Nowhere."

"I'm cutting you off," Nir said. "I think you've had enough to drink, Barashi."

"Nowhere," the old man whispered. The fight had gone out of him. "You know," he said, to Tirosh. "You've been there."

"Enough," Nir said. The old man waved his hand, dismissively. He eased himself off his stool and tottered away, towards a discreet door with a painting of a man in a tuxedo on it.

"Is he always like this?"

"He's harmless enough. He hears what we want him to hear and he files reports no one reads. It's not perfect, but it works."

Tirosh tried to smile but found himself shaken. He reached for his beer and emptied it and set the glass on the countertop. The foam at the bottom of the glass was like distant, dirty clouds. Outside, outside, he thought. He tried to picture Berlin, but all he could see were indistinct streets and indistinct people: it could have been anywhere, or nowhere at all.

(Isaac crawling on the bed, a relentless, human alarm clock, podgy little hands reaching for Tirosh's hair, pulling delightedly. "Dadad? Dadad!" and Tirosh burrowing deeper under the blanket. "Hush, Isaac, Daddy is trying to sleep, please—" followed by a groan, then turning and opening his eyes to see Isaac's smiling face, that quickening in the eyes when he sees him, and he can't help but smile back at his son, so perfect in every way.)

Behind him the door to the pub opened and closed, and the party by the window increased in size. Nir poured him a second shot of Waragi, unbidden, and placed on the counter a small bowl of peanuts. "Going to get busy," he said. Tirosh knocked back the drink.

"You said you tell him what he wants to hear," he said. "So what do you really say, when he's not listening?"

Nir shook his head. "If we wouldn't tell him, why would I tell you?" he said. "No offence."

"None taken," Tirosh said. "But someone is always listening. This is Palestina."

"We're not completely without the rule of law," Nir said. "Not yet."

Tirosh shrugged. "I'm looking for my niece," he said. "Deborah Glass. I was told she often comes here."

"Well, she's not here now."

"Do you know where I can find her? I don't care what you're involved in, I just want to make sure she's safe."

"I don't know what you think we do here," Nir said. "Sure, people talk. Politics. What else? Demonstrations, printing leaflets. That sort of thing. Civil disobedience, man. Old Barashi, I think he just likes the company. His wife died last year, and he has a son who lives in South Africa and never visits."

Tirosh, doggedly: "Well, have you seen her, recently?"

"Deborah? Now that you mention it, no. But she's always coming and going."

Tirosh pushed his chair back and stood. He needed air. He left a handful of change on the bar. He had not touched the peanuts.

Outside, the noise of the street and the hot, humid air acted to anchor him in reality. He walked away along streets remembered from childhood. He marvelled that they still existed, still smelled the same way. The makes of the cars were newer, and the old cinema had been turned into a fashionable boutique, but it was otherwise the same, as though no time had passed, as though the world had hung suspended, only waiting for him to come back.

Then he saw it.

Waxman's: a dirty and ramshackle hole-in-the-wall filled with old pocket books and magazines produced by the gutter press. Tirosh motionless still at the window. He could not believe it was still there. After their mother left the farm, they had gone with her to Ararat, Gideon and him, and it had not been easy. Tirosh had found solace in the refuge that Waxman's offered. He spent hours in the dark maze of the shop, reading the latest issue of *Yiddish Excitement Quarterly* or *Thrilling Hebrew Tales*. He followed the adventures of Sheriff Zeidelman as he hunted down the notorious bank robber Birnbaum, or squared off against the evil kidnappers Shlemiel and Shleimazal. He held his breath as Abe "Space Ace" Haisikowits found himself trapped inside the *Star of Zion*, the spaceship's atomic engines stalled somewhere off the Crab nebula. But most of all he loved the tales of Avrom Tarzan, the Judean Jungle Boy, as he battled Ugandan poachers, dove to the depths of Lake Victoria to find the missing diamonds of the Queen of Sheba, and searched for lost cities of gold in the depths of the Congo, all with the help of his trusted companion, Ephraim the elephant.

Now he stepped into the shop like an explorer venturing

into the dark unknown. The smells of his childhood hit him, the smell of old books, weathered paper, warm musty leather. Waxman sat on a stool as he always did, before the cash register, eating a sandwich. He was slightly older and his hair slightly whiter, but he was much as Tirosh remembered him.

Waxman glanced up as he noticed Tirosh. He nodded, mouth full of food. "Help you, young man?" he said.

"Just browsing," Tirosh said, and almost smiled; back when he was a kid, that was always his reply to Waxman's inquiry.

"Always with the browsing," Waxman said. He dabbed at his lips with a dirty handkerchief. "No one buys books anymore."

"Mr. Waxman, do you remember me?" Tirosh said. "Lior Tirosh, I used to come by your shop all the time when I was a boy."

"Tirosh, Tirosh," Waxman said. "Can't say that I do. Kids today, they don't go to bookshops, they have better things to do with their time."

"I'm a writer now," Tirosh said. Why he felt the need to explain himself to Waxman, an unkempt and slovenly man whose attitude to his customers was indifferent at best and downright hostile at worst, he didn't know. Waxman said, "Pffft," and made that wave of his hand, like the Unterlander on the plane; dismissing Tirosh and his aspirations like banishing an unruly child from his shop.

"Who isn't a writer, tell me," Waxman said. "Only yesterday I had that Amos Klausner fellow in here, asking for documents relating to the Wilbusch Expedition. Says he wants to write a novel about the early years of settlement. Everyone's writing a novel these days. Not me. All them words. What we need, Tirosh, is not writers. We need soldiers, farmers. Are you going to buy a book or not?"

"I told you I was just browsing."

"I'm going to close early," Waxman announced. "So make up your mind one way or the other."

It felt vaguely surreal for Tirosh to be inside the store. The books on their dark shelves whispered to him, each one a promise, each one a world. He let his fingers trail along the dusty spines; the dust tickled his nose and he held back a sneeze. He thought about that long-ago expedition: how the three men—the Jew, Wilbusch; the Swiss, Kaiser; and the British explorer, St. Hill Gibbons—met in Mombasa in that long ago January month, and from there set off by train heading to the Uasin Gishu plateau, a remote and unknown region of little interest to anyone but the desperate Jews. . . .

Their first port of call had been Nakuru, on the edge of the settlement.

Now Nakuru lay beyond the Green Line, as it was called. There was a heavy army encampment to keep the peace, and new settlements built in the fertile land round Lake Nakuru. Tirosh had memories of going there on school trips, of seeing thousands of pink flamingos dotting the serene waters like festive guests at the seaside, with rhinos standing by with their horns in the air, looking bemused at the cacophony of birds.

On their journey from Nairobi, the expedition passed through the fertile Kikuyu lands. In Nakuru they were stranded for some time, finding it difficult to hire porters. Eventually they began their journey into the territory. They did not know what to expect or what they'd find. They passed through thick, primeval forest, the land rising rapidly as they marched towards the proposed territory. Several days later, they reached the plateau.

"So?" Waxman said, startling Tirosh. "*Nu*? I'm going to close."

Tirosh made meaningless noises of appeasement. He cast about him and alighted on a small, slim volume: Baedeker's 1951 *Guide to British Judea and Its Environs.* Tirosh waved the book at Waxman, who took it from him with a slight sniff and said, "I guess Klausner missed that one." He thumbed to the front free endpaper, his lips pressed together in concentration as he studied the pencil-inscribed price and found it wanting.

"Twenty shillings," he said at last, reluctantly. Tirosh dug in his pocket. He did not remember changing money but was pleasantly surprised to discover he carried enough of the local currency on his person. He paid and accepted the book back from Waxman, feeling strangely protective of his purchase.

He stepped out of the shop and back onto the road.

My man who was following Tirosh was eating a chapati roll at a stall, and was not paying attention.

Tirosh turned, left or right it didn't matter.

Two men converged on him. They bumped into him as though in passing.

Tirosh began to say, "Excuse me—"

Something heavy and hard hit him on the back of the head.

It was a cosh, standard Internal Intelligence service issue, though the men were not working for us.

One man hit Tirosh on the back of the head. The other

caught him as he fell. It looked, if anyone was looking, as though they were merely helping a friend who had suddenly collapsed. Tirosh's face contorted in pain. He tried to speak but couldn't. The man, with a frown of irritation, hit him again with the cosh, and Tirosh slumped unconscious. It was all done with quiet efficiency.

By the time my man—juices running down his chin from the meat inside the chapati wrap—turned round, the two men and Tirosh were gone. Their car, an imported German make, black with tinted windows, had been idling at the curb. The men dragged Tirosh into the car and it took off immediately. My man saw nothing. It was the second time we had lost him.

Tirosh had that knack: however hard you watched him, he sooner or later just disappeared.

PART THREE

VOYAGES

11.

Towards afternoon, the minarets of Damascus cast down elongated shadows, like the masts of ships, across the city. You walk from shade to shade, hopping over hot pavement stones, between cool stone walls and under arches. The city rises from its afternoon sleep and shakes off the heat, slowly, by degrees. In the distance the muezzin call the faithful to prayer, green lights illuminating the rooftops. The air is scented with the bloom of sweet peas, the distant smell of the sea, with the pop and grind of roasted cardamom seeds, black coffee, men's aftershave, women's perfume. You walk without hurrying, with a precision of movement, hands swinging by your sides. You're humming a song, something old by Umm Kulthum. You wear a green summer dress.

In cool stone courtyards scholars gather to argue obscure theological points from the Quran and Zohar. In souks across the city traders display their wares much as they have done for thousands of years: bags of sun-bright turmeric, volcanic-ash paprika, rare pods of vanilla, saffron strands like delicate hair. You've missed Damascus, the mountains, the buzz of a thousand arguments; solar panels spread open like wings on the rooftops. The electric cars move silently through the streets. Under awnings the sheesha pipe cafés are open for business, and the smell of cherry tobacco and the hiss of hot coals send you back to an earlier, simpler time.

You pass quietly, unnoticed. Your reflections stare back at you from shop windows, cocking their heads, quizzical. Who are you today, Nur?

I am anyone and no one, you say to them, silently. You smile at your reflections and they smile back at you, but each one is slightly different, each one has a different smile. I can be anyone I want to be.

Past Hejaz Station, the grand terminus, and you remember when you first arrived in this city, taking the train from Haifa; how it ran through the Galilee, climbed the bridge over the Jordan River, how it led you here, a reserved young girl, stepping off the train with your suitcase in your hand, into the throng of languages and people. How exciting it was, to see Damascus that first time! It is a city one can never forget, no matter how long you've been away.

You think of that girl off the train, that country girl from Hebron, growing in the dark shade of Ursalim. You were her, once. It seems so distant now. You pass the train tracks, skirting the university where you gained your degree (that first one), making your way to the small and unassuming building on Anwar Sadat Street.

The building, like you, is misleading. It appears so plain. There are no signs outside. It could be anything: the office block of a shipping firm, perhaps.

Which, in a way, it is.

You step up to the doors and they open for you. Inside it is cool, the air conditioning is working. The air is dry. The building is filled with the quiet, busy sound of a library. It smells of paper. Here, borders are charted and maintained. A couple of people you recognise. They give you cautious nods as they pass you in the corridors. You follow the meandering path to the interview room.

"Please, come inside."

"Shut the door, will you?"

Your eyes are green like young mint leaves. They have a coldness that only manifests in rare moments, that is kept hidden from the world. You look at the room, which has no windows. The first speaker you know well: Professor Abdullah Hashimi, the agency's director. The other is his deputy, Bar-Hillel. Bar-Hillel closes the door after you, gives you an apologetic shrug. Professor Hashimi puffs irritably on an electronic cigarette.

"Well, sit down, sit down," he says.

You watch him. You remain standing. There is someone else in the room, a third person, but it takes you a moment to see her. In the shadows, and with that stillness that you, too, possess.

An agent.

She merges with her surroundings so perfectly, it is hard

to spot her at all. What did your ex-husband once call you, frustrated and angry? A chameleon. That night he left, he said he never felt he knew you at all.

You told yourself it was better that way, when he'd gone. You sat up until sunrise, in the apartment—you were living in Berlin at the time. One Berlin, at any rate, one of many. The sun rose sluggishly, hidden behind fog. You had sat up all night watching old movies on TV, nursing a single glass of wine. *Gone with the Wind*, with Errol Flynn and Paulette Goddard, followed by Jean Harlow in *King Kong*, the giant ape falling from a great tower to his death, then *M*, with Lugosi buying a balloon from a blind street vendor, whistling all the while. You hardly saw them. Sometimes you wonder what happened to him, to that man, your husband, who he was, if a version of him were still out there. He had been a doctoral candidate, like you.

"Well?" Hashimi demands. You look back at him. Your eyes are jade mirrors. He looks away.

"Who's she?" you say. You hear a chuckle, dry like old paper. The other woman pushes forward. She is old, older than you, but her face is curiously ageless, unlined, like yellowed paper stretched taut and thin. She could be you, in decades hence. Her eyes are amused, but you sense their coldness.

"Madame Méduse," you say, startled, though you cover it quickly. She smiles with teeth like fangs.

"They speak so highly of you," she says.

You say: "I thought you were dead."

Bar-Hillel squirms uncomfortably. He is not at home in this room, with people such as yourself. A civilian—though you remind yourself he is Hashimi's deputy, and that appearances, so often, can be deceiving—you of all people should know this well.

La Méduse, meanwhile, takes no offence to your bluntness.

"Perhaps I was," she says, "yes, perhaps I am. It is so hard to keep track, after a while."

Her tone invites your complicity. You resist it. Hashimi takes short angry puffs. "Sit, sit," he says. "We are already out of time."

"That we are, always," La Méduse says. "We have so little time, and so much . . ."

"I am not on active duty," you say, ignoring her. Doddering old fool, you think, but don't say. "I am on leave of absence."

"At the discretion of the service," Bar-Hillel offers, in that same apologetic tone. "And which has been withdrawn, as you are now aware. After all, you are here."

"I was happy," you say, "right where I was."

"In Haifa?"

"Yes."

A city on the edge of the sea, as old as the mountain it sits on, some say. Mount Carmel, evergreen, and the blue, sparkling sea in the distance . . . and the second-hand bookshops all along Wilbusch Street in the lower city, where you have spent all your time in recent months, continuing your research, for that book on Hebrew pulp writers you are never going to publish. . . .

Bar-Hillel sits. There's a thick paper folder on the table before him. Hashimi goes to the wall, as though drawn to a window, to a dream of one. La Méduse fades back into the background. Bar-Hillel wets a finger, turns a page. He looks at it in concentration.

"Nur Al-Hussaini," he says. You realise, too late, the trap they've laid for you. You thought this a routine visit, hoped to catch the night train back to Haifa, wanted nothing more than to clear up the confusion.

But there is none.

You are here to be given a task.

"Born in Hebron, in the thirty-fifth year after the Small Holocaust," he says.

"Yes."

"Graduated University of Damascus in '55, with a degree in Hebrew literature—"

"Yes."

He looks up at you.

"Why Hebrew?"

"Why not?"

He shrugs. "With a special interest in—what is that? science fiction?"

"It was a way of imagining futures," you say—a little defensively, perhaps. "Multiple futures."

"In my experience," Professor Hashimi says, "the future happens regardless of what you imagine."

"If you say so."

You can't really explain to him. To them. What it was like growing up in Hebron in the shadow of the Absence, long after the world changed. What it was like to read those strange, old stories, those vanished authors from the time Before. How differently they saw the world then.

"Tell me," Bar-Hillel says, seemingly at random. "Did any of them ever . . . *predict* what was to happen?"

Yes, you think. Yes, one. But they'd just been making up

stories; they made up a thousand futures and none of those had come to pass. Sometimes the stories served as warnings. Sometimes as entertainment. Thought experiments. That's all.

Yet in you, at the library, distanced from your surroundings—back then it was harder to pretend to belong, harder to blend in—they awoke something you hadn't even known you were missing.

A desperate need to ask, *What if?*

A question which finally led you here, to this building, this room, this city, or one much like it.

But Bar-Hillel does not pursue the question. He takes your silence for an answer, of a sort. He licks a finger, turns a page. "Postgraduate studies in Berlin, then Baghdad. You trained as a historian?"

"Yes."

For people in a hurry, you think, they are certainly taking their time.

"Then what?" he says.

"You know all this," you say, unwillingly. You were happy in Haifa. Happy with the hot Mediterranean wind, the hush of bookshops, the spoken mix of Hebrew and Arabic. Haifa is your haven, an oasis away from the greater world of Ursalim, and the worlds beyond it.

"She was identified as a possible candidate by one of our spotters," Hashimi says, addressing no one in particular, it seems. "Psych evals, the usual. You have no parents, do you?" he says, suddenly addressing you directly.

You say, mildly, "Everyone has parents."

"I mean, they died, when you were young."

"Yes."

"You were raised by an aunt."

Your aunt Aisha, a woman with the willpower and voice of a bull elephant.

"Yes," you say, smiling. Aunt Aisha would eat the director for her tea, you think. Men worshipped her. She used them like sponges. She'd have no time for the director, this officious man with his electronic cigarette and impatient manner. Yet you remember not to trust appearances; remember, too, that the director was a field agent once, just like you. To survive the sephirot one must be more than one thing at a time. We pass them like ants, crawling on the edge of a knife. A line from a film you must have once seen, you think.

"What happened to your parents?"

"I was told they died."

You see La Méduse lean forward then. Her face is an idolatrous mask.

"Told?"

You never really knew your parents. You remember your mother as a warm, all-engulfing presence, your father as a smell, a lift in the air, a squeal of delight. You yourself never had children. What had the poet said? The gate of the dead is open, and we pass?

"They vanished in the Blighted Zone," Bar-Hillel says. Licks a finger, turns a page. How you begin to loathe the man. "Is that correct?"

"So I was told. Later."

Ursalim. Jerusalem. Yerushalaim. The City of Peace. Which, in a way, is a name that became appropriate. You think of it then: the black hole of inexplicable devastation on its plateau, nestled between the mountains. A place of utter desolation where once a city stood, where once people lived and fought. A nothing now. A crack between the worlds.

"They'd lost their family in the Small Holocaust," you say, to fill in the silence. "They were obsessed with what had happened. Who was responsible. Where the people went. They kept going back, to the edges, the border. Maybe one day they went too far, and fell over the edge."

"It's what attracted us to you," Bar-Hillel says. "You were already living on the border, you just didn't know it."

You shrug. From the air, Ursalim is a black mirror of faultless volcanic glass. What caused it—who was behind the attack—nobody knows. Flights avoid it. The perimeter is supposed to be guarded, but how, or why? Only the desperate go to the border, and too many of them never come back.

There is peace now, all across this region: the city's last gift. All its holy places are gone.

"Who made the initial approach?" Bar-Hillel says; like it doesn't say so in his file. But you play along, of course. There are protocols. There are always protocols and they must always be observed.

"It was me, actually," Hashimi says, startled, perhaps, from some inner reverie. He glares at Bar-Hillel as though to say, *Can we speed this along?*

But Bar-Hillel is going nowhere fast. Licks a finger, turns a page. "Ah, yes," he says. "I see that is indeed so. The director himself?"

"He wasn't director then," you say.

"Up-and-coming," Bar-Hillel says, perhaps with a touch of bitterness in his voice. "He was up-and-coming."

You seem to remember Bar-Hillel was Hashimi's superior,

for a time. But Hashimi was well connected; he was a Hashemite, after all. Everyone knew he would be appointed, sooner or later.

And you remember his approach to you. That day at the university library, poring over ancient, crumbling pulp magazines, your fingers gloved in thin vinyl; staring at faded illustrations of spaceships landing on alien worlds, at words in that curious Hebrew block script, written in an obsolete typeface. His soft footsteps, the smell of French aftershave and cigarettes, his cough, until you looked up and he stared down at you, curious.

"Nur Al-Hussaini?" he said.

"Yes?"

"Could you come with me, please?"

That flash of his ID; a move you learned, later, yourself. It showed nothing, the ID. It was the gesture itself that signified.

You closed the magazine; carefully. You put it away. You removed your gloves. Finally, you stood. You looked him over, found nothing in him to stand out, to set him apart. He blended. In a strange way, it was like staring into a mirror.

You followed him out of curiosity. Into a quiet reading room, and he shut the door. "What is this about?" you said. He ignored you. He asked you questions, about yourself. You answered. You sensed that he already knew the answers, though he did not use folders, the way Bar-Hillel does.

Then he asked you if you thought the world was real.

12.

In the time since, you have seen many impossible things. You have seen the white towers of Kang Diz Huxt rise into the yellow sky under the broken moon, and you have navigated, masked and armed, the green gaseous swamps of Samaria where the Awful Ones live. You have a scar on your arm, from a knife attack: a drunken crusader at an inn in Outremer. You have heard the restless dead call to each other across the night in mist-shrouded Canaan, their voices like those of lost nightingales.

"What do you mean?" you asked Hashimi. You looked up at him with guileless eyes, though in your stomach ants crawled and gnawed at the delicate lining. You saw or heard in him something unknown yet half-remembered, like a dream you once had, which faded with the morning. How could the world not be real? You were born to it, its light met your eyes the first time you opened them and looked. The world is real, hermetically sealed upon itself. To imagine otherwise is to indulge in fantasy, to want escape.

And yet you never believed it. Not truly. You'd stare at walls and imagine them transparent, picture yourself crossing them as though they were nothing more than invisible lines. What lay beyond the walls? Anything. Everything.

And Professor Hashimi said, "I can't tell you. But I could show you."

Was there ever a worse line? Did you believe him? You looked into his eyes and saw nothing there.

La Méduse stirs. "She did what?" she says.

"She turned me down," Professor Hashimi says, by the window, his demeanour sour.

"Why, child?" La Méduse says. You stare at her with some hostility. Who is she to call you that, you who have been across the sephirot, you who have swum in the warm depths of the Middle Sea and heard the Nephilim cry, imprisoned in the volcanic vents, you who trekked across the Great Salt Marshes of the Egyptian Empire's province of once-great Retjenu?

Why? you think. Yet it is not uncommon. You yourself have done your share of recruitment approaches. Come up to a promising candidate, and looked at them with those same clear, guileless eyes, and offered them the question like a sacrifice.

Do you think the world is real?

To even ask the question, to acknowledge it, is to accept its possibility. One cannot live easily with the idea. It is better to put up walls. To draw borders. Walls to keep out. Walls to keep in. To *contain*.

"It is not uncommon," Bar-Hillel says, as though confirming your thoughts. Turns a page, looks up; gives you the ghost of a smile, meant to be reassuring.

"Yet we persevered," Professor Hashimi says.

"Why?" La Méduse says again, sharply. You get the feeling she does not entirely approve of you.

"I disappeared," you tell her. Your voice is soft and calm. It leaves no trace of itself. "On my way to the souq, to Al-Hamidiyah, the world suddenly tilted and changed. The street lay ruined, corpses littered the street. The sky turned red and there was heavy smoke, it was hard to see. I heard sirens in the distance, the sound of swift planes flying low overhead. A young boy ran to me. One of his arms was missing. He looked at me wordlessly, with a sort of wonder. 'My sister, my sister,' he kept saying. 'Uchti, uchti.' It only lasted a moment. Then he faded away and was gone."

"Six independent witnesses confirmed it," Professor Hashimi says. His voice has the tiniest tone of professional satisfaction. "She was gone for just over ten seconds. She was a natural. I said it, straightaway, when they wanted to remove her name from the candidacy lists. I said it, didn't I? She was a natural."

"You did," Bar-Hillel says, patiently. "That is on the record."

"I had your card," you say, with startled recall. You had all but forgotten it. Your first time. That careless slip, like a woman stepping on ice in the street. The moment of lost balance, the shock as you fall. This isn't supposed to happen. You remember it, the smell of that world: the smell you came to associate with war. A scent so foreign to you then. You looked around yourself in mute bewilderment. What was this place? The airplane flying overhead; for just a moment you caught sight of a flag on the engine: red, blue and white, a five-sided star in a circle, adorned with stripes. Why were they attacking? What had happened to turn Damascus into this battleground, this vision of the apocalypse? Then the boy, out of nowhere, that stump of an arm waving, pale face and dark hair stained with red dust, and those awful eyes that saw you and yet, perhaps, didn't: which seemed to impose upon your person someone else, some resident of this netherworld which you—hallucinated?

What happened? Did you fall in the street? Did you crack your head? For this can't be real, this vision of Damascus, this boy—who stares at you, with these strange, startling green eyes, eyes like yours, and his lips move, *my sister, my sister*, and you, you tried to ward him off, your hand raised, *no, no*, and he stared at you, and behind him the dust rose, outlining the ghostly shapes of masked men rising out of the ruined buildings with guns in their hands, and the boy—

Faded, silently, and the world rushed back in, the sound of birds and an old Diana Haddad song on a radio somewhere, nearby, and the hum of the cars on the road.

Did you think you were going mad?

"Excuse me?"

"Did you think you were going mad?" Bar-Hillel says, patiently.

"No."

"No?"

"No."

You stare at him coolly. Professor Hashimi chuckles. Even La Méduse forms a smile, though it is like a crack appearing in a cement wall, an alarming sight. Bar-Hillel frowns. Turns a page with a dry rustle.

Your life, bound into a single dossier.

"I had the director's—"

"Of course, he wasn't director then—"

"Yes, yes," Hashimi says, impatient. Puffs on his electronic device. Turns a disapproving eye on his deputy. "We've been through this, Bar-Hillel."

"Of course, sir."

"Professor Hashimi's card," you say. "No, I did not think I was mad. I believed in what happened. It was real. Somehow, I had stumbled into another world. A parallel one to ours. An alternate one. It was the same city, but different."

"So you came here."

"Ycs."

"And what happened?"

"This time," you say, with a faint smile, "I listened."

You're smiling, but you are beginning to grow impatient. What do they want? You wish they would get to the point.

"And then?" Bar-Hillel says.

"You know all this! It's all in there, in your, your *dossier*," you say.

"Indulge me," he says.

"What is this, a trip down memory lane?"

But of course you remember. You remember even as you try to forget.

13.

The training, first, though. The Border Agency has its facilities near Sidon, in the Lebanon. Here you were given no further answers, only tools. Arms, a thing for which your people had little use otherwise: how to fire a pistol, how to shoot a long-range rifle, how to assemble and disassemble a gun. You spent hours on the shooting range, you and these other, anonymous agents, as plain and unremarkable as you were. You discovered you were a fair shot with a gun, that you did not mind its weight in your hands, that you enjoyed the sense of recoil, the ping of a discarded cartridge, the smell of gunpowder. You knew, logically, that you might be required to use it, that there was a reason for this exercise. You contemplated the idea of wounding or killing another person. It should have been repugnant to you, you thought. Violence—arms—these were forbidden after the Small Holocaust, and you were taught to regard them in horror, with a special loathing like that reserved for carrion. And yet, when you pictured it, when you imagined aiming the gun, you felt nothing, or so, at least, you told yourself.

During this time, too, you underwent constant psychological evaluation. Others dropped out, disappeared day by day: each morning there were fewer of you in the dormitories. The mornings were cool and bright and the nights long and warm: you learned judo, karate, krav maga, Persian wrestling, Egyptian stick fighting. You learned to use a knife, construct a bomb, pick locks, use codes. You learned languages, but some of them were unknown and some strange, mutated: forms of Hebrew or Arabic strained through foreign filters, with unknown words, bizarre forms of speech.

You learned to read maps, even as they told you, repeatedly, that maps could not be trusted. You picked the locks off doors, only to be told that some doors mustn't be opened. You learned to fight, only to be told that fighting is ultimately futile.

"What is it all for?" you asked one of the instructors, a woman veiled in fine black silk.

"We're just trying to keep you alive," she told you. "Now, concentrate, please. Flowing punch, scissor punch, eagle hand, and kick, and again . . ."

That year you wintered in the Lebanon, as the leaves fell from the trees and the days grew short. The sunlight was white on the hills. In this light you began to see doubles; over the peaceful town of Sidon war planes appeared; in the old city, when you walked, a car bomb shook the ancient flagstones, screams cut the day to ribbons. When you blinked, all traces of such violence were gone, erased; in the sunlight the same schoolkids ran laughing who mere moments ago lay bloodied and still on the stones. A young man passed you, smiling, who moments before wore a vest of explosives. In the sky seagulls flew, crying, streaks of white against blue.

"History is not one thing," an instructor told you. It was spring, and the air was filled with the humming of bees. You had become better at holding the visions at bay, controlling them, so that at times it seemed to you that you could simply slip, from one reality to the next, almost without trying. "It is a tapestry, like an old Persian rug, multiple strands of stories, criss-crossing. Some are strong, central. Some fray at the ends, or fall off altogether. The places where they meet we call a crosshatch; they are peopled by shadows and doubles. They are places not to be trusted. Stories get muddled easily there."

"I don't understand," you said, and the instructor said, "You will have to go there."

At that a horror of a sort caught at your heart; but also excitement. There were only two of you left, by then.

The journey came in the summer. You took the slow train from Beirut to Jaffa, going inland past snow-capped Jabal Haramun, through forests of pine and oak, down to the hot shimmering haze of the Mediterranean coast. Here again Hebrew became prevalent in the air, and in Jaffa Harbour you sat at an outdoor fish restaurant run by a man from Syria, where tourists gathered in a cloud of foreign perfumes, a multiplicity of tongues. There was only you by then.

"I told them, didn't I?" Professor Hashimi says.

"Yes, yes already," Bar-Hillel says, sourly, and turns a page.

The next morning you travelled up, the land changing into hills, then mountains. You reached Bab al-Wad, the Gate of the Valley, a road that sharply ascends up to the Jerusalem mountains. Here there was a manned post, and a gate, barring your way.

You disembarked. The soldiers were young and seemed bored. Traffic seldom came this way, and when it did, it was politely but firmly turned away. You waited, in the shade of a pine tree whose needles lay soft as brush hairs on the ground.

"But it went wrong, didn't it?" La Méduse says. Her voice raises goosebumps on your arms. Her voice is as soft as pine needles. It demands your memory, everything you wanted gone, erased.

And you think: We all have the people we have lost in the passing.

"Yes," you say. "Yes, it went wrong."

But you do not think of what came later: the soldiers, Anwar's body shuddering as the bullets bit into his flesh, ravenously, like hungry dogs; you do not think of dark blood running down old white stone streets. You do not think of his shadow, cast against the wall in the setting sun, his shadow, falling.

You think of the smell of pine resin, and of a sky white with clouds, dotted blue, a sky like a comfortable blanket. Then he was there, as though he had always been there, moving so smoothly from one state of being to another that it took your breath away.

"I'm Anwar," he said. "You must be Nur."

His hair was cut short, his eyes a dark green. He was like a young olive tree, you thought then, a sapling. He took your hand and held it. His hand was warm, like bark. He said, "Are you ready?" and you nodded, with more confidence than you felt.

You slipped away like shadows. The soldiers were no longer there, their outpost gone as though it had never existed. Already you were slipping sidewise, shifting through fragment-worlds, splinter-shadows, adjacencies. The sensation of it was like passing through a cold fine mist. You walked on foot up the steep mountain road. Around you cars suddenly swarmed, a foreign make, the drivers honking furiously: then they were gone and in their place there was nothing, a single silence lying over hills on which no human foot had ever stepped, the sun shining brightly over coral peonies, Spanish brooms and Mesopotamian irises, until the sun fell suddenly and night came, and two moons hung, briefly, in the sky, then disappeared as the road expanded into an eight-lane highway where cars shark-finned and sleek roared in every direction at such speeds that sonic booms rocked the daytime—

On and on Anwar went and you followed, through would have beens and could have beens, until the rotting skeletons of old armoured cars began to appear on the sides of the road and the air filled with smoke and car exhaust, with drivers leaning out of their windows cursing, and a ruined fort came up on the hill, and you saw a van stop, and Jewish averchim clad in black poured out, placed giant speakers in the middle of the road and began to dance, to the echoing beat of machine music, dancing and clapping and running between the stalled cars, their zealous joy infectious—

Until they, too, were gone abruptly. A small red sun rose momentarily in the east and fell, too quickly, and for a moment you saw Ursalim as a city of white, delicate, towering stone, a city of the future with its minarets and skyscrapers reaching for the sky, and airships floated majestically between the buildings, like fat flies—but what flag they carried you did not know: you had never seen its like before and never did again.

Then all was gone, and you had crested the hill and looked down, on Ursalim: a terrible plain of black obsidian stone, smooth as a mirror, in which nothing lived and nothing moved, a black sea which had swallowed what had once been home to countless generations of humanity.

Jerusalem, the city to which all other cities are but imperfect acts of mimicry: a city in which stories are told. They are stories of bloodshed and stories of wars, of love, of faith—

Erased, in this world, with one awful act, turned into stone, a history suspended.

"Who did this?" you whispered. You held on to his hand.

Anwar turned, shrugged.

"We did. They did. Does it matter?"

"No," you said. Or perhaps you only thought you spoke. The sight of that barren plain silenced you. Slowly you made your way down into the city, and as you did the shifting began once more: in earnest this time.

"You were only meant to shift locally," La Méduse says, taking, you think, an unholy interest in all of this. "So what happened?"

Bar-Hillel coughs and turns a page. No one speaks. Hashimi stares out of the window.

It wasn't Anwar, you want to explain. It was you. It was your fault.

At first he led, through the borders between the sephirot: a cold tingling sensation, dry ice, resistance. Then you took the lead. All your training had come to this. You led, and Anwar followed, holding your hand like a child. You pushed through the membrane between worlds, wanting nothing more than to escape the black stone: it melted away and a rough village formed, and camels dozed in the shade of a palm tree; then came white stone walls, towers, the call of a muezzin from a mosque. A green sky and a fallow moon.

"Slow down," Anwar said, "slow down," but you kept pushing, exploring now, giddy with the power of it, this ability to move between worlds.

You willed it and it happened: things moved differently, time branched, and you passed rapidly onto a Jerusalem in which *Homo sapiens palestinus* built shelters in the mountain caves, a group of them rising suddenly out of snow and sleet and fog, so that you gasped and Anwar reached for a weapon, but they were not interested in you but in the Neanderthals behind you, small and squat, wrapped in furs, holding stone knives as the two humanoid species converged; this was history, you thought, this was real, not a fantasy: there had once been different species of men, but they all died; though in some other worlds they lived still.

You pushed through, and through, and *through*, until, for a moment, you glimpsed, from just the corner of your eye, the Ein Sof: the world beyond worlds, where the last door stands. But Anwar screamed, "Stop!" and you fell sidewise, jolted, and onto a city street; and time stopped, and started again—

"Oh, *that* place," La Méduse says. "The place where they never stopped fighting?"

"Which one," Professor Hashimi says, and unexpectedly laughs, a sound without humour, an academic scoring a point. And you think—they know which world it was, there is a purpose here—

Jerusalem, on a mid-afternoon outside the Dung Gate. Cars drove past, and people stared at you, suspiciously. Anwar looked left and right: his troubled face told you more than words.

"What is it?" you said, but then you saw the soldiers.

They wore olive-coloured uniforms and carried assault rifles, comfortably, as they searched the people coming in through the gate, going into the Old City.

Not all, you saw. But those who looked like you, perhaps.

You saw an old man stopped, carrying two bags of shopping. An argument ended with the man pushed on his stomach to the ground, his face pressed into the dirt. His bags fell from his hands and you saw an orange roll, roll until it came to a rest at your feet. The man was handcuffed, hauled away: a bruise was forming on his torn cheek and he was crying.

Anwar tugged your hand. "We need to go, now," he said, but it was too late. The soldiers saw you. You saw the bored contempt in their eyes, you wondered what they made of you. They were young, as young as you.

"Shift," Anwar said. "Hurry."

"Stop!" one of the soldiers called. "Raise your hands!"

You couldn't move. You stared down at the orange, fascinated. You wanted to pick it up. You were enchanted by everything around you, this real, living Jerusalem in the place where that terrible black rock had been. And the soldier spoke Hebrew.

"You messed up," La Méduse says.

"It wasn't her fault," Professor Hashimi objects, but mildly, without conviction. "She was a novice, Anwar was an experienced agent. He should have handled the situation."

"We keep making the mistake of thinking the sephirot are real," La Méduse says, a hint of contempt. "We let them trap us."

How could you have explained it then?

Already your memories were changing.

You were Nur, of Hebron, yes: a second-year student at Al-Quds University, studying literature and history; travelling from Hebron, you were used to police stops, army check posts, to the indignity of travel. You were used to feeling afraid for who you were, to avoiding crowds, to hiding your face. Your brother died in the Intifada; your father was home with a stroke, your mother taking care of him.

What was that other world, the fantasy world you sometimes dreamed of? Ursalim, where another Nur could travel freely by train from Haifa to Damascus, where she was free.

It was just a fantasy, a way of escaping a world where you were, eternally, a refugee.

You saw Anwar was affected, too. He knew this world. Later, you read his file.

You found out he had spent time there, had an identity, a past.

He tried to shift you. You resisted.

The soldiers came, boredom replaced with hostile suspicion. Anwar pushed you away as he pulled out his gun.

"He panicked," Professor Hashimi says. "It happens."

"He was wanted, wasn't he?" La Méduse says. "He was wanted, in that other place."

"It's on the forbidden list," Bar-Hillel says, primly.

"But we keep agents there," she says.

"To observe. To report. Nothing more."

"He got *involved*."

"Sooner or later," Professor Hashimi says, "we all have to get involved."

You remember the bark of the guns. Dark blood on white stone. The smell of an orange.

You barely even knew Anwar.

Yet his needless death marked you: only the first of many.

14.

"We need you to go back there," Professor Hashimi says. "Back to that place. For a little while, at least."

You stare at them, at each of them in turn, mute, waiting. La Méduse barks a laugh.

"Not to Jerusalem," she says. "To Berlin."

"Why?"

"There is a man there we want you to follow."

"Who is he?"

"He is a man who fell between the sephirot; now he is going back to his world, though he does not yet know it."

You are outwardly calm. Yet you think of that other world, how it reeks with hatred. But you have been to other sephirot, and you have seen that men and women are the same wherever in the alternities you go.

"Why would I agree to do that?" you say. They ignore you. Bar-Hillel wets his finger, turns a page, frowns.

"His name's Tirosh," Bar-Hillel says. "Lior Tirosh."

"So?" you say. "It's just a name."

"Your dissertation," Bar-Hillel says. "The one you abandoned. On those science fiction writers."

"Yes?"

"I asked you if any of them ever predicted the Small Holocaust. You didn't answer."

You bark a laugh. "What does it matter? They were just stories. I told you. They envisioned a thousand futures, all of them improbable. They were hacks, who worked for money and always stayed poor. Any sensible person would have quit and got a job. They just kept on dreaming, getting paid per page or per word or perhaps."

Hashimi chuckles, politely. Bar-Hillel frowns.

"They didn't predict the future," you say. "They wrote warnings about what the future could become."

And you think—were it not for the Small Holocaust, would your world be just like that other place?

"Still," Bar-Hillel says.

"What?"

"You still haven't answered my question."

"Yes," you say, unwillingly. Knowing you have been pushed into a trap. "One. He wrote a story called 'Unholy Land.' It was published in volume thirteen of a Hebrew science fiction magazine called *Grotesqa*."

"Published *Before*?" La Méduse says, sharply.

"Yes."

They already know all this, you think. They must have known all along.

"What happened to him After?"

"No one knows. He disappeared. So many disappeared, After."

"What was his name?" La Méduse says. They are all looking at you. Waiting. Judging.

You say, unwillingly: "His name was Tirosh," into their silence.

"Tirosh?" La Méduse says.

"Lior Tirosh," Bar-Hillel confirms, and turns a page, all but tutting.

Professor Hashimi turns to the wall, with great intensity; as though still hoping for a window.

And you remember Haifa, the second-hand bookshops, and Mr. Katz's apartment, on the hill above the ancient harbour. Mr. Katz's apartment was a temple of books. Old paperbacks hid in glass cabinets, piled on the floor in-between, sat in boxes, winked behind flowerpots, rested on the windowsill. The walls were covered in yellowing posters: of monsters and spaceships, djinns and bronzed Amazonian warriors, weird creatures and the views of strange, other worlds. . . .

You sat there for hours, as the sun chased the shadows across the books until it sank beyond the sea. Until you found it.

The story appeared in volume thirteen of *Grotesqa*.

In the story, you read of a woman who wanders across the Middle East, restless for a kind of truth. She travels back to Palestine, or Israel, the land of her birth, which she has not seen for many years. A kind of holocaust has taken place in the country's past; Tirosh avoided describing it in detail, but hinted that Jerusalem no longer existed, and that the nature of its destruction and the amount of pain it had caused brought, after a few years, a peace born of shared victimhood, creating in this way a new Middle East that collectively mourned Jerusalem. In a bookshop in Haifa the woman finds an old pulp magazine. Inside that magazine is a story, called "Unholy Land." She begins to read the story, but realises that her search was futile, that the tale's author never existed, that fantasy offers no real escape, and she lets the magazine drop, unread, from her fingers, and she leaves.

"What was the name of the woman in the story?" La Méduse says.

"Which one?" you say. "The first or the second?"

"Either. Both."

"Nur," you say. La Méduse smiles, the cat who got the cream. "She's called Nur."

"We need you to go to that other place, to Berlin," Professor Hashimi says, coming back to himself with alacrity. "Only for a short while. He's a slipper, we think. He is called back to his own world. We believe."

"We think," you say, aping him. "We believe. What do you *know*?"

"The sephirot are under threat," Hashimi says. "The borders are breaking down. They are becoming *porous*. We think this is by design. There is a mind at work here. We need you to find it."

"Where is he from, this Tirosh?" you say. "What is his world?"

Hashimi waves his hand, dismissively. "Some never-been," he says. "A place where the Jews had built themselves a country in Africa."

Bar-Hillel raises his head. The look in his eyes is vulnerable, wounded. La Méduse coughs. Hashimi mumbles something. Perhaps an apology.

"*Africa?*" you say.

"It would be like a holiday," Hashimi says, encouragingly. "The warm weather, the clean air. It would do you good to be back at it, Nur. You've been too long away."

"What happened in Smyrna was not your fault," Bar-Hillel says. La Méduse just stares at you, her ancient eyes. They remind you of the Sphinx, in that other place.

"What are they doing?" you say. Whoever *they* are.

"Death. Blood. They are fashioning a key, to open a gate."

"Why Tirosh?" you say.

"We don't know, but he is part of the pattern. Follow Tirosh, find the instigator."

"He is not the same Tirosh who lived here," you say. "At most he is a doppelgänger. A shadow."

"He writes, too."

You're not sure who says that. La Méduse stirs.

"I read one of his books," she says. "It was a mystery. A mystery why I read it!"

She laughs, a sound as dry as paint chipping off walls.

"Tirosh is not the issue here," Hashimi says, self-importantly. He repeats himself: "Follow Tirosh. Find the instigator."

"And then?" you say. Knowing you've lost. Knowing they've hooked you, that you would go back into the field, if only to prove what happened in Smyrna didn't matter, that everyone makes mistakes: even you.

They look at you, the three of them. Judges and jury.

"Find him," Hashimi says, and, simply: "then kill him."

"Doesn't it always come down to that?" La Méduse says.

Bar-Hillel says nothing. He jots down a note and tears off the page and hands it to you. You take it without looking.

"For Accounts," he says, with a slight apologetic air. "Make sure you keep the receipts. You know how they get, up there."

You pocket the slip. They look at you expectantly. You look for a window, find none.

There must always be a death, you think, now. Sooner or later we are all called to account.

"You better go," Professor Hashimi says. "Or you'll miss your flight."

15.

The world shifts as you sit on the plane. From Damascus to Berlin on a Lufthansa flight with the sky reddening in the west. From above, the world appears unchanged. You slip from one history to another as though changing your pyjamas. The passengers mutate and change, the seats become slightly more uncomfortable, the air hostesses remain more or less the same. It is a curious facet of alternity travel, the interchangeability of airplane staff. You recline in the seat, look out of the window at that world, one of the verboten spheres, where history took a wrong turn, somehow. The in-flight entertainment system is more primitive than that of where you come from. You turn on the news, on RTL a blonde presenter talks animatedly about the ongoing war in Syria, a car bomb in Iraq, American airplanes attacking targets near Mosul. When you land, security forces question you at length, your body and possessions scanned for weapons and contraband, but at last you are allowed to leave. Berlin, which you have seen in many iterations, where you studied, married, loved. Once you slipped, walking Friedrich-strasse, and saw the street in ruins, Russian tanks patrolling through a scene of apocalyptic devastation. Berlin fragments each time you cross its streets: when you pass the Brandenburg Gate a sidestep into a fragment world brings with it visions of the place lit up brightly, red swastika flags hanging from the gate's entablature, red-faced beefy men cheering at the sides of the road as a motorcade goes past. Mostly you have learned to control the slippage, though it is harder in Berlin, where many of the homeless that you pass, shivering in shop entrances, have the lost, hollow-eyed look of those who fell between the cracks, who woke up one morning in a world as like, yet so unlike, their own, in which everything that was once familiar had become alien and strange.

Your contact in Berlin, in this world, is Ahmed. A young art student, he occupies a crumbling old house in Kreuzberg turned into a sprawling commune. Outside there are coffee shops and bars and galleries, inside the house a permanent party seems to be in motion. In the kitchen a British punk band plays unplugged, the living room has been turned into a modern art installation by a Bulgarian artist, there's pop art in the toilets and the air's thick with hash.

You find shelter in a room occupied only by mannequins. Unclothed, they have perfect plastic skins. Their eyes stare at you. You ask Ahmed for a briefing.

"I heard about Smyrna," he says, sympathetically, and you try not to strangle him. "It wasn't your fault."

"Tell me about Tirosh," you say, and he nods.

"He's lived in Berlin for a number of years," he says. "Originally from Israel. He's well established here. A writer, mostly of detective novels. He won a small award a few years back, for a weird political novel called *Osama*. You know, after Osama bin Laden."

"Who?" you say, blankly.

"You know, Al-Qaeda and that?"

"Is that a band?"

"Never mind," Ahmed says, resigned. "Anyway, I don't know much else about him. I did get hold of his itinerary, though. That wasn't hard. He's flying to Tel Aviv tomorrow, or that's what my contact at the airport says. And he's giving a talk tonight at a bookshop just around the corner, as it happens, on Bergmannstrasse. A place called Otherland Bookshop. They specialise in science fiction and fantasy, that sort of thing. I got us a couple of tickets, if you wanted to go. They were free, anyway."

All you want to do right then is shower, change, lie down for a year or a thousand years. Ahmed's a sleeper agent; he's been in this world too long, has begun to accept it as a primary. While the Border Agency has decreed this place verboten, the term may be misleading. It means no unauthorised travel is allowed, but such places bear close attention, and for those purposes a small network of long-term agents—sleepers, moles—has been set up, to witness, report and provide assistance to active agents such as yourself, if and when the need arises. Reluctantly you study it—its September 11s and Gaza bombardments, Afghanistan invasions and Occupy demonstrations, private space flights and banker bonuses, its oil spills and Crimean wars, its doped up cyclists, software billionaires, Christianists and global epidemics and tsunamis and robots on Mars: in short, a world like any other world.

You watch TV. In all the worlds there is TV, and it is always the same, a way in which the world is told to its people. You watch bombings and destruction, but they are far away and on a screen, reduced, distanced; and after a time you do what all people do, and turn it off.

In the evening you stroll to Bergmannstrasse. This is a prosperous world of bright yellows and reds, cafés with their patrons spilling onto the pavement outside, jazz in the air, the smell of hashish—much as you remember your own sojourn in the other Berlin, the one in which the Nazis never came to power. Here they did, for a time. This is the nature of the sephirot, where a careless side-step away into a fragment-alternity would reveal a broken-down desolation where a bustling street, just a moment ago, stood. There are places where dinosaurs still roam the Earth. . . .

There is no queue outside the bookshop. Inside, shelves spill over with bright-coloured paperbacks in German and English, their lurid covers depicting mermaids and exploding suns, spaceships and dragons. A man stands on an alien planet under triple suns, a wide-brimmed hat covering his face, a futuristic ray-gun in his hand. Tirosh's own books, piled on a table by the entrance, have the dowdy appearance of a vagrant trying too hard to pass for a gentleman, as though the designers themselves could not quite decide if the books they were working on were literature or trash. You suppose the truth might be something in between, not nearly as literary as Tirosh perhaps likes to think, and yet not nearly entertaining enough to merit him the sort of commercial success enjoyed by those who truly embrace escapism.

The talk is sparsely attended. Chairs are arranged in rows at the back of the shop, and on them perch, in ones and twos, such people as could be expected to attend such an event, which is to say the misfits, the in-betweeners, those for whom life, on its own, is not fulfilling enough, who seek completion of a sort in fantasy: in books.

You sit at the back, perched for flight. You watch the people who are here to attend the talk, recognising in some of them, in their lost, bewildered looks, the mark of those who slipped away one day. People who do not belong, who lost their world.

A man in the corner looks vaguely familiar. Black, receding hair. A long face, unsmiling. A crazed, unhinged look in his eyes. But he should have had a moustache, you think, with a sudden shiver. He should have had a funny little moustache, but this man is clean-shaven. Just another lost soul, just another man out of history.

"Years ago," Tirosh says, "I dreamed I was in my father's house." He has a hesitant manner of speaking. His eyes don't quite meet the audience's. His fingers move constantly, as though untying imaginary notes. "I woke up and all was just as I remembered. It had been years since I last set foot in the house, and yet I knew each floorboard and windowsill, each creak and every groan in the pipes and in the walls. I woke up in my own bed. The moon shone through the window, casting the room in a silver glow. And I was afraid."

Tirosh takes a sip of water.

"Everything was the same," he says. "But everything was entirely different. I knew the house but it was not the same house. I became convinced of that. I got out of my bed though I was afraid. I could not say why I was afraid. I opened my door and stepped into the corridor. The same old floorboard creaked where it had always creaked. As a child I would step over it, carefully, and so I instinctively began to do so again, yet thought better of it. I listened to the house, to the whispering of the pipes, the creaks in the walls. They spoke a language, it seemed to me. It was a language I knew as intimately as my own, yet at the same time, I had never heard it before. The house I knew spoke a foreign tongue. I walked its corridors, opened and closed doors into rooms I knew and that yet were entirely foreign. This was not my house. Its occupants had departed, and the house lay still, waiting, as though it expected them to come back, though many years had passed since their exile. How could this be? I thought. How can there be one house, and yet two houses? How can there be one house, and two sets of memories, two languages, different names for every which thing that stood in that house?"

Tirosh takes another sip. Someone in the third row farts, quietly, and startles himself awake. Besides you, Ahmed fidgets.

"I searched for my father, but the house was large, and the rooms, though they seemed empty, echoed with the sounds of remembered departures and occupations. I wanted to ask my father, How have you come here? What price did you pay, for this house? But he didn't answer."

A blonde woman in the front row raises her hand. She has large bangles on her arm that shake and chime as they slide down. "You are speaking of the Israeli-Palestinian conflict, of course," she says, with authority.

Tirosh glances sideways, as though searching for a door.

"I am not sure if 'conflict' is the right word in this context," he says, but gently, "as it suggests two equal sides, which I am not sure is the case—but to answer your question, I am speaking metaphorically. Or rather, I am trying to explain what it is we do when we construct stories of alternative realities. What we do is literalise the metaphor, so to speak. We construct a world of make-believe in order to consider how our own world is constructed, is told. You see?"

"I think you are a self-hating Jew," the woman says, and her large earrings jingle in rebuke as she shakes her head in disapproval. Tirosh doesn't reply: he takes a sip of water, shrugs.

"Any other questions?" he says. There's a sorrow in his eyes, you think. Something private, nothing to do with literature or politics, but it is there in his every gesture, it is there in his eyes: pain, a loss.

"What motivates you to write?" asks a hedgehog-like man, leaning forward, hands folded neatly in his lap.

Tirosh hesitates.

"It used to be anger," he says, at last.

"And now?"

"Money," Tirosh says, with a small dispirited laugh. "That, and it's been too long since I've had a real job."

The hedgehog leans back, disappointed. Later, you wait in the small line as Tirosh signs his books. You pick up a couple—*The Bride Wore a Shroud*, and *Death Becomes the Executioner*—and hold them. They are printed on cheap paper and the lurid covers glare at you, the rotting corpse bride and the skeletal executioner both grinning with a sort of ferocious despair.

"To . . . ?" Tirosh says, not looking up. The pen hovers between his fingers.

"Nur," you say. He writes:

To Nur, Best wishes—

And signs his name intelligibly.

"Have you ever," you say, and hesitate, then plunge on, "have you ever written a story called 'Unholy Land'?"

"Maybe I would have, once," he says. "But no, I'm afraid I never did. Maybe you have me confused with somebody else. To . . . ?" and you realise he is already speaking to the next person in the line.

You leave, with Ahmed grumbling by your side. In the morning you catch a taxi to the airport. When you see Tirosh again, in the line for the flight, it is clear he has no idea who you are.

PART FOUR

INTERROGATIONS

16.

By the time I'd found Barashi, the old man was three sheets to the wind, as the English say. Palestina, being land-locked, is hardly a nautical nation, nor are its people great drinkers, as a rule. Barashi was perched at the bar in the Hare & Coconut; his false teeth had slipped out at some point and lay in a disgusting puddle on the floor, and his gums moved incessantly, masticating as he swallowed half his words.

The pub itself was a dingy shithole of the sort favoured by bar stool revolutionaries and spineless conscientious objectors, that is, it was mostly filled at this time of night with students. I was not surprised to see, intermingled amongst them, some faces known to me from the native population. Sedition takes many forms, but I had always believed it was best to give it space, to contain it where it could be watched.

The Hare & Coconut was such a place, but it had outlasted its own usefulness. They knew we were watching and we knew that they knew, and so the closed-circuit system had shortened itself until nothing of significance took place in the pub and the only watcher remaining was the currently drunk specimen of former sergeant Amos Barashi.

I stooped down and picked up his teeth and handed them to him, wordlessly. He grinned at me with that horrid pink gummy mouth and stuck the teeth back in, sloppily. The bartender looked over, saw me and my men, and wisely made himself scarce. I could feel the hostility from the assembled drinkers.

Good kids, mostly, from good families, who had done their army service before entering university, and now regrettably explored radical politics as a means of finding their way. Most of them would grow out of it: graduate, get a job, cut their hair, do their annual service in the army reserves, raise a family.

In time all memories of their little interlude of faux-rebellion would fade, and they would become productive, tax-paying citizens, who would take their families for weekend getaways to little B&Bs on the lake, cheat on their husbands or wives with similarly disaffected middle-aged citizens, in hotels neither too cheap nor too expensive, on the edge of town, and on weekends would take their children to watch the football—Ararat City vs. Kisumu Lions FC, perhaps.

Barashi didn't care for any of this. He was a washed out drunk, twice divorced, a disgrace to the force. His son was a tax accountant in Johannesburg. His daughter lived in the Nakuru settlements, beyond the Green Line. She never came to see him and he, so far as I knew, never usually left the city.

He had a justified fear of the Mau Forest, for he had been offered a glimpse of what lies on the border, and it had scared the living daylights out of him.

Now he stared up at me with bleary eyes and whimpered my name, "Bloom . . . Bloom, old fellow. What are, what are you, you doing here?"

"Where is he?" I said. "Where is Tirosh?"

"Tirosh, Tirosh, he's—" He hiccupped and the smell that wafted from him was nauseating. "He's . . . left."

"What did you talk about?"

"He said he was looking for his, his niece," Barashi said. His shoulders slumped in resignation and he looked at me in drunken misery. "Bloom, I didn't . . . you didn't say to *follow* him."

"What did you do?" I said, disgusted. "Did you tell him about the Mau Mau, Barashi? Did you tell him about the ghosts in the forest?"

"I *saw* them, Bloom," he said. "They came out of nowhere! One moment the forest was empty and the next, three men and a woman stepped out, dressed in khaki uniforms, carrying guns. I killed them, Bloom. I killed them all!"

"I know, Barashi," I said. "You told me before."

"Afterwards," he said, "I went looking at the bodies. What was left of them. I found a strip of cloth, left whole. An armband, Bloom. A blood-stained armband. A black swastika in a white circle, on a red, red cloth. What were they, Bloom?"

"They were Nazis, Barashi," I told him.

He looked at me and laughed. "But there are no Nazis," he said. "There have been no Nazis since the Hitler assassination, and that was in '48."

"They were Nazis," I told him, sadly. "It was just that they were not from around here."

He looked at me with eyes filled with misery. His face said he did not know what I meant, but his eyes betrayed him. There is a knowledge one cannot erase: the impossible cannot be ignored once seen.

"The old general was angry," he whispered. "He told me to bury the bodies where no one would find them. And to burn the cloth, to burn any other sign that they were ever there."

"But you didn't."

"I kept it, Bloom. I kept the armband. What are Nazis, anyway, Bloom? We were not involved with the war in Europe. The Nazis never did a thing to us."

"No," I said. "No, they didn't." I patted him on the shoulder. He was not a bad man, it's just that he should never have gone into the forest and, once he did, should never have been allowed out again. "Not here. Not in this time and place."

"I don't understand, Bloom."

"Perhaps it's better that way. About Tirosh. Where did he go?"

"I saw him step into the bookshop, across the road," he said. "Waxman's. I fucked his sister once. Waxman's." He barked a coarse, delighted laugh. "Ha! She had an ass on her, Bloom. That was some ass."

I waited him out. He traced lines of moisture in spilled beer on the countertop. "Died of the cancer, last I heard."

I motioned for the bartender. He was standing at the end of the bar answering questions in a tired, patient voice, like it was an unpleasant but routine task for him. He came over and brought Barashi a drink, wordlessly. He raised his eyebrows. I shook my head. He shrugged. I put a note on the counter and he took it and made it go away. I seldom drink, but I admire a man who can conduct his business in silence.

"Where *is* Deborah Glass?" I said.

"Sir?"

"Your name is Nir Clore," I said. "You served in Pelican Unit on the Maasai Mara border area, and later in the Disputed Zones?"

He sneered at me. "They are all Disputed Zones," he said.

"You were a good soldier," I said.

"We're all good soldiers," he said. "This is what Jews are now. This is what we've become. *Soldiers.*" He said it with contempt.

"So now you serve beer to drunks?" I said. "Is that how you want to make your living?"

"It's an honest living," he said. "It's better than some."

I let it go. I was used to their disdain.

"You know this Deborah?"

"It's the same I told your man earlier. She sometimes drinks here."

"He is not my man."

"No? Then what is he to you?"

"He is a person of interest," I said.

"Then God have mercy on his soul," he said, with fervour.

"I would like to find her," I said.

He shrugged. "Talk to the trees," he said. "They might tell you. Or ask the wind. I just work here."

"We both know that's not true, though, don't we," I said. "You're a Nandi sympathiser, Clore. You organise little political gatherings in your flat, when you think no one notices. It's in Golda Heights, isn't it? It's a nice area. On the outskirts of town, a green place, plenty of trees, a nice view of the sunset. You can sometimes see giraffes and rhinos in the distance."

He didn't say a word and I liked him for it.

"I couldn't afford it myself," I said. "Not on a public servant's salary. Your parents are rich?"

"That's none of your business," he said, tightly.

"No," I said. "But I was curious so I looked into it. You have a three-bedroom flat in Golda Heights, don't you, Nir?"

His fingers tightened on the bar, their tips growing white as the blood fled.

"It's a nice place to raise children," I said, quietly. He looked up at me then. I had his attention; all of it.

"Plenty of parks, swings to push the kids," I said. "Good schools."

"I suppose," he said. "I haven't given it much thought."

"Your girlfriend," I said. "Rose?"

He pulled back from the bar. His hand edged for a bottle. I watched his hand.

"She's positively glowing, these days," I said, quietly. I was ready for him when he raised the bottle. He smashed it on the bar and the sharp tang of alcohol filled the air. Broken glass showered Barashi, who yelped and fell off his stool.

Nir Clore raised the bottle, jagged edges pointed at my throat. He went in for the kill, but I'd been waiting. I punched him in the throat and brought my hand down hard, smashing his arm into the counter, breaking his wrist.

The bottle fell from his fingers and rolled to the floor and shattered. I grabbed the back of his head and threw his face on the counter, hard. When he came up the countertop was covered in broken glass and fresh blood. He stood there for a moment, swaying, winded, then he dropped to the floor.

Every man has a breaking point.

My men went behind the counter and propped him up. He wasn't good for much anymore.

I said, "Clean him up and take him to the cells. Barashi, you come with me."

I turned on my heels. Behind me I could hear Nir Clore moaning, faintly, and Barashi's resigned sigh as he pushed himself up from the floor.

"But I liked him, Bloom," he said, sadly, as he limped outside after me. "He was a nice boy."

"Nice boys don't help terrorists," I said.

Barashi hacked a cough. "It didn't have to be this way," he said.

For some reason, the implicit rebuke hurt.

Where I came from we had no insolence such as this, no criminality of any kind!

Ours was a clean, well-ordered place.

17.

My men took the boy, Clore, away. He'd spend a night in the cells. I had already put him out of my mind.

We next interviewed Waxman, a dour old man who refused to admit he knew or saw anything, for all that Tirosh was kidnapped right outside his store. Moreover, he then attempted to sell us a book. I told him what I thought of him and his like in so many words, at which he bristled, and made a comment as to the Jews being called, in vain, "the people of the book." I ignored him but could not help notice Barashi hastily pocket an old and well-thumbed issue of *Zaftig*, a magazine that featured large, naked women on its cover.

Sergeant Katz was at the Congress building, where the first round of peace talks had only just begun. Sometimes I suspected that for all his servility to me, he had been secretly sent to observe me on behalf of my superiors. For all my loyalty to Palestina, still some suspected me of being an outsider, though few knew what it really meant. I was efficient, and tolerated; yet I was not liked.

This did not bother me unduly. Personal like or dislike did not matter to me, only my job, and the safety of this little haven of the Jews. A Nachtasyl, some of us called it. A night shelter, a place of refuge for the Jews. It was my duty and my privilege to protect it. With Katz elsewhere, however, I was stuck with Barashi. We stopped at an all-night shack, where I purchased strong, black coffee, and made Barashi drink it until his eyes began to water and at last he stood up and said, "Enough, enough!"

"Go clean yourself up," I said. "We have a busy night ahead of us."

"I was happy where I was," he said. "I was happy watching the bar, and eavesdropping on the students."

"I know you, Amos Barashi," I said. "And I know you hear more than you put in your reports. Go. Clean up. The night is young and we have work to do."

"Aye, aye, Special Investigator Bloom," he said. I watched him head to the bathrooms, the rolled up magazine poking from the pocket of his jacket. I turned back to the counter and motioned Beiga to pour me another coffee. There's good coffee grown in Palestina; the climate is ideal, and it was Baron Rothschild's initiative that financed the first plantations back in the 1920s. It was the English baron of that name, not the French one who invested his efforts futilely in Ottoman Palestine.

This one, Lionel Rothschild, was a keen zoologist. The Rothschild Zoo in Ararat City, as well, of course, as the Rothschild Game Reserve, are named in his honour, as is our local species of giraffe, the five-horned *Giraffa camelopardis rothschildi*, or the Rothschild giraffe. He once rode a carriage pulled by six zebras to Buckingham Palace, both to prove their suitability for being tamed and to publicize the efforts of the settlers in the newly formed British Judea. He is buried near Lake Nakuru, close to his beloved giraffes.

"Planning a late night?" Beiga said. He was a big man with hairy arms and a pot belly that stretched the material of his chequered shirt. I gave a non-committal nod.

The Tea Hut, as the place was informally called, seldom served tea, but it did serve a loose alliance of nightbirds: truckers, taxi drivers, chauffeurs, police and security personnel, and late stragglers from the city's nightclubs and bars. It sat on the edge of the city, on the Tchernichovsky Bypass, near the old tea packing district, a warren of old warehouses that now served as the city's main nightlife area for the young. At this hour it was not yet busy.

A Ugandan trucker sat in one corner, nursing a Coke; at a table two police officers, a man and a woman, were silently smoking clove cigarettes; along the window counter three employees of Lansky Limousines were talking animatedly with many hand gestures, and I listened to them talk.

The Tea Hut was a good place to listen to conversations. Within its walls there was a truce even I dared not disturb.

"And they don't bloody tip," one of the drivers said. They were three in a row, two wearing yarmulkes, one without. "They don't tip and they insist on speaking English to you, or worse, they only talk through the interpreter."

"We trained half of these guys and the other half went to university here," another driver said, the yarmulke sitting awkwardly on what little was left of his hair. "Now they suddenly don't speak Judean."

"It's pride, isn't it," the third one said. "It's face. It's all about face with them."

"Face," the first one said, and made a rude gesture. "They should be coming as beggars, cap in hand, asking for our grace. Not making demands. Not like *they* want to see the Nandi and that lot in their own country. Look at the Kenyans. They could have taken the refugees in. Or the Tanzanians. They're not *our* problem. It's just that no one else wants them so we're stuck with them."

"And the British sticking their nose in like they still own the place," the third one said. He was getting quite worked up—they were talking about the latest round of peace talks, of course. "Send them to Uganda, to Amin and his gang. He's funding half the terrorist organisations beyond the line, anyway."

"Amin just wants to make trouble for us, he doesn't want *them* coming over. And who trained *him* in the first place? We did. Got his paratrooper wings with the PDF. Ungrateful shit."

"That's why we need the wall," the second one said. "You seen that bomb on the bus the other day? We need to stop them where they are. No more coming and going, no more sneaking over the line."

"What are we going to do for workers, though?" the third one said. "You know they're the cheapest, and they work hard. Palestinians don't want to do the dirty work anymore. This isn't the settlement time."

"Are we short of foreign workers?" the first one said. "We'll bring them over from—" he waved a hand, "Egypt or Angola. Asia, even. Got to be lots of people looking for work in Asia. Cheaper, too. Good work ethics."

"Still," the third one said, dubiously. "Got to be careful they don't stay."

"This is a Jewish country, for Jewish people," the first one said.

"Still."

"I just wish they'd tip better," the second one said.

Presently Barashi came back from the men's room, the magazine out of sight. His walk was steadier. He slid onto a stool and Beiga served him coffee without saying a word. Barashi downed it in one. He turned to me.

"Well, boychik?" he said.

"Call me that again, and I'll show you what hell really looks like," I told him. He just grinned at me, the old goat.

"Come on," I said. I left some money on the counter and rose to my feet. "We have a long night ahead."

"Sir, yes sir," Barashi said.

Beiga looked after us mournfully as we left the Tea Hut. He was married to a Ugandan woman, from beyond the line; an illegal. He knew what we were about, but he wouldn't say anything, not to me.

We got back in the car.

"I hope you remember how to use a truncheon, Barashi," I told him as he strapped himself in. "Tonight, we raid Golgotha."

He blanched at that, but he said nothing; and a new determined expression settled on his face. I put the car in gear and roared into the night, heading beyond the Green Line: heading to the camps.

18.

For a long time Tirosh did not know where he was.

He awakened in the dark. Pain sent sparks of light behind his eyes: the only thing he could see. After a time he realised he was tied to a chair, and there was a sack of black cloth over his head. The cloth smelled of laundry detergent. It was not unpleasant. His hands and legs had been tied securely but comfortably. The ropes did not cut into his circulation unless he tried to move, and so he sat still, awash in the scent of the laundry, and tried to picture himself elsewhere.

This came naturally easy for Tirosh, for whom life was one long attempt to escape into other, better, imaginary lands. He pictured himself on a beach in Zanzibar, somewhere on the east coast of the island. The sand was pale, fine-grained like powdered whalebones. A line of coconut trees demarcated beach from land proper. The sea was a calm azure, and on the tideline the sand was covered in brightly coloured shells. There are no seashells as beautiful as those found on the shores of Zanzibar, and Tirosh, in his mind, wandered happily along the beach as the sun set, slowly, over the horizon. He picked each shell and admired it in the light of the setting sun. Sometimes, the shells were empty, and he pocketed them. At other times they were inhabited, still, by their native molluscs, and at such times he watched the little creatures struggle and wriggle in their homes before he tossed them back, gently, into the sea.

The sun never seemed to set entirely and the beach never seemed to end. When he imagined himself thirsty, Tirosh picked fallen coconuts and tore their green encasing open, cracking the hard nut within against a rock until it broke. Then he drank the water, though it never seemed to truly satisfy him, and he grew more thirsty with every passing hour. His bladder, too, pressed very painfully, and he imagined himself urinating, luxuriously and at great length, against the trees or into the sea, but every time that relief, too, proved illusory, and he was pushed deeper into the horizon, until he looked back and saw Isaac trailing behind him.

The boy had only recently got his first pair of shoes, and he walked almost crab-like (though Tirosh was vague on exactly how crabs actually moved). That is to say he moved not like a crab at all, but with halting steps, his upper body pulling forward faster than his little legs, so that he was constantly in imminent danger of falling. The boy retained his balance, however, as he followed with a determined purpose, and only his hand, reaching forward and up, towards his father, signalled how desperately he wanted to be picked up. Tirosh walked faster, but the boy kept pace, somehow, until at last Tirosh was forced to turn and reach out his arms for him. The boy clung to Tirosh as though he were drowning, and indeed the water must have been reaching higher up to the sand, for Tirosh could not see the boy's footsteps in the sand at all. For a moment he held Isaac close to him. His son's warmth overwhelmed him, and he stroked Isaac's delicate light hair, gently, feeling the little uneven bumps in the boy's skull.

"Dadad," the boy said. He couldn't yet speak but had taken to babbling animatedly when the mood took him, jabbing his chubby little finger to point at things, speaking a nonsense language only he understood.

"Hush, Isaac," Tirosh said. "We'll be home soon."

The boy felt very light in his arms. He carried him across the warm sand as the sun set and the world grew dark, and the pressure in his head intensified. "Dadad, dadad," the boy said; then the darkness was abruptly gone and with it the sea and the sand and the boy, and Tirosh blinked back tears as the light hit his eyes. He coughed. He was very thirsty.

"I need to pee," he said.

"Then pee," someone said, and laughed—it was a cruel sound.

"We are not animals, Mushon. Help the man up."

A grunt. Tirosh blinked, saw shadows standing over him, but he could not make out their faces. Someone cut the ropes that bound him. Pain flared as blood was released. The man helped Tirosh stand, none too gently. Tirosh almost fell. He was like a child, learning to walk. The man led him away to a toilet cubicle and waited with the door open as Tirosh unfastened his pants and urinated. The relief was overwhelming. How long had he been kept here? He was profoundly grateful he had not pissed his pants. Somehow the thought of doing that was mortifying, unbecoming.

"Finished?"

"Thank you."

When Tirosh turned he could see the man's face more clearly. It was a lumpy face on top of a lumpy body, which towered over Tirosh. He had the ears of a boxer. Cauliflower ears, Tirosh thought. It was an expression he'd often used in his books.

"What are you looking at?" the man demanded.

"Nothing."

"Come on."

He grabbed Tirosh by the arm and led him away. They were in some sort of warehouse, Tirosh saw. It was a vast hall, filled with sacks of cement, mixing machines, tractors and bulldozers. One other figure, round and small, was merely a shadow ahead. Mushon led Tirosh through the silent machines, to the warehouse's doors. They stepped outside.

In the light of the moon, Tirosh saw the land of his youth.

Mount Elgon rose in the distance, though it was not as large as he recalled it when he was a boy. The land around it was green and pleasant, though of a dark shade in the night, the vibrant green turned almost rusted, like old blood. Somewhere to the southeast would be his father's farm, the farm on which he grew up, but he could not see it from up here. He was on a hill, and the hill had been taken over entirely by a vast construction site. Warehouses sat hastily built, and with them tractors and bulldozers and cement bags and kilns, and he saw local people milling about, none paying him the slightest attention, all busy at their tasks. There must have been hundreds in that camp. Lights had been strung up on poles everywhere. A road led down from the hill and cut through the greenery and the night, leading to Elgon, yet as it approached the mountain it skirted it, forking into two paths, as though wary of the volcano. Tirosh could see campfires burning in the distance, and hundreds more men on the slopes below, as small as ants.

A white line cut through the greenery, a neat and orderly form, like a surgical cut in the land.

The wall.

Even as he watched he could hear the distant grunt of great earth-moving machines, and the shouted calls of overseers, speaking in the languages of the Nandi and other Kalenjin. Judean was barely heard but for where he stood, with the big man, Mushon, and the other one.

Now Tirosh turned, and looked at the other with new interest, for this was his first opportunity to examine his captor.

The man was short and ran to fat. He wore sunglasses pushed over his forehead, and a chequered shirt open at the neck, under which his hairy chest showed proudly. His arms were wide and the watch he wore expensive—it was a European import, from far-off Switzerland. He glared at Tirosh with the irritable look of a busy man confronted with an unwanted obstacle.

"You have been asking *questions*," he said; an accusation Tirosh found hard to deny.

"I do not believe I have had the pleasure," he said, "Mr. . . . ?"

"Gross. It's Gross, you little *ku fartzer*," the man said. He waved his hand, encompassing the building site, and Tirosh could indeed see a sign prominently displayed, which read GROSS CONSTRUCTION CO. LTD.—NO PROJECT TOO BIG!

"I'm sorry," he said. "I don't understand." He touched the

back of his head, tenderly. It was sore, still, to the touch. "You had me kidnapped?"

"I felt we should have a little chat, yes," Gross said. He looked ill at ease, bristling with a secret sorrow. Tirosh saw how none of the workers dared glance their way; they may as well have been invisible. And he was suddenly afraid of this man.

"What about?"

"There he goes again!" Gross said, agitated. "Always with the questions."

"You want I should tap him again?" the big man, Mushon, said. "Just a little tap, to give him manners."

"Listen," the man, Gross, said. He jabbed his finger in Tirosh's chest. "Why are you going around asking questions about Deborah Glass? Did you *do* something to her?"

"Did *I*?" Tirosh was momentarily taken aback. "She's gone missing," he said.

"I *know* that!" Gross said. Tirosh took a step back; the man's demeanour, it occurred to him suddenly, looked less intimidating than deeply concerned. Something did not add up.

"Deborah was looking into the wall's construction when she disappeared," Tirosh said. His head was pounding and his mouth was dry; it was hard to swallow. He took a step forward, pleased to realise he could tower over Gross. "She was against the building of the wall, she was an activist."

He glared down at Gross.

"You're the one *building* it, for God's sake. It would have been in *your* interest to make her disappear," he said. "I swear, if you did anything to my niece I'll—"

"Your *niece*?" A look of confusion filled Gross's eyes. "Who exactly *are* you?" he said.

"Tirosh! Lior Tirosh! I'm a writer. I live in Berlin but I came back, my father—"

"Tirosh?" The look of confusion in Gross's eyes intensified. "You're her *uncle*?" His shoulders slumped. "Well, this is *fakakta*," he said. "I thought you were . . ." He didn't complete the sentence.

Tirosh was breathing hard. All around them the workers worked, carrying bags of cement, quarry stones, digging tools. The wall in the distance was white, so white.

"What is this about?" he said, more quietly. "Why did you kidnap me, and how do you know my niece?"

Gross waved a hairy arm. "This is not what I expected at all," he said. "I think we should have a chat. I mean, a proper one, this time. Can I offer you a cup of tea?"

Tirosh rubbed the tender back of his head, tiredly. "I suppose that you could, at that," he said.

He followed Gross to a large tent that was set up, as a sort of command centre, near the edge of the camp. On a portable gas stove Gross boiled water, measured out tea leaves into a strainer, prepared biscuits on a silver tray. Tirosh watched him, this curious, powerful man, and again he thought how little he understood the people of his own land and the things they were capable of.

Gross wasn't at all what Tirosh had expected. He looked worried, as though he'd made a mistake but was the kind of a man who never made mistakes, not in his own mind. As Gross prepared the tea service he told Tirosh a little of his life. How he started out as a runner boy, trading in the Nakuru

Market. How he'd made friends with the Swahili traders and learned their language. How he'd been accused of smuggling, of having his own routes into the territory—"But they never had anything on me. They never did." Finally how he'd figured there was more money and less headache in construction.

"In this land we always build, build, build," he said.

Tirosh nodded, politely.

Gross served the tea. He poured the milk first, Tirosh noticed—the sign of a man who had not grown up wealthy. Mushon stood at the entrance, looking out on the night. Construction never stopped, and Tirosh saw trucks come and go, and men march—it was like a military operation.

"You're making them build the walls to their own prison," Tirosh said.

Gross looked hurt at the suggestion. "I pay them well," he said. "These people are my friends."

"Friends," Tirosh said.

"You!" Gross shouted. "Moses Tanui! Are we not friends?"

A man, one of the workers, turned his head at the sound. "Yes, boss," he said, and turned back to his task.

"See?" Gross said. "I went to his wedding."

"Why did you kidnap me?" Tirosh said. "What was your connection to Deborah?"

"I didn't know who you were," Gross said. "All I knew was there was some *schmutznik* going around poking his nose in my business. I thought you might have had something to do with her disappearance."

"She's gone? How do you know?" Tirosh said. "Her professor said—"

"Her professor!" Gross snorted, and his large hand slammed

the rickety table, upsetting the tea service that was resting there, until Tirosh had to act quickly to rescue his cup. "Listen to me, Tirosh. Deborah Glassner was working for *me*."

"I don't understand."

"What is there to understand!" His eyes softened. That same curious countenance, that secret sorrow, suffused his face for just a moment. "She's a beautiful girl. I don't mean in the conventional sense, maybe. But a beautiful person, inside. People judge me, do you know that, Tirosh? I'm not one of those *nogids* born into money and power, those whose parents sent them to Paris or London for education, the old families. I'm a self-made man. I'm Nakuru born and bred. These workers *know* me, Tirosh. But for the colour of my skin I'd be one of them. So don't you think, too, to judge me. Deborah didn't."

Tirosh took a sip of the tea. He thought of this man, his speech, peppered with too much Yiddish as though he'd picked it up from some cheap romance sold at the kiosks of his youth. He knew what Gross meant. Through his father he, too, had got to know the upper echelons, those from the old banking and trading families, who vacationed in Switzerland or Pemba, spoke French and German with only a hint of Judean accent, who bred horses on private farms away from the plateau. They, too, had respected his father, but only because the old man could not be bought. They'd look down on a man like Gross, with his loud voice and his pulp fiction Yiddish, with his market manners. He would never be welcome in their club.

"How did you meet Deborah?" he said.

"She came to me," Gross said. "At first, of course, I was suspicious. I do not like the activists, Tirosh. Sofa revolutionaries who've never spoken to a Kalenjin but are outraged on their behalf. The wall, the wall! Let me tell you something, Tirosh. Walls mean nothing to me. Is this right? Is this wrong? That's for others to decide. I just build it. This is what I get paid to do. Who's to say there won't be peace if we build the wall? My grandparents lived and died behind walls back in Europe. Perhaps the walls protected them from the world outside. At the end of the day, you've got to choose who your people are. You can't be of one place and another, you must be one thing. We are Jews. The Kalenjin are my friends, yes, but they are of themselves, and this is as it should be. They must do what is right for them, and we must do what is right for us. Do you understand?"

Tirosh nodded. Outside, the electric lights ran in straight lines, illuminating the workers as they trudged to and fro with their cargo.

Tirosh looked at Gross. He was like a man who'd got everything he'd ever wanted, yet still felt like a fraud. As though he were having to justify himself, to Tirosh, to whoever would listen. And he thought, this was what Deborah must have been to him, in the end. His Western Wall. She was someone who listened.

"She came to you," he said to Gross, then. "Why did she come?"

"She was nosing about near my construction site," Gross said, and unexpectedly smiled; a tender look which transformed his face. "At first she was with those protester groups, you know how they come near, chanting and waving placards and all that *dreck*, mostly for the cameras, though the media's hardly interested in them anymore. My men just told them to keep their distance. I mean, it's a free country." He looked at Tirosh defensively. "I won't say nobody ever got hurt if they got out of line, and the cameras weren't there . . . but that's just actions and consequences, isn't it?"

"Sure," Tirosh said. "Sure."

"Deborah wasn't like the others," Gross said. "She started coming round, on her own. Making friends with the workers. She speaks Kalenjin, did you know that? Not many Palestinians do."

"My father does," Tirosh said, remembering. He thought of his father, marching through a Nandi village as though he were its chief: how the children followed behind him wherever he went.

He always seemed to have more time for other people's children than his own, Tirosh thought, and had to push down the bitterness.

"Your father, of course," Gross said. "The general. He always respected the land, I'll give him that. How is the old man?"

"Dying," Tirosh said.

"I'm sorry to hear it."

Tirosh shrugged.

"Do you have any children, yourself?" Gross said.

"Me?" Tirosh said, in confusion. "No."

For a moment, Gross looked at him curiously. Then he said, "Well, I got to know her, gradually. She was just persistent. She wouldn't take no for an answer. I liked her, Tirosh. She was smart and she was funny. Ultimately, we disagreed on pretty much everything, but we liked each other all the same. Is that very hard to believe?"

Tirosh looked at the other man. There was something soft,

something vulnerable under Gross's hard exterior. Tirosh wasn't sure he entirely believed him, but he did not think it ridiculous that it could be so, that this man and his niece had formed some sort of relationship. It occurred to him he did not know Deborah at all—barely remembered the little girl she had been. His memory had been playing tricks on him recently. He was remembering things out of sequence, and things that never occurred.

He said, "No, I don't think it is that hard to believe."

Gross, he thought, looked at him with something like gratitude. Gross said, "I figured we could help each other. Do you see?"

"How so?" Tirosh said. He was discomfited by the view of Mount Elgon always in the background. As a child, it had been a constant, there the whole while until his mother uprooted him from his life and took him to the city. The mountain didn't care if Tirosh had gone or had returned. The mountain just was. It'd seen humans come and go, with lives as brief as those of elephants or ants. Once it had been a conduit of fire from the earth. Now it lay dormant, its flames extinct, but something of that early power remained in the soil.

"She was researching folklore. Old stories. Silly stuff, but you know what the natives are like." Gross scratched his nose. "I mean, sometimes, you know, you do wonder. You grew up around here?"

"Sure."

"You do wonder. An old volcano, and the caves and all that . . . You do sometimes see strange lights at night. Hear sounds you maybe shouldn't be hearing. I don't know. Stories sometimes have a kernel of truth in them, don't you think?"

"Sure," Tirosh said, again. It seemed easiest to agree with whatever train of thought Gross was following. "Sure."

"You maybe don't know this, but we've been having problems with the workers," Gross said. "Good people. Hard workers. Usually. But they refuse to work round Elgon. That whole area's a fucking *breach*, Tirosh."

"Why won't they work there?"

"They say there's a bad place. I've never heard of it. There never used to be. Something us Jews brought with us, in the Settlement, they say. Or something woken up, by the construction. . . . Honestly, I can make no sense of it. I don't know. My expenses are running high and my workers are mutinous, Tirosh. I can't afford not to finish this job."

Their tea was long gone. Tirosh watched the lit road to the mountain, and how it forked, how it skirted the darkness of the old volcano. It was an island of shadow in all that light, something older and more real than those makeshift roads, that ephemeral wall. Gross talked like a man who needed to talk, who wanted to unburden himself. In Tirosh he had found a willing confessor.

His man, Mushon, stood motionless at the tent's entrance, as immovable and dark as the mountain.

"I don't see how Deborah could help you?" Tirosh said at last.

Gross stirred in his chair. "I thought she could find someone to convince them," he said. "I tried money, I tried threats . . . maybe I needed a different approach. It couldn't hurt, could it? Look at it!" he said, pointing, forcing Tirosh's eyes to follow again those dark contours to which he was both attracted and from which he was repelled. "Look at the damn thing!"

"Why not just build around it?" Tirosh said, and "It's not even on the Green Line, that's Uganda on the other side."

"It's not that, it's spreading everywhere," Gross said. "The bombings, the destruction. It's not been on the news, but we've had several attacks, sabotage attempts. People died. It's all over the line, Tirosh. It's all along the wall, it's everywhere." He pointed at the mountain again. "But that's the source."

"It's just a mountain," Tirosh said.

"I know that!"

"What was Deborah doing?" Tirosh said. It was hard to get a straight answer out of Gross. Tirosh suspected that, for all the man's protestations, he was not that bothered about the problems with the workers, and his tirade was merely a sort of protective noise that he was raising over himself; that what he wanted to hide was less clear, but may have been his feelings for the girl, which were deep enough to have had Tirosh abducted and brought here. Which meant, too, that Gross was not above breaking the law; that he could and did resort to the use of violence; and that he could therefore be very much a suspect in Deborah's disappearance, if indeed there had been ill design behind it. Tirosh needed to step cautiously around this man, and yet he felt the need to press, to rattle a truth out of him.

"What did you ask her to do?"

"I needed her to come up with a story," Gross said, "something to pacify the Kalenjin and the others. I thought she had it, then. She went off to the lake."

"Her professor said that," Tirosh said. "She was looking for something, but the professor didn't know what."

"An object from the first expedition," Gross said, and

unexpectedly smiled. His moods shifted like the clouds over the plateau, rapidly and without warning. "Wilbusch's theodolite."

"What the fuck is a theodolite?" Tirosh said.

"It's a surveying tool," Gross said. "They were surveying the land, weren't they."

"Why would Deborah go looking for that?"

Gross shrugged. He looked uncomfortable. The night was hot and a mosquito settled on Gross's wide neck. Gross slapped it without blinking, then flicked the tiny, bloodied corpse away.

"It was like a, what do you call it," he said. "A totem? No, she told me. A *fetish*. An object believed to have supernatural power. She'd found scraps of information, I don't know where. She was always in and out of old libraries. There was this belief that it was connected to the bad place. It was lost, but then it surfaced on the other side of the border. Fucking Uganda, man. She thought if she could bring it back it would be what I needed to convince the workers they were safe. That's what she thought."

"What she thought, or what you wanted?" Tirosh said.

"I don't know," Gross said. He stood up. "All I know is that she never came back, or if she did, she never came to see me. I'm worried about her. I just want to make sure she's safe."

"Sure," Tirosh said. He, too, stood up.

"You understand, don't you?"

"Sure."

"Listen," Gross said. "You're looking for her. I can help you. I've got money, resources. How much do you charge, a day?"

"Charge? I'm not a detective, I told you, I'm a novelist."

"Yeah, sure, but that's not your *job*, is it," Gross said. "*Arbet iz keyn shand*, you know?"

"What?"

"Work is no shame, is what I'm saying, Tirosh."

"Two hundred," Tirosh said. It was what his heroes always charged, in his novels.

Gross looked at him blankly.

"Two hundred what?" he said.

"Two hundred Palestinian pounds, a day. Plus expenses."

"I'll give you a week up front, is that all right?"

Tirosh shrugged. Gross reached into his pocket and came out with a big dirty wad of cash and peeled off a bunch of notes and handed them to Tirosh. Tirosh didn't count the money. He wasn't entirely sure what had just happened.

"And Mushon can take you down to Kisumu," Gross said. "That's where Deborah told me she was heading. You can leave right now."

"But I must deliver my lecture," Tirosh said.

"Your what?"

"At the university. Elsa—"

The name momentarily stopped him in his tracks. He knew Elsa—didn't he? His memory of Berlin, of life outside, was fading, somehow. "My agent," he said, lamely. "She arranged it."

"Forget your lecture," Gross said. "This is far more important than any second-hand thoughts you may have about literature, Tirosh. You! Kipngeny!" he bellowed. Down on the slope a man turned and grinned sheepishly, having stopped to roll a cigarette while a bag of cement was balanced over his head. "Watch how you go, you little bugger!"

"Yes, boss, Mr. Gross," Kipngeny said; but he didn't look

particularly concerned, and he finished rolling and then lit the cigarette with a match before he continued on his way. When Gross turned back to Tirosh, he looked like he had already forgotten Tirosh's presence. A look of surprise fleetingly suffused his face. Then he put his hand on Tirosh's shoulder, and leaned close, and he said, "You'll find her, won't you? I just want her to be safe."

"Sure," Tirosh said. Mushon led him away, to a waiting car parked a little way down the hill.

"I'll drive you to Kisumu," Mushon said.

"Sure," Tirosh said, in a daze. "Sure." When he looked back he saw Gross in silhouette under the moon, and he thought you never saw the moon so close and so large as you did in Palestina. He had forgotten that, too. He had forgotten a lot of things.

19.

There are few places as beautiful as Lake Nakuru at dusk; the sky is suffused with hues of crimson and amaranth and vermillion, and down below, the pink flamingos gather like a tribe of wise, ancient people, deep in a group discussion. But when we got there it was late at night, and so I missed the view.

When I arrived at the wall I was pleased to see the new Eretz Crossing was up and running. We called it Eretz, *land*, but in truth it was no land at all but the liminal point between one world and another: between ours and theirs.

Concrete boulders blocked the way to vehicles, preventing

the possibility of a car bomb attack. I parked and exited. Barashi snored in the passenger seat. The soldiers knew I was coming. Even at this late hour, Nandi workers and families were queuing up on either side of the barrier, waiting with bowed heads to enter or leave Palestina. I did not hate them. It was just that they weren't my people.

I conferred briefly with Captain Blau of the Nakuru Protectorate Civilian Administration Command. Captain Blau was an upstanding Palestinian patriot and a man I had worked with before. He had short cropped hair greying at the sides, keen hazel eyes and a harassed manner.

"It won't be easy," he said. "Listen, Bloom. We go in quick, we hit them hard. It's the only way. What exactly are we looking for?"

"An Orkoiyot," I said.

"Their spiritual leader? But—"

"Not an official one," I said, with hatred. "Just round them up, Blau. He'd be an older man, but we can't take any chances."

"The Nandi won't like it, sir."

"What the Nandi don't like they can submit in writing to the United Nations," I said, and he grimaced, a momentary expression of displeasure that disappeared so swiftly I wondered if I'd imagined it.

"Is there a problem, Captain Blau?"

"No, sir. It's just—"

"Just *what*, Captain Blau!"

"We'll have to go hard and fast," he said, "it's the only way."

"Then that's the way we'll do it," I said, smiling at him pleasantly until he got the message and walked away.

I did not like those camps beyond the Green Line. I did not like Nakuru, the slums, the way the streets were all crowded, the broken roads and the concrete blocks, where families huddled ten to a room, where the terrorists lurked, hiding in the civilian population. These people called themselves refugees, but the reality was that they had lived and they would die in those camps, that these were their homes, that the land they claimed was one given to us by covenant. Kenya should have taken them, but wouldn't. Tanzania balked. And so they remained, forever on the doorstep, growing more desperate with every passing year. And desperate people are dangerous. They may not have meant to become what they've become, but historical processes have made them into weapons, an enemy of the state.

I was merely doing my job!

Crossing the wall was like going over into another world. Overhead the stars dominated the sky, the galaxy stretching its arms from one horizon to another. I loved the stars over Palestina, their pure, cold beauty.

The camps pressed against the wall. On our side it remained pristine, untouched. On theirs the wall was filthy, filled with graffiti. Slogans spray painted on the wall. A grotesque illusion: a stencilled man pulling a curtain open, revealing another world, of blue skies, white clouds, innocence. A road cut through the camp, leading from the gate. We drove down it in convoy, five armoured trucks, and turned into the warren of dirt roads that ran like an infection through the camp.

They knew we were coming. They always knew. I saw boys race ahead, to warn their people. Women watched us behind curtains as we drove past. We moved slow, encountering debris, thrown junk, an open fire burning in a disused oil drum. There were so many of them, in the shadows, in the corners, watching. The first stone came out of nowhere, and then another, and another.

"Don't shoot!" Blau ordered. I remained mute. The stones hit the sides of our vehicles with hollow thuds. There was no justice here, no police, no civil order. There was only us.

We were deep inside the camp when we stopped. Blau shouted, "Go, go, go!"

The soldiers deployed rapidly. They were veterans of this war, in which the enemy moved unseen. It could be a young boy, a kindly grandmother, an old man smoking a pipe. You couldn't trust anyone because no one was innocent. They hated us and they wanted to do us harm.

My job was to stop it.

I knew more than they did, more than Blau, more than most people do. People think of reality as immutable: solid and reassuring, that it is true merely because it is *there*.

But I knew better. Even Tirosh, that hack, had a sense of the real truth of it, in all his wild inventions and his torrid fictions. The world is the sum of what it could be, what it might have been and how it could have been.

I *knew* how fragile the borders are between the worlds, how quickly madness settles, and fiction becomes fact. The world is always stranger, after all, than we imagine. You can call it quantum mechanics, you can call it Kaballah, but either way, it was my job to stop it from happening. People *need* to believe that the world is solid and real, and here, in this time and place, we had established something true and precious, this night shelter for the Jews.

I did not hate the inmates of the camps; I pitied them. But I had been tasked with protecting this land, and protect it I would.

We streamed, therefore, out of the vehicles. The soldiers moved rapidly, in unison. Their guns were drawn. They were equipped with live ammunition. I myself carried only my side weapon, which was always on me.

"Break down the doors."

"Sir—"

"And never challenge my orders again, Blau!" I said. I made a mental note at that moment to speak to his commanding officer. I once had high hopes for Blau, but his service here had changed him, had made him weaker, as though even he, a good Palestinian soldier, had become somehow sympathetic to the plight of the people he was forced to operate against.

He was not like me. My intentions were pure, had always been pure. In the place I come from, we had no dissent.

I heard screams, as doors were battered down and my soldiers went into the tenements, dragging the inhabitants out. Several of the soldiers spoke some of the native tongue. They shouted questions, threatened imprisonment, confiscation, destruction.

"Make them understand," I said, calmly. "Make them understand."

"Sir."

I approached one large house. "Secured?"

"Secured, sir."

I went inside. A family huddled in a corner next to a large television. The soldiers moved methodically, quickly through the house, searching it. They knocked on the walls and tore open drawers, ripped carpets, moving room to room, searching for contraband. It was the house of a relatively wealthy family, I saw. A ten-year-old boy glared at me defiantly from behind his father's robe. I pointed my finger at him, imitating a gun, like in the movies, and said, "Pow."

He blanched and hid, as well he should.

"Where is he?" I said to the father.

"Sir?"

"Where is the old man? The Orkoiyot."

"Sir, we don't know—"

"Don't know what?"

"We know nothing!" the woman, his wife, interjected. "We are innocent people, we have done nothing wrong!"

"Keep your mouth shut!" I shouted. I took out my gun and pointed it at the woman's forehead. "Where is he!"

"I don't . . . I don't . . ." She began to cry.

I did not enjoy humiliating her. I was merely carrying out my duties. I was a *professional.*

"Please. We know nothing, sir," the husband said.

The soldiers returned, their sergeant shaking his head. "Nothing, sir."

I motioned at the family. "Take them outside."

"Sir. Yes, sir."

I walked out of the house. I paced the street. Everywhere that had electricity, lights were lit. Families were being force-gathered outside, pulled out of doors, confused, frightened, dressed for sleep. The soldiers stood guard, but they looked nervous. In the camps, an attack could come suddenly, out of nowhere.

When the first shot rang out it came from the rooftops.

A soldier collapsed. They wore bulletproof vests but the hidden sniper had aimed for the head, and the soldier fell, a red flower blooming in the centre of her forehead. Then hell erupted all around us as the soldiers began firing, and Blau grabbed me and pulled me down low. "Sir, you need to take shelter!"

"Get your hands off me, Blau!"

I ran in a crouch, hugging the walls, my pistol raised. Frightened people shied away from me.

"I know you're there, old man," I said. "I know it, I can feel it."

More shots rang out. Another soldier collapsed to the ground, hit in the leg.

"Catch them and bring them back to me!" I screamed. "I want these men alive!"

The soldiers split into smaller units, separated. I stood upright in the middle of the road, breathing heavily. I waved the gun in the air.

"Is this what you want?" I shouted. "Take a shot if you feel you can get it!"

I looked around me. I saw the boy, the one who had glared at me. A dark stain of urine marred his pants. I stalked up to him. I whipped him with the pistol. It caught him on the cheek and he cried out in pain. The mother tried to attack me and I kicked her savagely, and she fell sobbing to the ground. I picked up a handful of dirt and brought it to the boy's mouth. "Is this what you want? This land? This land!"

"Please . . . please . . ."

"Then tell me. Tell me where he is. The one who wishes

harm on my people. The man who can see beyond this world, into the next. Where is he!"

"Not here! Not here! They're hiding in the Mau Forest!"

I did not even know who said it. The cry came out of one of them; it didn't matter who. There was always someone who would talk.

I stood there, not saying anything.

Not the forest, I thought. Not that, not again.

But of course it was there. I should have known, I think I must have known all along.

"Bloom? Bloom!"

"Secure the area," I said. I reached for the boy but he shied from me like a wounded animal. I took his hand, nevertheless. I helped him to his feet. I patted his head.

"Good boy," I said. "Good boy."

The mother kept crying, but I no longer heard her. "Secure the area. Bring me the shooters. Do not fail me, Blau."

I turned to the boy's father. "Your house," I said.

"Sir?"

"Set up a command post in this man's house," I told Blau. He nodded, tight-lipped.

"Sir," the father said. "Please, use my home, only, please, do not destroy my property."

"It will be in the hands of the Palestinian Defence Force," I told him, stiffly. "There will be no safer house than this in all of Nakuru."

He nodded, meekly enough; but do you know, I do not think he was convinced.

PART FIVE
BORDERS

20.

The borders of what had been British Judea and is now the Republic of Palestina have been drawn and redrawn several times. You watch it on the view screen of the plane, the dotted lines of borders, the slow, unceasing movement of the aircraft on the flight path.

The transition from one world to the next is subtle when one is in the air. The sky remains the same sky. The clouds continue to reflect back at you your own preoccupations, like a set of Rorschach blots. It is only when you land that the world resolves in its little differences, the arrival on a new and unfamiliar shore magnified by tiny wrongnesses: the worlds are much the same, but the details differ.

You land and the sun beats down on the tarmac. You are glad of the airport's cool interior. You see Tirosh. Has he noticed you? Already, your mind clouds with new, false memories. It is a disorienting experience, as though you are two people in one, and you find it hard to separate one from the other, know which of you is which.

You go through immigration and customs, and this, at least, is like in any other place. There are always borders, and there are always those who guard them lest they fracture. Outside, you hail a cab. Tirosh is there, he watches. But you have people in this town, and they will keep track of his movements. For you, it is important to first familiarise yourself. You are a good, experienced field agent. You have survived Smyrna. You have seen the mechanical warriors under the banner of the Crimson Emperor in Jund Filastin. You have seen the fish-frog men abominations of Ash-Sham.

You learn to survey. You learn to study the lay of the land. Joshua sent spies to Jericho in Biblical times, and you, that is, your superiors at the Border Agency of Ursalim, have done the same. You hole up in a cheap pension on Adaf Street, near the market, and explore the city. It is a curious place, this Jewish town transplanted into the heart of Africa, and you are caught unawares when you suddenly hear the Arabic words peppering Swahili in the market. You see black-clad Unterlanders walking along pavements beside Nandi workers, Jewish girls in light summer dresses imported from Paris and Rome, soldiers in baobab-grey uniforms and black guns. You taste ugali. Your interest is in the hidden denizens of this city, this world. This is a place where the Jews won.

But you notice, everywhere, too, the signs of their occupation. In a city park you see the Nandi women who care for the elderly: brightly dressed and laughing they congregate under the shade of the wide palm trees, talking softly in their mother tongue, while the elders in their wheelchairs sit dozing in the sun. A street cleaner sweeps away the day's debris, his bald head shiny in the heat. Black nannies push the prams of curly haired boys adorned with peyes. Drivers in peaked caps wait patiently at the gates.

Yet it is much the same everywhere, you think, even in your world. Always there are the servants, and those who are being served.

You just observe these things. Sometimes they trouble you. You watch all the invisible people and wonder where they go when night descends. Later, in your pension, you fall asleep to the radio, and news of a bus exploding: here, it's just another terrorist attack.

The next day you see Tirosh, by accident, as you climb off the bus on Herzl Avenue. He goes one way. You go another, at a brisk pace. Down a side street, Der Nister, which means "the hidden" and is named after the Yiddish author, who is buried in the cemetery nearby.

Away from Herzl's busy sprawl of shops and traffic, Der Nister is a palm tree–lined, shaded avenue of modest, mid-century buildings. There are haberdasheries here, barbershops where the barbers are neat, little old men in white smocks, wielding scissors with an old-world dexterity, side by side with cheap stores blaring out the latest Afropop hit from Nairobi or Cape Town, where one can buy cheap plastic toys, or knock-off fishing rods, or second-hand tyres. You make your way, cautiously, to Abu Ramzi's Emporium & Grand Bazaar which, despite its name, occupies but a small and unassuming corner unit next to a bicycle shop on the one side, and a small, public square on the other, adorned with wilted grass and centred around the marble statue of Isaac Luria, the renowned Safed Kabbalist.

Balloons, bells, fans, balls, cushions, notebooks, pens, seed packets, pipe tobacco, hats, scarves, sweets, soap, mysterious bottles and a plethora of other, manufactured and imported objects litter every available space. Shelves are crammed into the small, dim interior. A fan overhead turns slowly, stirring the air and pushing the drowsing flies this way and that on the currents. A long counter runs against one wall, shelves of sweets and cigarettes behind it, jars of tea and spices. On the counter are a scale and a cash register, both old but dignified, and behind it is a young, serious-looking man, who is busy reading the *Palestina Times*. You approach the counter and unwind the scarf from around your neck.

"Yes? Can I help you?" the young man says.

"I am your cousin, Nur. From Al-Quds."

His eyes widen. He looks out of the window as though checking for a tail. He sees no one, only a man walking his dog.

"I am Ramzi," he says.

"Yes," you say.

"My father was expecting your arrival yesterday."

"Yes," you say; and only that.

The truth is you need time; time to acclimatise, time to remember who you are.

It would be different for Tirosh, you think. For him it is slipping back into something known if forgotten, pushed into the back of the mind and recalled easily; he fits.

For you it is different. You remember now the time before your arrival, but it is blurred, hazy. Your memories conflict. You had arrived on a flight from Berlin the day before. It was a connecting flight. You had left Jerusalem early in the morning, with the call of the muezzin rising eerily through the fog, and driven to Jaffa for the airport. Your plan was to visit your distant cousins, Abu Ramzi and his family, who had settled first in Tanganyika and then, later, in Ararat City, Palestina. You are a historian. You are interested in—in what, exactly? The words run through your mind—*Hebrew pulp writers, alternate worlds*—but they make no real sense.

You do not *belong*. The world is merely trying to squeeze you in, building a protective shell over an irritant embedded it in the host body. You remember your childhood in Jerusalem, then as now a part of Ottoman Syria; your studies first in Istanbul and then at Heidelberg, where you gained your doctorate; your return to Jerusalem, where you taught German to the children of rich parents, while trying and failing to write a great book of literary criticism. At last, the death of an aunt who had unexpectedly left you a modest sum of money, and the decision, equally unexpected, to undertake this voyage to this remote backwater of the world, to see relatives not seen for many years.

These memories are like the pages of a book left too long on the beach, stuck together with salt water and sand. Yet they cohere, they force themselves on you the longer you stay, the longer you live as though they are real. It is a struggle to think. Pain has built behind your eyes all day, and it is only getting worse. You aren't here at all, this woman you think you are. You are someone else, from a place unimaginably distant.

"Are you all right?" the man, Ramzi, says. Hesitates: "Cousin?"

"It's just a headache," you say. "I've been travelling a long time."

"Of course, of course." He comes round the counter. "Please. My mother is upstairs. She wants to hear all about life in the old country."

"Do you have the . . . equipment I asked for?"

He raises his hands. "I know nothing," he says. "You must speak to my father."

"I will."

You follow him upstairs meekly enough. There'll be time for you to regroup and plan. You have a job to do, and you intend to follow it through to the end.

Later, you wait for the arrival of Abu Ramzi. You sit in the spacious living room of the family upstairs. They are watching the television. An anchorwoman in a tailored jacket speaks of the terrible tragedy of the suicide bombing of the night before. Clips show Palestinian Defence Force soldiers going door to door shouting orders, rousing frightened families of what the anchorwoman says are known subversives. Umm Ramzi tutts with disapproval and turns her round eyes on this foreign niece of her husband's.

"Almond cake?" she says.

"No, thank you," you say. You drink white coffee, sweet with condensed milk, and the thought of another slice of almond cake fills you with a quiet horror. On the screen, the anchorwoman now cuts to a new segment and a reporter in the field. The man stands against the background of an imposing, roughly circular white building, whose east and west wings spread out like the open pages of a book. Wide stone steps lead up to a raised courtyard where people are milling like chickens before a feed.

"As the Congress assembles here today for its first session," the reporter says, "delegates from neighbouring Uganda, Tanzania and Kenya, as well as representatives of the Kalenjin *oreet*, or clans, from the Disputed Territories, have gathered here today for the commencement of the Regional Peace Summit. As you can see behind me, everyone is waiting for the doors to open shortly, and security is heavy."

The camera pans across the assembled dignitaries, a mix of suits, robes, Orthodox garb and the occasional short-sleeved, chequered shirt. Each has their own security detail, armed discreetly, with wires trailing from behind their ears into the jackets of their suits.

"Also present are delegates from His Majesty's government, here to facilitate the talks, and observers from the German Reich, the Sultanate of Zanzibar and the Kingdom of Swaziland. Ah, the doors have opened, and everyone is shuffling forward, as you can see. Representatives from all over Palestina are here today, for the assembly of the Congress, first founded by Theodor Herzl in Basel in 1897. We now go back to the studio, where we will be speaking with Chief Kirongo of the Nandi Council of Elders about the forthcoming talks. . . ."

The words wash over you. The television screen flickers, the family sit spellbound in its entrapping light. It is with a sense of profound relief that you spring up as a short, balding man comes in through the door. He has grown a paunch in his time here, where he was younger and leaner when you once saw him. Black hairs bristle on his thick arms. He engulfs you warmly, lifts you off your feet.

"Niece Nur!"

"Abu Ramzi."

"You have met my son."

"You must be very proud."

"I am, Nur. I am."

He abruptly releases you. When he scans your face you see the shrewdness you expected, that calculating coldness that is the mark of a veteran agent. He wasn't always called Abu Ramzi, this man. He is of that legendary generation to which La Méduse belongs. They fought in skirmishes that have no name, in the days when the borders were more porous and each slippage and transition could be your last. Abu Ramzi fought in the ill-fated battle of the Mukhraka, against the combined might of the mutant priests of Ba'al and Suleiman's djinns.

"Let us walk outside," Abu Ramzi suggests. You follow him, glad to be out of that house, the droning of the television and the sickly sweet cakes. Outside, he turns to you and says, "Sooner or later, a man must have a home."

He's a sleeper agent, in semi-retirement, sent here on a sort of extended holiday, really. This backwater place, as the Agency considered it, where nothing much ever happened. A good place to settle down, raise a family, begin to remember how to forget. He sounds apologetic.

"Is it home?" you say. "Here?"

"My son is here. My wife."

"Abu Ramzi, a shopkeeper."

He smiles; indulging you. "I have always been a shopkeeper," he says. "Everyone talks to a merchant."

"I saw you," you say. "In Outremer. In Antioch under the stone arches, where the crusaders built their Kingdom of Heaven . . ."

"I was there," he says. "I was there a long time."

"How do you manage it?" you say. "How do you *remember*?"

"You are struggling," he says. "But you are young. For me, it is like putting on or taking off a suit of clothes, nothing more. Who am I? I am me. Everything else is merely . . ." He hesitates.

"Camouflage?"

"Scenery." He smiles again. Takes your arm in his. Together you walk down Der Nister, past the statue of Isaac Luria, the Kabbalist.

"They remember him here," you say, with surprise.

"Here," he says, "travel between the sephirot is not a science like it is back—"

"Home?"

"Back in Ursalim," he says. "But that is not to say there are no slippers, and it is not to say that the knowledge is entirely unknown. You must tread carefully, Nur. There are forces at work here which remain hidden from me. The borders are thinning. It was I who raised the alarm."

"Then tell me what I must look for," you say. Then, "The man, Tirosh."

He sighs. "My men followed him but lost him a couple of hours ago."

"Lost him? Lost him how?"

"They believe he may have been abducted. By who, we don't yet know."

"If he dies—"

"The pattern grows. I know. But I cannot discern the pattern here, Nur. I do not know the sequence. Someone is coordinating death as a means of opening a gate between the worlds. Remember the rule: one cures at the source. Do not be distracted by what are mere symptoms."

"You're cold," you say. You look at him again, this pleasant, mild-mannered man. "This is a man's death we speak of."

"One man. One death." He shrugs. "Perhaps he'll turn up. Or perhaps he'll be the next link in the chain, and thus reveal to us more of the one fashioning the key. Your path lies elsewhere."

"Where?"

"Beyond the wall."

"What is this wall?" you ask.

He merely shrugs again. "Another symptom."

"It seems wrong," you say, "to cleave a land."

"People like walls. They make them feel safe."

You think of other walls, in Berlin, in Pakistan, in Mexico, in Korea. In this and other worlds than these. Always there are walls to keep people in, or keep people out. You shrug. This is not your fight, and this is not your home. You are merely here to carry out the job at hand.

"What's beyond the wall?"

"Knowledge. I hope. I have arranged the paperwork for you. There is a woman there, a German from the Reich. She has set up a free health clinic for the refugees. You will visit her. She is not one of us, of course, but she will extend to you the hospitality. To her you are just a tourist from Al-Quds." He laughs. "The other Palestine. The rest you must find out on your own. There is a man, too. Bloom. He is high up in their internal security apparatus, but he is not of this place. Do you understand?"

"Yes."

"Outsider calls to outsider. Be careful."

"The equipment I asked for—"

"You will not be allowed a weapon through the checkpoint."

"Then what do I do?"

He smiles, thinly.

"Improvise," he says.

21.

The crossing of Eretz is an exercise in misery. You queue for hours, in single file, shuffling through a corridor of wire mesh and steel, as bored soldiers watch you with their weapons always at the ready. In the centre of this facility is an examination room, a space into which you enter alone, and machines scan you as unseen security officers examine your person. If you are carrying an explosive device, you get no chance to activate it on this route. Concrete slabs surround you. In this room, bombs have gone off before.

You're told to go through. You're clean. More of the twisting metal corridors until you emerge, at last, on the other side, allowed to collect your belongings, given back your Ottoman passport. You pass one final gate, out of the perimeter, and there the world changes.

Here markets stalls are set up, on rickety wood tables sit bananas and pineapples, fried chicken, hard-boiled eggs, cooked corn. A teenage boy squats in the dirt beside an open fire, cooking sticks of meat over the flames, frowning in concentration. The soldiers are more relaxed here, they buy some of the food, and the people returning from Palestina are welcomed with their cargo, which is opened and pored over and distributed and resold over the self-same tables.

Children stare at you, this foreigner, neither from here nor from there. You pass a stall selling batiks, and hand-carved masks and statues, voices beseeching you to buy, buy, buy. Your pocket is full of Palestinian pounds. You see carved handguns, a carved double-decker bus, a bowl for washing faces. You buy a stick of meat from the boy and chew on it as you pass. This is a world like any other world. The refugee camp is teeming. Vehicles pass on the main road, army convoys escorting settlers to their lands, local cars passing with asthmatic wheezes, their license plates grey with dust, marked with an N—for Nakuru or Nandi, or something else entirely, you don't know.

This is not your land. These are not your people. And you think of other marketplaces, other borders—the teeming crusader towns of Antioch and Tripoli, the bark of crazed dogs under the broken moon of Kang Diz Huxt, the whispered bargaining in the green swamp villages of Samaria where the Awful Ones live—and you are not sure where you are anymore, as though you've lost your way amidst the sephirot, and become unanchored from reality. Then a voice hails you, saying, "Nur? Nur Al-Hussaini?" and you turn, and the world is whole again.

"Yes?"

She is a youngish, blonde woman, tall and leggy in white, with the discreet swastika flag on the breast pocket of what must be a nurse's uniform: and you remember that in this world, things turned out differently.

"I'm Astrid. Astrid Bormann." She smiles, easily. "No relation," she says.

"No relation to what?"

"I mean to . . . Oh, never mind." She takes your hand in hers. She has a friendly, outgoing nature; so different from the likes of us. "Abu Ramzi phoned ahead to say you were coming. What a wonderful man. He has been *so* helpful with our work here."

She leads you to a jeep parked by the leaning wall of a house, on a dirt track. The jeep seems brand-new, spotlessly clean, in marked contrast to the local vehicles. Astrid seems oblivious. On the side of the vehicle is a red swastika.

"I'll take you to the clinic," Astrid says. She hops inside and you follow more cautiously. Astrid starts the jeep and begins navigating her way with confidence, through narrow, twisting dirt tracks. The oppression of the camp settles on you, the way the rickety buildings seem to lean in towards you, how they obscure the skies, where only the sinister moon glows, its light casting shadows everywhere you look. Children shout and wave and old women smile and some men leer and others look defiant, and Astrid talks as she drives, an endless stream of words.

"We set up about two years ago," she says. "We had plenty of funding to begin with, but it's becoming hard to raise the money, the ministry's redirecting funds to the Chinese colonies, you know what is happening at the moment in Tsingtau . . . It's terrible, really, but donors have simply given up on work in the Disputed Territories. We do what we can, but I worry. There's only really me, and Dirk and Hans, and there are so many people in need, and every day there seem to be more. . . ."

You let her drone on. She is driving you through the camp when the two of you become aware of the sound of gunshots.

A battle has erupted in a nearby street. You hear the shouted orders of PDF soldiers, doors banging, dogs barking—in all of the worlds, you suddenly think, there is always a dog, barking. Astrid's mouth becomes a thin line, her lips are pressed, her eyes are focused on the road. In time the sounds recede as you move away, though you notice the sudden tension in the streets, the shut doors, extinguished lights, the sound of fleeting feet beyond your sight, the rising of a pressing silence. It's eerie, driving through those endless habitats, and you wonder if the children born along these roads will ever know the scent of grass, the touch of an uninhibited sun, the crystal joy that comes with an unexpected spray of foam and salt water. You think, with sadness, that they might never be free.

The jeep comes to a halt outside a low prefab building surrounded by a fence. Chickens cluck nearby. The building's painted white, and a red swastika marks the door. Two sleepy men—the clinic's indifferent security guards—look you up and down without much interest, then turn away as you follow Astrid through the door. Inside it is quiet, a little dirty, with the smell of used nappies, medicinal alcohol, ammonia and iodoform, mixed in with the smell of cooking, garlic and fat, and the hint of cigarette smoke. Astrid looks apologetic, but leads you, anyway, to her office, and sets about making you both a cup of tea. You marvel at this woman, self-assured, so confident of her place in the world, so confident of the *world*, its tenets, its unshakeable foundations. If only you could tell her how quickly it can all disappear.

"So tell me," Astrid says, "what it is you're after. Abu Ramzi said you are an academic? From the Caliphate."

It takes you a moment to realise this is just a name some use, in this world, for Ottoman rule—and that *you*, the other you, indeed live there. Abu Ramzi was right, you think. In time, it gets easier to remember to forget.

"I'm researching old stories, really," you say, "magic systems, odd customs, stories of what might have been . . ."

"He said you wanted to speak to a . . . one of the, how do you say? *Nachtvolk*?"

You mull the word. "Night folk," you say, curious.

"Yes."

"I was not aware of the term," you say.

Astrid shrugs, suddenly uncomfortable. "It just popped into my head."

"You work in the local community. You must meet a lot of people. You must hear a lot of talk."

"Talk. What of it?"

"I'm just curious."

"Look," she says. "I'm not political. I'm here to help the people in the clinic, not to fight this war against the Palestinians."

"Still, you must hear stuff."

"I'm in a very precarious position. The clinic is here on sufferance of the Protectorate authorities."

"Astrid," you say, gently. "I am not the army or the police. I have no stake in this. Whatever it is you know, you can tell me."

For a moment she looks miserable. Then she says, "There are factions, you know they're fighting for independence. There are all the regular ones, but what I keep hearing is about the *nachtvolk*, the night people. Some new faction, with serious funding, a training camp in the Mau Forest. I heard they were behind that bus attack, and some of the others. It's strange, because usually someone would claim the credit for an attack, but they didn't. No one even knows who they really are. The reason I thought of that is, well, they say they're, you know." She laughs, self-consciously. "That they have supernatural powers."

"I see."

And you do. And you sit up straight. And you listen because, really, this is what you came here to do. There is a wrongness in the sephirot, there is a *thinning*.

"And you know no one?" you say; and her cheeks flush.

"There is one man. . . ," she says.

Of course there is, you think, but do not say. And she agrees to take you to him, one Ephraim Keino, a local bricklayer.

You drive again, from the silent clinic, through nighttime streets in which there is no traffic. Perversely, Astrid chooses the ring road, passing by the wall, and for a moment you get a glimpse of the other Nakuru, the one below: the lake, gleaming in the gentle moonlight, the pink flamingos all asleep, and on the shores the settlements, prosperous, green, lit with electric lights behind their windows. So close and yet so far the worlds become, here one sleeps and here another is awake, but which is one, which is the other?

Astrid says, "He lives right through here," pointing at a dark alleyway, a fondness in her voice—but you're uneasy. There is a silence here which isn't natural, that you have heard before, if silence can be said to be a thing one hears. It is an absence, and not even a dog barks. You try to warn her, but she doesn't really listen, and the wheels crunch against the dirt as she parks the jeep.

You climb out cautiously. Every sense you have whispers you should run.

Astrid, meanwhile, is oblivious. Where are the dogs? you think. She leads you to a ramshackle house, a lean-to with a door of corrugated metal sheet.

"Ephraim?" she says. "Ephraim, it's me!"

She pushes the door. It is unlocked. She frowns.

"That's weird," she says.

She disappears inside. It's dark.

You follow.

"There should be a lantern somewhere here," she says. You hear her moving about, knocking things. "Ah, there it is. Hold on."

She strikes a match.

For a moment its brightness flares up in the room, and you see: a Kabbalistic Tree of Life inscribed in charcoal over one whole wall; a map of Palestina, with the wall marked through in red; a face.

The face stares back at you; the eyes are bright and wild. Then the lantern falls and breaks with the sound of exploding glass, and Astrid screams.

Suddenly the room is filled with light. You blink back tears. You find yourself in the middle of the room, surrounded by PDF soldiers with blackened faces, all staring back at you.

Their guns are trained unwaveringly on your chest.

"What is the meaning of this? What did you *do*?" Astrid says. The soldiers turn you, cuff you, take you away.

But you remember what you saw in that room.

The signs of *incursion*.

It is all part of the pattern, you think.

They take you away. What they do with Astrid, you don't know.

They drive you to a rich man's house and put you in a child's room.

They lock the door.

You wait.

22.

There is in Judaism the concept of *Tikkun Olam*, the healing of the world. Kabbalah teaches that there are many worlds, or *olamot*, emanations of light from the infinite, what we call, in Hebrew, the Ein Sof.

I have been there. There is a place where the lone and level sands stretch far away. . . .

Meanwhile I was already back on the road. The men who attacked us had escaped but for one who, when questioned with enough persuasive force, revealed a name: Ephraim Keino.

This Ephraim Keino was not at his address, but what I

found within disturbed me. The Tree of Life, the books of Luria, as well as Cordovero, Isaac the Blind, de León and the Baal Shem of Worms. There were objects there, too, historical artefacts, predating settlement: a pith helmet crusted with rust and dirt and age, which must have belonged to Alfred St. Hill Gibbons, the explorer; a train ticket stub from Mombasa, rusted and water-stained, which had somehow yet survived from those long ago days; a brass pot the explorers' porters must have carried.

It was troubling that such objects had been assembled together, and all without my knowledge. Such a thing should not have been possible.

I was filled with a new fury. I left the soldiers at the place and returned to Eretz Crossing, where I found Barashi awake and complaining, and mostly sober. He wanted to know why I'd left him there. I told him a drunk was no use to me, but an ex-soldier might be. When he learned I meant to return to the Mau Forest he reacted with understandable horror, but soon subsided when he realised that he had no choice. I let him drive this time. As for me, I sat in the passenger seat and brooded.

There are, nowadays, clear roads leading up into the forest, and even some of the way inside it. There are even picnic areas, where Palestinians like to come on the holidays, when the air fills with coal smoke and the smell of grilled meats. The drive is not long from Nakuru but, after a time, one runs out of road and must venture deeper into the forest on foot. We left the car parked by a parasol tree and ventured into the dark.

Neither of us wanted to be there.

We were both armed. I hated the forest, the dark, the call

of Hunter's cisticolas in the trees. There were thick clouds overhead and we could not see the sky. It began to rain, it always rained in the damned forest, and the water ran down the tree trunks and into the mulch. It was a hot, humid, stinking environment to wade through. The trees made our progress slow, and the wet, rotting leaves made every step uncertain. I wasn't sure exactly where we were going, merely that we had to penetrate deeper into the forest. It is one of those curious places that can be larger on the inside; I have heard there is a forest in England that is much the same, though I must confess I had never desired to enquire further on the subject.

For what seemed like hours we trudged through the mulch and the rain and the clouds of mosquitoes. Barashi shivered beside me but did not speak. He was a good soldier, and he knew this wood, had seen some of its mysteries.

We first noticed the shifting of the border when we heard a noise ahead, and both froze.

Barashi's hand strayed to his gun, but I halted him with a gesture.

The sound came again. It was a growl.

Slowly, slowly, we crept ahead. It was foolish, but I had to *see.* The clouds parted, and silvery moonlight fell down on a clearing ahead. I watched through the branches of a peacock flower tree.

The creature that stood there resembled something between a hyena and a bear. It had high front shoulders and a sloping back. It had an elongated skull, and its head turned this way and that, slowly, as it sniffed the air. Then it opened its jaws wide and growled again, and it took all my strength not to bolt.

How I hated that awful place!

Once, long ago and in another place, I had visited a muscum of natural history and there, behind glass, observed the skeletal remains of a prehistoric creature called a *Chalicothere*, long before, of course, extinct into oblivion. The creature before me then was of a similar species, perhaps, but this one—I knew only too well—was carnivorous, and deadly.

The local people called it a *kerit*. It was better known as the Nandi bear.

The creature ambled forward. Its odd, sloping gait was nevertheless powerful, commanding of the space it took. Behind it, then, came another, and then another.

It only lasted a moment, but it felt much longer. The creatures traversed the clearing in the moonlight, a sight not seen on this Earth for millions of years. There was something wild and majestic and free about them, and as much as I hated the sight I could not help but be moved by it, too. Then the clouds returned and the light died, and the creatures were gone.

We waited, a long moment more. When we pressed cautiously ahead, the clearing was free of any creatures. Had they sensed us? If so, they were wise enough to leave us alone.

I knew then that we had penetrated deep into the wood. This was the border, and beyond it things shifted, and I was afraid. I had loved this, my adopted home. I did not want to lose it.

Yet the rebels must be there, I thought. If I were to find what I sought it would be here, in the heart of the Mau Forest, where the sephirot intersect.

As quietly as we could, we kept going. Deeper and deeper into the wood.

They found us before we found them.

There had been no warning.

One moment we were in the mulch, amidst the trees, crawling forward bone-weary and tired. Then they were upon us.

Faces in the undergrowth, bright eyes the only clue to their presence. We were grabbed and our hands pressed back and bound before we had a chance to speak. Barashi struggled beside me and was silenced with a blow to the head. He collapsed to the ground. I remained still. They picked him up and dragged him along, easily. They prodded me forward. No one spoke.

We had seen other things in that forest, that night. Earlier, we had passed a patrol of Wehrmacht soldiers, from another history. At one place we found the bones of a British explorer under a tree, his uniform rotting, a sun helmet still sitting on his bleached white skull. A diary was still clutched in his bony fingers. When I leafed through it I saw the detailed anatomical drawings of impossible creatures, a map showing an entryway in a cave, deep into a hidden world in the centre of the earth. The paper crumbled in my hand. Later still, I saw a bright object in the ground and, bending down to retrieve it, discovered a coin bearing the profile of a Zulu king on one side, the image of a shining rocket ship on the other. It was contemporarily dated. I looked at it for a long moment before I let it drop from my fingers, back to the ground.

Our captors pushed us along narrow forest trails I would never have found on my own. They formed a complex network between the thick vegetation, and seemed well trodden. Not long after, we emerged into a hidden camp. Semi-permanent structures had been erected amidst the trees, cunningly hidden. Guards stood on the perimeter, young men with rifles slung over their shoulders. They stared at us, expressionless, as we passed.

The camp expanded around us. It was bigger than I'd thought. The houses stretched on, storage sheds, a firing range, kitchens, latrines. It was well organised. We were led to a round house in the middle of the camp and escorted inside. Barashi, thrown on the floor, began to stir. He groaned and then threw up on the clean ground. The smell of his bile reeked, and I was vindictively glad that he had soiled this place.

It was dark inside. My eyes had grown accustomed to the darkness and yet it still took me long moments to begin to discern features. I heard a match strike a moment before it flared, blinding me. Then it was applied to the wick of a kerosene lamp and a steady white flame began to burn.

I saw the walls adorned with maps showing the territory of Palestina and the Disputed Zones; a Tree of Life and a more fantastical map, of many intersecting geometries, which must have been an attempt to chart the amorphous borders of the sephirot, emanating from a central point in the Mau Forest.

"Special Investigator Bloom," a voice said. I started, for I had not seen him.

A man rose from the floor where he had been sitting cross-legged, watching us. He was neither tall nor short, old nor young. He was just a man, and I thought that, like all men, he could die.

"I am the Orkoiyot."

"You, sir, are a terrorist," I said, coolly.

He smiled. "I fear you will never make a good diplomat, Bloom," he said.

"That is not my job."

"No," he agreed; a little sadly, I thought. "You are a weapon, fashioned to a different purpose. In many ways I admire your bluntness. You are like the blade which Alexander used to cut through the Gordian knot. But you are not the wielder of the sword, Bloom. You *are* the sword."

His words, his calm poise, discomforted me. He went to Barashi and gently helped him to sit. He wiped the ground with a cloth, soaking up Barashi's sick. Then he disposed of it, neatly, and offered the older man a glass of water, which Barashi took without a word. Then the Orkoiyot addressed me again.

"It is not that you have made refugees of my people," he said. "It is that you will then deny it. It was not enough to do a bad deed: but you would retell history, so that in the telling, it had never happened. You cast yourselves as the wronged party, and thus we can never progress, can only fight. You have your victories, and we have ours, but . . . we do not see what's there, only that which is unseen."

"We can agree to disagree," I said, stiffly.

"You're in my hands," he pointed out, with that same patient, gentle tone. "For now, at least, I have the advantage."

I looked at him. "Untie me," I said.

He shook his head. "No."

"If I am a weapon it is only because I had been fashioned that way," I said. I hated myself for sounding plaintive. For trying to explain myself to this man, my enemy.

"I know."

"I do what must be done."

"I know," he said again. "I count on that, Special Investigator."

He said my title as though it were a mockery.

"You know why I have come," I said.

"Why don't you tell me?"

"These attacks," I said. "You know who I am. You know what my role is. There is no place for pretence on this score. Not between us."

"No," he agreed.

"The bus bomb, the murder in the Queen of Sheba hotel. Each taken on its own is but a physical act of death. But they add up, you and I both know. A pattern. A key."

"Yes."

"To destroy the border."

"So it would seem."

"Why?" I said—demanded. "Why do you do it?"

"Tell me," he said. "The man you captured—Joseph. He worked at the Queen of Sheba hotel."

"Yes."

"What happened to him?"

He looked at me mildly. He was a mild sort of man. I did not reply.

"You are a fool, Bloom."

Barashi groaned on the floor. We both ignored him.

I stared at the Orkoiyot.

"You are the man behind the attacks . . ."

"You are a fool, Bloom."

I had the sense then that I had made a terrible mistake somewhere.

"The man who died at the hotel, what was his name?"

"Menhaim," I said.

"And why would he be killed? What purpose would he serve?"

"I don't know."

"You are a fool," he said, a third time. "Menhaim was not the target, it was the other one, the outsider."

I said, "Tirosh." The name stuck in my throat.

"It was not Menhaim's death that extended the pattern," he said. He looked at me almost with kindness. "It was the murder of Joseph."

"No," I said. "No."

"He *is* dead, isn't he, Bloom? What was it, exactly?" He pretended to consult an imaginary report. "The subject exhibited a fatal response to routine investigation techniques? That *is* what you call it these days, isn't it?"

"No," I said, "it can't be."

"Everything *you* do," the Orkoiyot continued, remorselessly, "seems designed to extend the pattern. Your murder of Joseph. Your savage and unprovoked attack on the camp tonight on the pretext of searching for me, or someone like me." He went and returned. He was holding a gun. He put it to my forehead and stared at me hard. "Give me a reason not to shoot you, Special Investigator."

"I am trying to *halt* the pattern!" I screamed. "It's you, it's always been *you*, you . . ."

I subsided under his gaze.

"Shoot me, then," I said.

"We want our land back," he said. "We want our home. We want our children to grow free, in a world where they can walk proud, a world without soldiers holding guns on them, Bloom. It is a small thing to want, and yet it is a whole world." He sighed, and seemed to grow smaller then. "But we want *this* world, we want *our* world, Bloom. I do not desire to breach the walls of creation. Do you?"

I shook my head. The fear and the anger all drained out of me then. I felt empty and lost.

I had made a mistake.

"The sequence *must* be stopped," the Orkoiyot said. "Someone is manipulating our moves, both yours and mine. Do you understand?"

"Yes," I said—whispered.

"Do you agree?"

"Yes, damn you!"

He removed the gun from my forehead. The pressure eased and he holstered the weapon.

"Untie them," he said.

Hands grabbed me and in moments I was let loose. Beside me Barashi straightened slowly.

"I don't know what you two were talking about," he said, "but I wouldn't say no to a drink."

The Orkoiyot smiled, without much humour. He turned back to me.

"The man you seek isn't here, Special Investigator. Whoever is behind the attacks is back in Palestina. It is to your own people you need to look, not to us. Find him, and stop the sequence. Stop it before it destroys the worlds."

He turned away. He was a slight man, and soft-spoken, and he was a terrorist and my enemy. I knew if I tried to come back to find him the camp would be gone, and I would find no trace of it. The men took us back through the undergrowth, through narrow trails that twisted and turned impossibly. In a very short time we found ourselves back by the car. Dawn had broken, and the clearing sky was filled with shards of coloured glass. I loved the skies over Palestina.

PART SIX
DIVERSIONS

23.

"People lie," Tirosh said. Back at the university, the students waited in vain for his appearance. Beside him, in the driver's seat, Mushon grunted, uninterested. But Tirosh had a lecture to deliver, and deliver it he will.

"People lie, to each other, to themselves," Tirosh said. "Which is really just another way of saying, people tell stories." He stared out of the window of the car, at the dark asphalt and the rolling hills. They were heading down from the plateau, towards the distant water.

"The detective, like the historian, must go around asking questions, banging on doors, interrogating unwilling witnesses. They must piece together a story from conflicting tales, from clues. There are things that are not in dispute—the bloodstained knife found by the corpse, a battle that took place—but what do they mean? *Someone's* fingerprints have been left on the kitchen wall in blood, but whose, and why?"

"What blood?" Mushon said. He was staring straight out of the windshield, at the open road, his fingers tightened over the steering wheel. "What the fuck are you going on about, Tirosh?"

But Tirosh wasn't listening. In his mind the argument fled, nebulous. What was history, he thought, if not a human attempt to impose order on chaos, to give meaning to a series of what were, essentially, just meaningless events? Causality was hidden from him. In detective fiction, as in history, order had to be imposed: clues sifted, witnesses interviewed, conspirators unmasked, murderers brought to justice. The problem was that everyone had a different story. The same place could have multiple names: Jerusalem, Ursalim, Yerushalaim. Each name came with a different and competing history. What happened, he thought, when a different peoples had to share the same land? The same places with different names, the same battles with different outcomes. His mind fled from the implications, and as his head rested against the glass a memory rose instead, of Isaac, reaching out fat little fingers to tug at Tirosh's ear, squealing with delight; and another, of Tirosh lifting Isaac out from the bath and placing him, gently, on the change table: and his son, unexpectedly, reaching out his arms, urgently, and grabbing hold of Tirosh's shirt as he pulled him down. Tirosh, overwhelmed, leaned over his son and hugged him, the boy's face nestled into Tirosh's throat, so that Tirosh could feel his son's breath on his skin, and the boy's comforted sigh. For a long moment he held him like this, the boy unwilling to let go, and Tirosh would have happily stayed that way forever, as though he could forever mask his son from the world and keep him safe.

"Daddy's here," he murmured, his breath fogging the glass. "Hush, Isaac, Daddy's here."

This was how he fell asleep; against the window. Mushon drove on. Tirosh's lecture was forgotten. He was not much of a writer, of detective tales or otherwise. Outside the dawn lengthened across the sky, but Tirosh missed it. He was fast asleep, escaped into that dark chasm which is like a prelude to what awaits us all.

When he awoke the world had once again shifted; he forgot all about Berlin, about the boy, all that which came before. Tirosh awoke instead to a deep blue sky, a bright sun that illuminated gentle white clouds in the distance against the lakeshore. He knew then where he was, for one never forgets the sight of Lake Victoria. The car drove smoothly over asphalt, descending from the highlands to the port. Tirosh watched, enraptured, the play of sunlight on the calm blue inland sea. Then the city hovered into view.

Its official name was and remained Port Florence, since the time it was founded as a modern town by the British. But everyone called it by its original name, Kisumu, which simply means a place of trade.

It was not a pretty town. The old colonial architecture had not been replaced but added to with ugly, functional buildings. The docks extended into the lake, where heavy cargo ships laid anchor, and warehouses lined up on the shore, and with them came cranes, trucks, forklifts and the workers who operated them. The port was never entirely silent, and the ships came and departed from Kisumu to Mwanza, Entebbe, Port Bell and Jinja. Linked to the port there stood the great railway station of Kisumu, from which the lines rose up and back towards the highlands, crossing Palestina, linking it through Kenya to the seaport in Mombasa.

It was not a pretty town, but Tirosh liked it all the same. Beyond the city, on the more pristine sand beaches, stood the weekend mansions of the Palestinian rich. In the town itself, beyond the port that gave it the reason for being, there were the usual amenities of hotels and restaurants, heavy with a transient population of travellers, as well as small shops, nightclubs, housing estates, bars and shebeens. It was not a pretty town, just a place to pass through and do business in, unless you were unfortunate enough to have to live there.

Mushon drove them through the town. They passed the small Arab souk that had stood there for generations, a remnant of the days when Arabs traded ivory and spice here, and other, less palatable merchandise. He stopped outside the Arnold Rothstein, a grungy two-storey hotel in downtown Kisumu, between the British Old Town and the harbour.

The air was humid when Tirosh climbed out of the car. Storks and herons called in the distance while, on the green trees lining the old English avenues, kingfishers and green parrots chattered to each other.

"Where will you start?" Mushon said.

Tirosh stared at him. The thought came to his mind that this was all a game; that he was merely avoiding the inevitable, the visit to his father. "I'll ask around," he said. "I'll see what I can find."

"Any idiot can do that," Mushon said.

Tirosh just shrugged. He wished he smoked. It seemed appropriate to sneer at the bigger man with a cigarette dangling from the corner of his mouth. But Mushon didn't care one way or the other.

"Any idiot," he said again. Then he slammed the door and pressed on the accelerator and was gone from there; back to his master.

The hotel, when Tirosh entered, was dusty and dark. A brass bell rested on the counter and, seeing no one, Tirosh pressed it.

"Yes, yes," an irritated voice said. A large woman emerged from a door marked OFFICE and stared at him accusingly. "What can I do for you?"

"I'd like a room."

"And I'd like a second white wedding," the woman said. "But we don't always get what we want."

"You don't have a room?"

"I didn't say that. Do you take everything so seriously? Here." She went to the row of hooks on the wall and took down a key. "Happy?"

Tirosh looked at her in confusion. "I don't know," he said, helplessly.

She sighed, audibly, and pushed a form across the counter. "Fill this in, will you? And pay is up-front, if you don't mind."

Tirosh filled in the registration and pushed cash across the counter and collected the key. All he really wanted was a shower. He was relieved when he entered the room and failed to find a corpse. He'd had enough of dead men in hotel rooms. He wasn't sure what he was doing in Kisumu, or what Deborah had got up to, or why his memories were so clogged up, as though he were two incomplete persons. He stripped and stepped into the shower. A stream of cold, rust-coloured water eventually emerged, and he shivered as he scrubbed himself clean.

He didn't go to sleep. The cold water had awakened him somewhat, and after he dressed he stepped out of the hotel and onto the street. Cars were already in motion along the road, Susitas and Sabra minis and large trucks all throwing dust into the air. He walked through the Old Town and its neat grid and its tended trees, heading in the direction of the lake, but entered instead into the maze of the old Arab market. Here, amidst the curio stands and the shops selling tat for the tourists, and men feeding imported sugarcane into a crushing machine, the bark stripped, there were other, more specialised shops.

Here, in this unassuming commercial hub between Palestina and the rest of Africa, there stood the old world shops aimed at the obscure collector. The first shop Tirosh tried specialised in stamps and coins. It was dim inside, the air still. A dark-grained wooden counter was piled high with stamp albums, jars of neatly labelled coins and other, less easily distinguished objets d'art. It was an old town in an old town part of the world, and the lake it sat nestled against had played host to numerous wars and trades. Here there were German army helmets from the Great War, old Arab curios and ancient British maps, hand-carved statues from a dozen tribes and nations, amulets, bao boards, gold pendants, bayonets, old guns: history to some, the unwanted junk of centuries to others.

Tirosh's attention wandered. His hand ran along the spines of books. His eyes were drawn to a giant carved Nyami Nyami from the distant Zambezi; to an ivory-inlaid ebony pipe; to a cigarette case engraved with a Prussian eagle; to a First Day Cover bearing the first Palestinian stamp, of a smiling Albert Einstein, apparently signed—

"Don't touch that!" a voice said, sharply. Tirosh raised his head to see a tokoloshe-like man stand up from behind the counter, where he must have been dozing. His bulbous eyes stared querulously at Tirosh.

"I'm just browsing," Tirosh said, defensively.

"You don't need your hands to browse, do you?" the man said. "What do you want? Did you make an appointment? I don't have time for time-wasters."

The man's hair was mussed from sleep and his eyes blinked myopically at Tirosh before he reached for a pair of glasses held on a string around his neck. Putting them on, he peered more closely at Tirosh.

"Well?"

Tirosh wasn't sure how to progress, exactly. He said, "I'm interested in the first expedition."

"Burton and Speke? Livingstone? Shaka Zulu? Ernst Schäfer? Which one, *yungerman*?"

"Er, no," Tirosh said. "I mean, the first Zionist expedition to the Territory. I'm sorry, I didn't catch your name? I'm Tirosh. Lior Tirosh?"

The man blinked at him. "I'm Fledermaus," he said. "Mr. Fledermaus." He looked somewhat mollified. "The first expedition, you say? I have a wonderful set of commemorative stamps issued just post-Independence. It should suit your pocket—" The look he gave Tirosh clearly indicated what he thought of Tirosh's spending power.

"Money's not an object," Tirosh said, thinking of the cash Gross had given him. Also, he had to admit he had always wanted to say that particular line.

Mr. Fledermaus stared at him with a little more interest. "Hmmm, well, well, yes," he said. He cleared his throat. "For the more *discerning* collector," he said, "I have here, with me, an almost unique specimen, the Yellow Inverted Wilbusch five-penny stamp from '34. That will set you back five hundred pounds. That's Palestinian, not Ugandan, Mr. Tirosh—" And he laughed softly at his own joke.

Tirosh looked at him coolly. "I am not after stamps," he said.

"No?"

"I'm interested in . . . artefacts."

"Ah . . ." the old man said. He rubbed his hands together, as though using a washcloth. His eyes blinked behind the thick lenses, rapidly. "What *sort* of artefacts, exactly?"

The note of caution in his voice did not escape Tirosh.

"You tell me," he said.

"Well, well," Mr. Fledermaus said nervously, "I think maybe you came to the wrong place, yes, yes, thinking about it, I do not deal in *artefacts*, no, no, curios, yes, stamps, coins, not . . ." He stopped, helpless.

"Not what?"

"*Those* things," Mr. Fledermaus whispered, distraught. Tirosh smiled, unpleasantly. This new role suited him, he felt. He was playacting a character he had long known and longed to be.

"Listen to me, old man," he said, advancing, somewhat threateningly, on the wooden counter and the precariously balanced stamp albums. "If you don't, then who does?"

"No, you listen to me, *boychik*," Mr. Fledermaus said, rallying round, and fixing his gaze unnervingly on Tirosh. "I fought in the Ugandan War when you were still a *pisher* in nappies, so don't you think you can push me around. I told you I don't deal in these . . . artefacts," he spat out the word, "and I want nothing to do with that sort of thing."

"What sort of thing?"

"*Muti*," Mr. Fledermaus said, using the southern word, then repeating himself in Yiddish: "*Kishef*."

"Witchcraft? But they're just old . . . things," Tirosh said. He tried to laugh, though the old man unnerved him. "You don't really think they—"

The old man regarded him sadly. "Listen to me, boychik. I don't know what you got yourself into, but you clearly don't know what you're about. Have you even read the *Zohar*? *The Book of Creation*? *The Book of Secrets*? *Illumination*?"

"No," Tirosh said. "I mostly read crime novels."

"Well, then," Mr. Fledermaus said. "Don't go sticking your nose where it don't belong, that'd be my advice."

"And if I needed to, anyway?" Tirosh said. "Where would I go?"

"Away from here," the old man said.

Tirosh took out his wallet and peeled off two fifty-pound notes and laid them on the counter. "I just want the information," he said.

Mr. Fledermaus looked at the money. Then he looked round his empty shop. He seemed to make up his mind. He leaned forward, and spoke softly.

"There's a man," he said. "A Ugandan. He only comes over now and then. You know how it is with us and the Ugandans.

Anyway he's a trader, a specialist. He calls himself Cohen—he's a big Judeophile, you see."

"Do you know where I can find him?"

Mr. Fledermaus shook his head. "You could try the casino," he said.

"The Pink Pelican?"

"Why, do you know another one?"

Tirosh shook his head. He had distant memories of being taken there by his father once. He and Gideon were excited by the illicit atmosphere, the sound of the slot machines, the men smoking cigars and the sound of ice tinkling in glasses. They had played in the hotel pool while their father was ensconced in a series of meetings with the other generals and their counterparts from Uganda. Then, it had seemed a world away from the farm and the everyday, a place where the thick carpet swallowed sound and it was always dusk: it was like something out of a European novel, filled with impossible promise and glamour.

He left Mr. Fledermaus's shop. Outside it was already growing hot and the humidity soaked his clothes. He tried the next shop and the next but got no further, and so, with a sense of nothing to lose, he hailed a cab and rode it the short distance to the Pink Pelican.

"What do you think of these peace talks?" the driver said. He was a Luo, from the tribe that lived mostly around the shores of the lake. He drove with easy abandon through the thronged streets, beeping on the horn every now and then to scare away pedestrians who remained indifferent. "Think it will amount to something, this time?"

"What peace talks?" Tirosh, who had not really been

paying much attention, said, and the driver grinned and said, "Exactly."

The traffic was bad, and it took longer than it should have to reach the casino. The radio was on, and after a song by Hamlet Zhou, the Jewish-Zimbabwean musician, it segued to the news. The radio announcer was a crisply spoken woman with the clear vowels of formal Judean, and each syllable fell out of the transmitter as clear as crystal shards.

"The time is one o'clock and this is the Palestine news from Ararat City. Tensions remain high today along the separation barrier, as Palestinian Defence Forces continue to conduct an extensive manhunt in pursuit of suspected terrorists following the recent bus bomb attack which claimed over twenty lives. In Ararat City, talks are continuing between the Kalenjin representatives and the Zionist Congress—"

"Ha!" the driver said.

"—as Sultan Al-Said of Zanzibar has urged the two sides to reach a long-lasting solution in the ongoing debate over the Nakuru Protectorate's independence and the so-called Right of Return. The weather is expected to remain hot, with bursts of rain. In international news, unrest continues in the Central African Republic as French mercenaries—"

The driver turned down the radio and opened the window. A hot wind hit Tirosh's face and with it the smell of the lake, frying fish, exhaust fumes and uncollected rubbish. He closed his eyes, remembering long ago trips to the beach with his mother and father, when they had still been together: they'd drive down from the highlands in his father's beat-up old Susita, their camping gear packed in the back, and his mother would put on the radio, which played the music one seldom heard anymore, of the old, Beautiful Palestina of yesteryear, melodious and earnest. His father would have the window open and be smoking a cigarette, one arm hanging over the side of the car, and Tirosh and Gideon would squabble in the back seat. Then the lake would hover into view and they'd skirt the town, make their way to the nearby beach with the palm trees lining up on the shore, and they'd set up camp. There was always something to do on those small excursions, and he and Gideon would often put together makeshift rods with wooden sticks and fishing line, and they'd spend hours trying to catch fish, though they seldom did. He wondered where those days had gone, and how they had once seemed as though they would last forever. Yet they had so quickly faded away. He wondered at the dull ache in his chest, when he thought about it. Some memories had become so clear to Tirosh, and yet others were unattainable, like film that had been overexposed to the sun. He could sense, vaguely, that they were there, but he could no longer bring them to the front of his mind.

The casino sat on the edge of town, away from the docks. It had its own private sand beach, and its servers glided through the corridors in their liveried uniforms. The staff was mostly black. The taxi discharged Tirosh outside the gates. It was an old colonial building, and palm trees lined the road, and sprinklers made a soft woosh-woosh-woosh sound as they watered the pristine and manicured grass.

A blast of cold air hit Tirosh as he entered the Pink Pelican Casino & Hotel Resort. For a moment he stood there, and was transported in his mind's eye to his long ago childhood, when he and Gideon roamed those self-same corridors, and darted into the gaming rooms to play the slots when the attendants weren't looking. Then, it had seemed a sort of wonderland. Now, however, as he advanced farther inside the casino, he could not help but feel a growing sense of disappointment. There were burn marks on the once-lush carpets, and the walls were smudged with dark stains and dust. One of the overhead lights was broken, and another, as he passed under it, kept flashing, on and off, on and off, distracting Tirosh. An air of genteel disuse lay over the old casino, and the few gamblers there seemed captive in the brightness of the slot machines, sitting before them on raised chairs as though they were witnesses at a trial. A dilapidated sign pointed Tirosh to the hotel reception, and he waited as a group of Tanzanian Catholic priests checked in. When at last they were done he approached the desk. A harassed-looking clerk welcomed him cautiously. Tirosh said, "I'm looking for a Mr. Cohen, from Uganda?"

The clerk's face brightened and he nodded, twice, before he said, "Mr. Cohen, yes, of course. Who shall I say is calling?"

Tirosh hesitated. He said, "Just tell him it's about the theodolite."

The clerk, it seemed, was not unused to such requests. He lifted the phone and dialled a number and waited for two short rings.

"Mr. Cohen? There's a man at reception who would like to see you. Yes. Yes. Of course. He says it's about a theodolite, sir. Yes, I see. Very kind, sir. Yes, of course. I'll tell him."

He put down the receiver.

"Mr. Cohen regrets that he is unable to come down in person right now," the clerk said. "But he suggests you return tonight. Would eight p.m. suit? Mr. Cohen has a private table reserved at our Lake View Restaurant when he stays here with us. You're quite lucky to catch him, sir. Mr. Cohen is often absent as he goes on his travels."

"I thought he lived in Uganda, and only visited here," Tirosh said, and the clerk gave him a pitying glance.

"We prefer to think of this as Mr. Cohen's primary residence. A valued guest, certainly. Would there be anything else, sir?"

"No," Tirosh said. "Thank you."

"You're welcome, sir. Please do enjoy our state-of-the-art gaming facilities. The poker room only opens in a couple of hours, but if sir would like to book a seat at the table I could—"

"No," Tirosh said. "Thank you. I am not much into gambling."

"Of course. Well, have a good day, sir."

"You, too."

When Tirosh left, a man emerged from the elevator and approached the desk. The clerk nodded in Tirosh's direction, and the man who had come down nodded to the clerk before following Tirosh with unhurried steps. Tirosh did not notice. He stopped only once, to put a pound coin into a slot machine. When he pulled the lever the machine whirred, and the colourful symbols on the dials spun, fast at first and then slowing down, a whirl of coconuts and cherries, melons and papayas. Then it stopped, and a row of three identical melons came into alignment, and with it the ding-ding-ding of a winning bell, and a handful of pound coins clattered noisily into the cash tray. Tirosh scooped them up and looked at them in his palm, as though they were archaeological artefacts he had uncovered, but try as he might he could not, or so it seemed, discern their meaning.

He pocketed the coins and left the casino.

He was not aware of being followed.

24.

Tirosh's phone rang outside. When he answered it there was a hiss of static and then a woman saying, "Tirosh? Tirosh, where the hell are you?"

"Elsa?" he said, though the name sounded unfamiliar, and he wondered why it had come into his head.

"Tirosh, I don't know where you are, you never showed up at the university, the hotel says they have no record of you checking in. Where did you disappear to?"

She sounded distraught.

"But I'm here," he said, wonderingly.

"Here where!"

"Home," he said, as though it were the most obvious thing in the world. "I'm getting close, Elsa. Things are becoming clearer. There's a missing girl, you see," he said earnestly. "And it's all to do with this wall, somehow. I'm on the trail. I'm pursuing a lead—" He said it with self-importance.

"Tirosh, have you gone mad? Are you even in Tel Aviv anymore?"

"Tel Aviv?" he said, trying out the unfamiliar name. And, "I'm sorry, who did you say you were again?"

She was shouting at him down the phone, from far away, clearly concerned, whoever she was; and he felt a pang of pity for her. It was then, crossing the street to his hotel, that he ran into Melody Rosenberg.

"Lior?" He heard his name spoken, and before he knew it she was bearing down on him. "Lior Tirosh, is that *you*?"

The phone, with that unknown woman shouting desperately at him, was shut now like a glasses case and in his pocket, forgotten. Coming towards him, along the wide pavement, was a woman of Tirosh's age, though she looked younger. She wore the very latest fashions from Paris, a dress and a shawl over her slim shoulders, and she was carrying delicate bags of duty-free shopping, and as she approached he could smell her expensive perfume, Judean Rose by Dior. He thought she looked very beautiful, and that she had barely aged since he'd last seen her, which seemed an eternity ago. And he said, "Melody? Is that *you*?" as she gave him a very grown-up hug.

"I don't *believe* it!" she said. "I thought you lived in Paris."

"Berlin," he said. "I'm a writer now."

"You were always a bit daydreamy," she said, smiling. She had very nice, very even white teeth, and Tirosh thought they looked expensive. He'd always had a small crush on Melody Rosenberg, of the Rosenberg diamond dynasty, ever since he'd seen her on his first day at school, when they had moved from the farm to Ararat City. The Rosenbergs were as close as you could get to real aristocracy in Palestina. The family did business with the de Beers in South Africa and the Hasidic diamantaires in Antwerp, and were distantly related to the French branch of the Rothschilds by marriage; and Tirosh's brother, Gideon, had gone out with Melody's sister Tamara for a while.

"It's been so *long*!" Melody said. "I've just come back from the mines in Tanzania myself." She smiled, a little self-consciously. "I ended up studying at the Sorbonne for three years, but now I'm in the family business. My sister got married and moved to America, of all places—that backwater!—and my father's been ill for a long time, so . . ." She shrugged. "It turns out I'm pretty good at it," she said.

"I'm sorry to hear about your father," Tirosh said.

"He's doing as well as can be expected," Melody said. "Lior, it really *is* good to see you! Listen, I can't stop—I'm on my way to a meeting with some Congolese diamond traders—but I'd love to catch up properly. It's been so *long*!" She said it with the slight hesitation of a person unwilling to admit quite how long ago their childhood had been. "Why don't you come over tonight to the villa? We're having a small party, just a little gathering really, you remember where it is, don't you?"

Tirosh did. They'd gone there, just the once, Gideon with Tamara and Tirosh dragging along for the weekend. The Rosenbergs had their own private beach. . . . He suddenly remembered, with acute embarrassment, that he had tried to kiss Melody that weekend, and how she'd turned her head away and then said, delicately, that she didn't think of him in *that* way, and how they should just be friends. His cheeks burned at the memory. Melody had always been grown up, whereas he never seemed to have grown comfortably into an adult. Tirosh was the kind of guy who never felt very comfortable in his body. Perhaps that's why he became a writer, and why forgetting came naturally to him. He was always the kind of guy to escape easily into daydreams.

"I'd like that," he said, feeling shy. Melody hugged him again, her perfume enveloping Tirosh.

"I'll see you tonight," she said, and then, with a clicking of heels, she was gone, down the street until she turned and disappeared from sight.

Tirosh looked after her, longingly. When he turned back he saw a man watching him from the other side of the street, but he thought nothing of it, not then. He went back to the hotel and up to his room, where he stripped and showered before lying on the bed.

When he slept, he dreamed. In his dream he was married. They were living in a small apartment in Berlin near Görlitzer Park and they were happy, for a time. It was a small apartment and it was cold in winter. Tirosh had a desk facing the window, where he wrote. In the dream his wife was sitting on the toilet and Tirosh was standing in the door. His wife held a home pregnancy test stick in her hand and it was blue. She looked up at him and smiled. In the dream she was radiant, and he had to look away, and blink back tears, from the glare.

"Oh, Lior," she said. "We're going to be so happy."

He woke up drenched in sweat, tangled in the sheets. The window was open, and a hot, damp wind stirred the dirty curtains. He washed his face in the sink and stared at himself in the mirror. He didn't know the person who stared back at him. He wondered if he was happy.

When he stepped back out onto the street night had fallen, and the electric street lights burned with a cheery yellow glow. He walked to the Pink Pelican, enjoying the cooler air and the calls of the sugarcane sellers and the smell of grilled beef. Judean reggae blared out of loudspeakers on Sir Andrew Cohen Square, and couples strolled arm in arm along the promenade.

He must have been happy, he thought.

"Daddy, daddy," a voice said, but when he looked back in alarm it was just some toddler, running after his parent, who lifted him up with seeming ease and carried him away. The boy looked contented.

The Lake View Restaurant, when he arrived, was already filling with tourists, but when Tirosh mentioned Mr. Cohen's name he was ushered inside almost immediately, and escorted past the public dining room, along another carpeted corridor, and at last to a private room with floor-to-ceiling glass windows that overlooked the lake. The room was dark, and for a moment Tirosh's eyes were drawn to the distant pier and the incoming ships and the glare of the port's floodlights. The server who escorted him departed silently and shut the door. There was a large round table in the centre of the room and three shadows, two standing and one sitting down.

"Marcel, a light, please."

One of the large standing shadows struck a match and lit a candle on the table. In its light, Tirosh saw Mr. Cohen. He was a short, thin man, quite elderly, but with large, animated eyes. When he stood to shake Tirosh's hand he moved with a quick agility. His skin felt dry and warm in Tirosh's palm.

"I'm intrigued, Mr. . . . ?"

"Tirosh. Lior Tirosh."

"Ah . . . I did wonder what mystery man came calling this morning. But my door is always open, eh, Marcel? Eh?"

"Yes, Mr. Cohen," the large man said. He took position by the door, standing with his arms crossed, and the look he gave Tirosh was indifferent—Mr. Cohen, the look seemed to suggest, received many dubious callers, and Tirosh was merely one of them, and soon to be thrown out with the rest.

There was a bottle of wine on the table, which had been set for one. Mr. Cohen motioned for Tirosh to sit down and resumed his own seat. He poured wine into his glass but did not offer any to Tirosh. Mr. Cohen took a sip, nodded in apparent satisfaction, and examined Tirosh.

"Tirosh, Tirosh, I have heard that name recently," he said.

"It's a common enough name," Tirosh said, cautiously.

"What did you want to see me about, Mr. Tirosh?"

"I understand you specialise in antiquities," Tirosh said. "Curios. Especially, items relating to the first expedition."

"Ah . . ." Mr. Cohen said. "Yes, yes, indeed. I am no expert, you understand. Merely a keen amateur. I grew up in Entebbe under the British, you know. From an early age I apprenticed with an old trader, a Mr. Simpson. At the time we were shipping carvings and suchlike to folks back in Europe, but every now and then Mr. Simpson would travel across to Judea, as it was then, and I'd accompany him. Do you know, I am fascinated by the tale of that first expedition. How easily things could have turned out differently, had Mr. Wilbusch only returned a negative report to the Zionist Congress back in Europe. How prophetic of him it must have been, to envision this land so transformed, a Jewish homeland—not a holy land, but a land all the same."

"An unholy land," Tirosh said, and Mr. Cohen chuckled appreciatively.

"Yes, yes. Quite, Mr. Tirosh."

"I did not realise they had left much behind them," Tirosh said.

"Oh, plenty!" Mr. Cohen said. "Don't forget the three men travelled with much equipment, and many porters. Many porters. Then there was the matter of the attack, of course."

"The attack?"

"Mr. Wilbusch was pursued by indigenous Nandi," Mr. Cohen said, and chuckled again. "Quite prescient of them, really, don't you think?"

"I heard Wilbusch was working for the Holy Landers," Tirosh said. "That he was set from the start to return a negative report."

"Perhaps, perhaps."

"Until something changed his mind. Something he saw, in a sacred place."

"I would not know about that, Mr. Tirosh. No, I am sure I won't. I am not a superstitious man, merely a curious one. I love the past. And it provides me with a modest living. Yes, it does. Now, how can I help you, exactly?"

"I was told you may have an object of Wilbusch's in your possession," Tirosh said. Mr. Cohen regarded him gravely, his fingers entwined over the stem of the wine glass. "His theodolite."

"Ah, yes," Mr. Cohen said, "the theodolite. I'm—"

There was a knock on the door and he turned his head. "Marcel?"

The large man opened the door. A white waiter glided in, pushing a cart laden with food. The cart was covered in a starched cloth. "Your dinner, sir."

"Ah, excellent!" Mr. Cohen said.

It was, however, the last thing he said.

The waiter was dressed in a white jacket and black trousers. He was himself, it seemed, a Palestinian, like Tirosh.

He removed an automatic handgun equipped with a silencer from under the cloth.

Marcel moved towards him, but the assassin coolly fired at him, twice in close range, and the big man dropped to the ground. Tirosh ducked as the assassin turned and shot the other bodyguard in the forehead.

Mr. Cohen opened his mouth, perhaps to protest, perhaps to plead. Tirosh never found out. The assassin fired two short bursts, a part of Mr. Cohen's head disappeared in a burst of blood and bone, and then it was done, and three men lay dead in the room.

Tirosh faced up to the assassin. He was just a young man, with hair cut short and a pleasant enough face. He could have been a waiter or a soldier. He could have been anyone.

Tirosh raised his hands, protectively. The assassin never spoke. He reached over almost casually. Tirosh could just see the arm holding the gun rising, then falling towards him.

A pain exploded in the side of his head and he sank to his feet.

Through the pain he saw the assassin do something curious.

With the blood of the fallen man he drew a symbol on the wall, a sort of tree or map; and, it must have been Tirosh's imagination, the blood seemed to flare, for just one second, as though it had been set on fire.

He tried to crawl away. Dimly he heard the assassin's footsteps.

The man knelt beside him. He took Tirosh's fingers gently, then eased the gun he had used into Tirosh's hand.

He placed Tirosh's finger on the trigger and squeezed out a shot. It hit the wall above Mr. Cohen's table.

"Hush," the assassin said. "Easy now."

Tirosh tried to move the gun, to point it at the assassin. The man pushed it down with his boot.

Tirosh saw that he held another, clean gun.

The assassin's arm descended a second time and a second time Tirosh experienced a blow to the head.

This time, mercifully, he lost consciousness.

25.

In that place the mind escapes to when confronted by trauma it was dark. It was a place well known to Tirosh, who tended to spend much of his time in his own head. His mind was a warm, dark cell.

In between consciousness and dream, Tirosh began to discern blades of light. There was a teenaged boy who bore Tirosh's face, clambering up a mountain. The mountain was Elgon, and the boy was Tirosh, and he knew this mountain well. It was the summer holidays and he was staying with his father on the farm, away from the city. The Rosenbergs had gone to the lake and Gideon had gone with them and so it was only Tirosh and his father on the farm.

The boy who was Tirosh took to hiking much of the day on his own. Mostly he daydreamed, of the stories he would one day write (though he was not yet sure how one went about writing such stories), and of the adventures of Avrom Tarzan, the Judean Jungle Boy, and his battles against the Ugandan poachers and South African mercenaries, and his expedition into the Hollow Earth.

It was this last story (which Tirosh had devoured avidly only the month before) that led him to explore the caves on Elgon, despite his father's warning. Now he climbed, hand and feet, over the rise. When he stood he could look down and see how far he'd come, Ararat City far in the distance, its white houses against the blue sky, and there the farm, and the villages, and there a giraffe reaching the high branches for the leaves of a tree.

But the young Tirosh did not care for the view. The mouth of the cave yawned ahead of him. He pushed through shrubberies and saw tiny insects scuttle away in distress as he passed. Inside the hollow of the mountain the air turned still and humid, and he could smell distant running water, lichen, and a certain fetid air that came and went without warning.

His father had often told him not to go near the caves. The elephants went there, and other things: there could be snakes there, or Ugandan raiders, and stories abounded that, back in the early struggle for independence from the British, some Palestinian freedom fighters had hidden caches of arms and munitions in the Elgon caves.

Tirosh was well equipped for this exploratory journey, with a flashlight and a thermos and a bag of sandwiches and a compass, and he marked his passage on the walls of the caves, the better to know his way out again, and as he did he noticed old, similar symbols etched in the stone.

There had certainly been people there before him. He found

traces of their passing, some more recent than others. When he emerged into a large cave he found the remains of a small fire, ringed by stones, and farther on his way he saw discarded sugarcane bark and, later still, a bullet casing.

His heart raced when he picked up the casing. Did it mean someone had been shot, or was being shot at, in the caves? He had been going for quite some time, and he was no longer sure what the time was outside. The caves seemed to go on forever, branching off from one another and turning back upon themselves unexpectedly, and more than once he'd come across a sign on the wall he was sure he himself had drawn, though he could not remember being there.

Though the paths he followed went up and down, up and down, then sideways and round, he began to sense that his ultimate direction was deeper and lower into the mountain. What propelled him to go on he didn't know.

He began to imagine he could hear voices, whispering in his ears, hurrying him along. The sound of water grew louder in his ear. The cave walls expanded around him for a time, and he found himself walking through a series of rooms where the walls were filled with fantastical art, showing long-extinct beasts and small graceful hunters, and symbols he could not quite comprehend, though they evoked in him unpleasant feelings when he stopped to study them.

More and more he saw trees etched into the walls of the cave, and some of them seemed grotesque to him and almost alive. Then the sound of water grew louder and the light all but disappeared so that the blade of his torchlight's beam shone weakly into the darkness, and he moved slowly and cautiously, and wondered if he would die there, or if he would ever find his way back and whether his father would miss him and come looking for him. But it did not stop him, and he thought nothing would.

When he came at last to the place he almost slipped and fell on wet stone, and it was with panic that he put out his hands and held on to the walls. His torchlight fell and tumbled down and away from him, the beam of light spinning in the dark. Then it hit not the ground but a body of black water, with a splash, and disappeared.

Tirosh crawled forward and down. At first it was very dark and he dared not move much, but as his eyes grew accustomed to the dark he began to discern thin threads of sunlight falling down from far overhead and, raising his face, saw that he was in a vast cave or hollow that must have reached all the way to the top of Mount Elgon, allowing some sunlight in through hidden slits or cuts in the roof; and slowly, slowly, he could see.

He stood very still, his heart beating to the sound of rushing water. When he looked around him everything seemed ghostly. He could see the black river, and he followed along the slippery bank until it fed into a large black pool. Tirosh knelt by the pool and put his hand into the black water and gasped—it was icy cold. He was thirsty, and he cupped water in his palm and drank from it—just a little. It tasted pure and clear, but it was foolish to do so. One does not lightly drink from the black waters of the Sambatyon.

At this point Tirosh's dream recollection became confused. He was not sure, afterwards, what had happened or how he had emerged from those subterranean depths back into the world; in his memory there was a series of narrow tunnels that he traversed, emerging into sudden, bright sunlight, as though no time at all had passed outside, and the chilling memory, which must have been an illusion, of a dark tree in a secluded spot, stark against the mountain, from which hung not fruit but dozens and dozens of ancient human skulls.

Now, in his dazed state, he seemed to recall something else, too. For a long time he had forgotten this episode, as indeed he had forgotten many other things. But now he seemed to think he had been there once more; and with this uncomfortable realisation Tirosh woke up.

His head hurt indomitably. He blinked and looked at the room. Mr. Cohen with half his head missing was lying on the floor behind the dining room table. His bodyguards were slumped down against the walls. Tirosh looked down at his hand.

There was a gun in his hand.

That moment, unfortunately, the door opened. A woman in a server's uniform stood there. She had began to say, "Mr. Cohen, there's a—" then stopped, suddenly, and saw the room.

Her hand rose to her mouth, stifling a scream.

Her eyes met Tirosh's.

"Please," she said. "Please, don't—"

"No, no," Tirosh said, earnestly. "You don't understand."

The gun was still in his hand. His fingerprints were all over the gun. He stared at her in confusion, until she turned and ran.

He stood up. He was beginning to realise his predicament then. There were three dead men in the room with him, and he was the only, and very likely, suspect.

He thought he should stay there until someone came, so he could explain. The police would be there soon.

It occurred to him that this would be the second time he was accused of murder in the space of so many days.

What he should have done is stay where he was and put down the weapon.

Instead he kept the gun and he ran.

26.

Tirosh fled. He took comfort in the fact he had never given his name, but of course, that would hardly matter. He walked out of the restaurant without running, and once outside he began to walk, quickly but without drawing attention to himself. He bought himself a suit on the way, from a cheap stall still open at that hour, where they didn't ask any questions about his appearance. He went back to his hotel room and washed and changed rapidly and then left. He had no luggage. Everything he'd brought with him, which wasn't much, had been left in Ararat.

What he did next was pretty smart of him, I think. He hailed down a taxi and gave the driver the address for the Rosenbergs' place.

By this time the police had been summoned to the Lake View Restaurant and the first call for me had been made, but I wasn't there.

No one would have thought to look for the killer in one of the wealthiest addresses in all of Palestina.

It wasn't a long drive. The cab went along the coastal road until it had left the town and the port behind it, and the darkness grew more profound, and Tirosh could see the stars overhead when he looked out of the cab window.

As they drove away from the town silence descended, and with it came the peaceful sound of waves beating gently against the lakeshore, and the call of birds and the hum of insects. The houses grew larger and farther apart from one another, set in their own plots of land. Presently he heard faint music, which grew louder as the cab slowed down and then came to a halt outside a large gate that stood open. Tirosh paid and the cab drove away, leaving him standing there.

He took a deep breath of fresh air.

Rows of trees led up to the entrance, and cars were parked every which way outside. They were the sort of cars writers like Tirosh often wrote about but could never afford: Ferraris and Maseratis from Italy, Rolls-Royces from England, Mercedes vehicles from the Reich . . . The cars gleamed in the light spilling out from the windows of the beach house.

Tirosh went up to the house, where a silent server welcomed him in with a nod when he offered his name.

Melody had mentioned a small gathering, but what welcomed Tirosh as he stepped in was a full-blown party, and seemed to include anyone who was anyone in the upper strata of the Palestinian social world. Tirosh remembered some of them from school, and others from the television or the newspapers.

There were Arisons and Adelsons, Salomons and Abramoviches, Ephrussis and Blavatniks, Soroses and Brins. They were like so many fish swimming around each other: the men in suits and the women in furs and dresses, and their kids cool in jeans and T-shirts that must have cost more than a workman's annual salary. There was no Gross amongst them, and Tirosh felt a pang of sympathy for the construction magnate, who for all his money clearly did not belong in this world of old and inherited money. He saw members of the ancient, European nobility there: von Oppenheims and von Löwenthals and de Morpurgos, Rothschilds and Auerbachs. Some had grown up in Palestina, but many held dual nationalities, retained the old bases back in Europe, the seats of trade. They did not bear those new-fangled names like "Tirosh."

But he didn't really have time to be resentful. Melody found him standing there, and once again her scent enveloped him, and she looked at him and said, "Lior, you look like shit!"

"Sorry," Tirosh said. "I had a rough day."

"Let's get you changed. You can't walk around like this." She threaded her arm through his and escorted him along. "My brother's clothes might fit you."

She took him to a room with a walk-in closet. The room was bigger than Tirosh's apartment had been back in Berlin.

"Well?"

"What?"

"Well, take them off!"

Melody made a face. Tirosh obeyed, reluctantly. He felt exposed standing there, under her gaze. He unbuttoned the cheap shirt, then let it fall to the floor.

"Take it all off," Melody said. She came closer and lifted his vest, pushing it up and over his head. She was standing quite close, he thought.

"Lior?"

"Yes, Melody?"

Her fingers traced a line, very lightly, on his stomach. "You've changed," she said. She said it with some wonder.

"I was away, for a long time."

"I remember when you left. Everyone just thought you disappeared. I think they even sent out search parties to look for you, then your father said you were fine, and you'd gone overseas to study."

Her hand kept moving across his body. He found it hard to swallow.

"What do you mean?" he said. "What search parties?"

He remembered leaving. His mother and father both together, for once, at the airport. His mother's hug, his father's rough handshake. Remembered boarding the plane, which took off into the clear air, and climbed above the clouds. . . .

"When you went missing," she said, as though it were obvious. "Everyone was worried sick, they thought you fell and broke your leg or something, near the caves. Apparently you were always going into the caves there, even though you knew it wasn't safe."

"But I didn't," he protested. "I never . . ."

It was hard to think. There was a heat in his body that he'd almost forgotten, and Melody's hands were both moving now, up and down his torso.

"Melody . . ."

"In here," she said. There was a hungry urgency in her voice. She pushed him into the closet and came in after him and shut the door. She laughed, softly, and the sound sent a shiver down his spine.

"You smell different," she said. "You smell of gunpowder and blood. That was blood on your vest, wasn't it?"

"I don't . . ."

"It's funny how people change," she said. Then she was in his arms, warm and willing, pushing him amidst bespoke suits from Savile Row and Milan, amidst cashmere and linen, silk, tweed and wool. Then her lips were on his, soft and plump, and he thought with an aching loneliness of that summer long ago when he had tried to kiss her and they agreed to be just friends.

But they were grown up, and they were different people now.

"Oh, Lior . . ."

"But I didn't," he said. "I never went missing. There was never . . ."

She silenced him with her lips. Her hands were on him and he stopped talking, there was nothing more to say. He held her, it was like a dream or a fantasy. He kissed her then, they were hidden amidst all the clothes, like a couple of teenagers in a forest. She slid her dress off and Tirosh held his breath and she laughed, gaily and easily—it seemed so simple to her, and so strange to Tirosh. He had never really lived the life of his storybook heroes, until now.

They moved against each other, with each other. He remembered cold black water, flowing. Why was he thinking of that? He did not want to think of that, not now. He held Melody desperately, burying his face in the crook of her neck. His lips tasted salt, a sweet scent. He remembered falling.

The water had been so cold.

He was drowning.

Melody said his name. A shiver ran through him. He held on to her like a desperate man. She gasped and pulled him deeper, deeper and down. Tirosh's thrashing had a desperate quality, he was cold and then hot, he held on to her as she called out his name and as she cried out and as she raked his naked back with her nails. Then the awful black water fell away from him and he dropped.

He was falling, through warm air, into another place

They lay there, still entwined, for a long moment, amidst the suits and the coats. The sounds of the party slowly penetrated into their private world. At last Melody disentangled herself. She smiled at him, a little dreamily.

"That was nice," she said.

"Yes," Tirosh said. He had broken through the black water, he thought, he was safe, there was air, and light. He smiled then, shyly. "I always wanted to—"

"I know," she said. She stroked his cheek. "You're in some kind of trouble, aren't you, Lior."

"Yes," he said. "Yes, I think I am."

"I like it," she said. Then she rose and put the dress back on and reached down. He took her hand and stood.

"I should get back to the party," she said.

"Melody—"

"You're sweet," she said, distractedly. Tirosh sat up and pulled on the expensive shirt she offered him. The silk felt cool against his skin. Dressed in someone else's clothes he followed her back into the party. Melody moved away with a final, affectionate squeeze of Tirosh's hand. He thought it had meant very little to her, what had happened. Tirosh walked amongst the partygoers, a glass of wine in his hand. He stepped out of doors, onto the Rosenbergs' private beach.

It was then, standing on the manicured lawns, looking out at the lake with the moon overhead, that he saw something impossible.

A woman materialised in the air above the lake.

For a moment she seemed to hover there, then she plunged down and fell with a splash into the sea.

When she emerged she stepped out of the water and stood there on the beach.

She raised her head and their eyes met. She was slight of frame and her wet dark hair clung to her face.

He knew her.

It was the woman from the airplane.

PART SEVEN
VOYAGES

27.

When you wake up it is early morning, it must be. You are still held captive by the PDA soldiers, in the house belonging to that Nandi businessman temporarily turfed out of his home. You hear a car, returning. You do not know why you're being held, or not exactly. These people who have captured you are crude; this world has very little understanding of the fundamental physics that underlie travel between the sephirot, merely a dim glimpse or recollection of it, some obscure Kabbalist texts—mysticism, not science.

It is different in your world.

Yet though this world is crude, it is not entirely without knowledge. Moreover—there are slippages. Which is to say: you expect what is coming, you expect the dishevelled man and his shambling assistant as they come in through the door.

You recognise him, vaguely. You've seen him at the airport, an official without a title. He had detained Tirosh. You are trained to notice that kind of thing.

And hadn't Abu Ramzi warned you?

There is a man. Bloom.

"Barashi, bring us some coffee," the man says. He is not an exceptional-looking man. He has that sort of anonymity that you and Tirosh also possess. You could pass for natives in half a dozen worlds and be privileged outsiders in a dozen others. The assistant shrugs at you, apologetically it seems, and withdraws. You are left alone with this man.

He looks at you. He searches your face, for what, you cannot tell. You look back, cautious. He says, "My name is Bloom."

You nod. He is important, you think. Willingly or not he is a part of the pattern being made here, the one you have to stop.

An outsider. And you're curious, so curious, as to how he got here, and from which improbable history it is that he came.

"Your name," he says, this man, this Bloom, "your name is Nur, according to your papers. Nur Al-Hussaini."

You nod, yes.

"With an Ottoman passport, and an address in Jerusalem, in the Holy Land."

You nod again.

"In Palestina to visit relatives."

You nod, a third time.

"Well?" this Bloom says, unexpectedly, and smiles. "What do you think of our little country?"

"It's very interesting," you say.

"Interesting?" He seems disappointed in your reply.

"Very beautiful," you say.

"That it is."

"It feels like a historical accident," you say, unable to help yourself, perhaps; or perhaps you want to test him, this man, you throw him a line and bait, to see how he reacts.

"What do you mean?" he says. Still that reasonable voice, that hospitable tone, as though you're not a prisoner, as though this is not an occupied house in an occupied territory. As though he does not wear a gun.

"Jews," you say. "In Africa."

"Jews," he says, "are everywhere."

You nod, conceding the truth of it. Your memories of *this* world—false memories, perhaps, but true just enough—rise to the surface of your mind and you use them.

"We have Jews under the Ottomans, too," you say. "In Jerusalem, in Jaffa. Only a minority, but to them, there is no other place to live but the Holy Land. So why do you live here, so far from where you came, in a foreign land?"

The words, you think, pain this man, a private sorrow, but he replies, nevertheless, with courtesy. "We do not need a holy land," he says, and you think he must be quoting or misquoting someone else's words, "but merely a land of our own, in which we can be free."

You nod. Do they know, in this world, how lucky they've been, that the expedition returned a positive report, that the great Jewish migration to Africa began in the first decades of the twentieth century? In this world there was still a Hitler, but it had escaped a Final Solution.

And you wonder what Jews are like when they are not defined by the great Holocaust that shaped them, the survivors, that formed of them creatures of power and guilt: more easy in their ways, perhaps, more comfortable in their skins, or perhaps just a nation as all other nations, with the same natural impulses to assert themselves, to be masters in their kingdoms. And you think of the wall they are still building, and of the Displaced, and you know the lesson learned the hard way on your missions for the Border Agency: that no matter what we do, human history always attempts to repeat itself.

"I am curious," this man, Bloom, says, "why an innocent tourist such as yourself would be caught by my men, visiting the house of a known terrorist."

"Astrid—" you say, and he waves his hand.

"She's not been harmed. She is of no concern to us. You, however . . ."

"I am just a tourist. I was just curious to see the refugee camps, the works being done here. All my papers are in order—"

"They would be," he says.

"I don't understand."

"Oh," he says. "But I think you do."

The door opens. His man, Barashi, enters with a tray of coffee. He hands you a mug with a look of sympathy. The coffee's black, bitter, and you're grateful for it. You sip as you try to think.

Which side is this man on? Could he be behind the breaching of the walls, the forming of the pattern? You had expected to be captured, at some point, you think, in a way you are forming your own pattern here, but he doesn't—yet—know it.

"There were strange things on the walls of that house," you say—feeding him a line again.

"Yes?"

"Don't you think?"

He waves his hand, dismissively. "Black magic. Mumbo jumbo."

"Then what's the harm in them?" you ask.

You've reached a temporary stalemate. Bloom drinks his coffee in one gulp. You sip at yours. Bloom says, "Barashi, leave us."

"Sir, yes, sir."

He's done tiptoeing. Without warning, he throws his mug at the wall and it shatters, making you jump despite yourself. The broken china collects on the floor. He leans towards you, aggressively, his veins bulging, and you can see the rage that is always, must always be there just underneath his skin. You think: how tightly wound he is. His bloodshot eyes glare at you.

"Where do you come from? What is your purpose here? Don't lie to me!"

You sip your coffee. It takes control. He's close. Close now. There is only one quick way to do this, but it will hurt: it always does.

"I am here to fix a breach," you say. And before he can react you shoot forward, catching him by surprise. You grab him by the shoulders, you hold on to him tight. His chair topples over and you both

. . .

Fall . . .

. . .

From high above the world, the great African lakes shine with a thousand thousand lights. What great technological civilization had arisen here, over and over through the millennia, you never get a chance to discover, but their shining artefacts, their elaborate cities and great monuments, their libraries and flying craft are all about you as you and Bloom

. . .

Fall . . .

. . .

Onto a world that had never known *Homo sapiens.* Along the shores of the lake stand the camps of *Homo erectus,* smoke rising into the clear blue sky, and you see a small child drawing stars in the dirt, and looking up at you with a wondering gaze, you and Bloom, these two aliens out of time and place, stepping where there is no road, and

. . .

Slip, sidewise, through time—

. . .

Into a world at war, where Wehrmacht tanks overrun the villages along the lake and the fires burn, day and night, and humans beyond count are herded by the soldiers into makeshift concentration camps—

A soldier spots you and shouts, and you and Bloom *duck*—
As a volley of bullets flies overhead and you

. . .

Shift

. . .

Away from there, away from easily comprehensible worlds, into the realms of could-have-beens and never-beens, into fragment worlds and fraction-possibilities:

Here the moon has been burst in half, and its two separate halves hang in the night sky as you pass under a plethora of bright stars, in a world where humanity had never even evolved, where the meteorite never landed, where a herd of brontosauruses graze, peacefully, under the twin moons—

As you shift further, into a world where the gods dominate the Earth, tiny Tokoloshe swish by your feet, startling you, and the Nyami Nyami rises, immense, in the distance, from its kingdom by the Smoke That Thunders, and the young, virile Eshurides rides past, while Mawu gives birth in the sky . . .

. . .

To a world in darkness, the sun is absent and you grope your way in the freezing cold, the air barely breathable, what lives in this world, what terrible catastrophe has engulfed it, you never find out as you press on, and on, and I am afraid,

Nur, I am afraid. I have fallen off the edge of the world once before and I fear falling again, and yet we press on, through the dark, the ground a black shard of glass against which our feet make no sound, for days or hours I know not now, for time has no meaning in that place, but things *do* live there, awful, sentient things, cold and hungry they reach grasping tentacles through the eternal night, whispering, *Leng* . . .

. . .

And we *shift*

. . .

There is a little stone hut that stands here, on the edge of a sea of stars. There is no Earth, no land, only the stars all about and, on their shore, this stone hut, which had stood here for eternity and will stand here for an eternity more. There you kneel, you and the man who is Bloom, the man who is me. There, in that tiny sea of reality on the edge of the stars, there is a packed earth floor, and an altar. The altar is devoid of deities. It is bare. To this altar you offer your silence.

Who built this place, this bubble outside of space and time? I do not know. There are other, older beings than us who have travelled between the sephirot. There are mysteries even you don't know.

In that place we take shelter from the night. In that place one realises how small humanity is, how insignificant its wars, its victories and losses. We are but a blink in the eye of a creator.

It is a terrible place, there on the edge of the stars. And yet there, too, there is life. There is vibrant green moss growing in the cracks in the walls, and in the corner there is a circle of stones in which coals had, until recently, burned. The stones are still warm to the touch. And I think perhaps this is where God lives, and that he had merely stepped out for a time, a fisherman there on the sea of stars, and that soon he would return . . . and I'm afraid, for I do not want to meet him.

Why did you bring me here, I say. Words do not take shape in that place. Words do not form out of air and vibrations; in all this time we do not make a sound. Why did you bring me here to this waste between the stars?

But you have been here before, you say, and I say No, no. You take my hand in yours. Your hand is cold, and I am cold, I shudder. And I know you then, I know you and you know me, entire, for in that place there are no borders, and one's mind is but a part of the whole, and all is known, all is light.

Gently you take my hand and gently you lead me out of that stone hut which had stood there for eternity, and on the sea of stars I think I glimpse, for just a moment, a fisherman's canoe, dark against the sea, gliding towards us, and its occupant's face is shaded. I do not wish to see its face. Gently you take my hand in yours and gently you lead me to the shore of that tiny island of reality, and we look down into the sea, we look down, you and I, we look down into a sky full of stars and we

. . .

Jump.

28.

It is the feet one notices first. Those colossal lion's feet of yellow sandstone, towering above you, for the creature—if that is what it is—is vast indeed, and it stands alone in that place, where the lone and level sands stretch far away. Shelley had the measure of it, and he must have caught a glimpse of it, in daymare or night gaunt, and the great Kabbalists knew this place well. The sun beats down, harshly, allowing no shadows, yet this is no earthly sun but something far more alien, an eye, a radiance which is the first light, which is God's light, the emanations of which beat forth and form the lower worlds of the sephirot. All is known under that light, for this is the penultimate world, the *Ein Sof*—the ancient Hebrew for infinity.

It is the feet I notice first, and only then, reluctantly, do I look up and see the rest of it, the creature—if that's what it is—its lion's body and its eagle's wings and its serpent's tail. And only then, at last, I reach the head, which is human, and regal, and alive: and it looks down on me with a cold and alien amusement in those deep and golden eyes, which hold me in their gaze, until I'm lost forever. . . .

"Snap out of it, Bloom," you say. And I blink, and turn from that monstrous gaze.

The sands stretch far away. There are no other details, nothing but this featureless, endless plane, but for one, so small under the sphinx's gaze that it is easily missed.

A door stands in the sands, unsupported, closed.

A small and featureless door.

And the eyes move away from it, the mind shies from its glare, for it leads beyond.

"I know your mind now," I say.

"And I know yours."

"Then you must realise we share a purpose."

You look at me with slight distaste. "But not a methodology."

"What I do, I do for a higher purpose!"

I look at you. I say, "We're not so different, you and I."

"Oh, spare me the rhetoric."

"We should work together."

At that you shrug. And all the while we stand in the gaze of the sphinx and the door it guards. You look tired, I think. It must take a lot out of you, to make this journey. I have been here, once before.

That you are able to do so at will impresses me as much as it scares me, though I try not to show it.

"This Tirosh," you say, and I almost sigh with relief. We are to be partners after all. "He is the key, yes?"

"It would certainly seem that way."

"But why? What is so special about him?" you say, and you sound confused.

"Perhaps it is that he casts shadows," I say. "There are imperfect reflections of him, across the sephirot, I saw it in your mind. There had been a Tirosh in your own reality. Isn't this why you agreed to take the mission?"

But you frown. "No, that is not it," you say. "No, I don't . . ."

But what it is you were going to say, I do not know.

"Ask the sphinx," I say. You glare at me.

"That," you say, "would be very unwise."

There is a rumble overhead. The giant human head above the lion's body moves, and masonry falls down on us so that we must duck and pull back lest we are crushed beneath.

"Who dares disturb—" it says, in a terrible voice, then the head moves lower still and those impossible eyes blink and the sphinx says, "Oh, Nur, it's you."

"Sphinx."

"I'm bored," the sphinx complains. "How go things in the lower worlds? I feel the threads of light which bind the sephirot shudder, and I grow curious of the affairs of women and men. Who dares meddle with Creation?"

"Who doesn't?" you say, and the sphinx laughs.

"You humans," it says, not unkindly. "You conjure up such wonderful lies, spinning tales of the world, every sentence you speak is a fantasy. You try so hard to believe you are the book of the world, the words that tell its story. And all the while you know in your heart of hearts that you are nought but the ephemera."

My eyes are drawn to the door; that door; that terrible door that stands there on the terrible desolate sands.

It is a door even you dare not open.

I draw my gaze away and look at you. Under the shadow of the sphinx we square up to each other like gunslingers in an old western. The lonely sands stretch far away. I know your mind and you know mine. We have no secrets from each other.

"Well?"

You nod, reluctantly. I smile. The light is very bright. The sphinx's head lowers.

His breath, warm and scented with cardamom seeds, blows against us.

The light is very bright. We grow apart.
You step into the light and

. . .

Fall . . .

. . .

While I am thrown violently sideways and hit the wall. I am back in the commandeered house in the tenements of Nakuru. Barashi stands in the room, staring at me with an unreadable expression. The prisoner is gone. You

. . .

Fall, through endless worlds, from Keter to Yetzirah, from Crown to Creation . . .

. . .

Into the warm waters of Lake Victoria. Overhead, the sky has darkened, and the stars are out. Ahead of you is an unfamiliar house where a party is in progress. You rise out of the water, dripping. You see him then, Tirosh, your quarry. Your eyes meet. He startles, takes a step towards you, and another. You see shadows gathering, the glint of moonlight on a metal object . . .

You shout, "Get down!"

A gunshot, prosaically, rings out.

PART EIGHT

ESCAPES

29.

It is hard for me to pick up the thread of the story at this point. Things become confused. By the time I arrived at the scene of the attack both targets and perpetrators were long gone. It had taken Barashi and myself over two hours of frantic driving, along badly lit roads, to reach the Rosenbergs' villa. Witness testimonies were confused. They described men dressed in black, with an obvious military bearing, emerging out of the shadows, guns drawn. There was a woman in the lake—how she got there, or who she was, no one could tell, though I knew, of course. There was Tirosh, in someone else's clothes and the smell of blood and sex still on him—the smell of pulp, the smell of garish plots—ducking as guns were fired. There was the woman in the lake rising onto land, and somehow, she disarmed one of the attackers.

Their target appeared to be Tirosh.

There had been a short, and mostly silent, battle. The woman fled, taking Tirosh with her. The attackers retreated, melting into the shadows the way they'd come. My men found their car abandoned a short distance away on the lake road. Only a corpse remained on the manicured lawns, and though the man carried no ID it was Barashi, of all people, who identified him. His name was Misha Gomel, and he had served, with distinction, in one of the PDF's elite units, but had since become a mercenary, as many of our young men did, selling his skills to the highest bidders across Africa.

"Last I heard," Barashi said, prodding the corpse with his foot, "he was fighting a war over in Equatorial Guinea—some rich British baronet trying to execute a coup d'état with CIA funding. What he was doing back here I really have no idea."

"Getting himself killed?" I said.

Barashi shrugged. "Well, that *is* an occupational hazard," he said.

I didn't like this very much. I didn't know where Tirosh had gone to or who was behind this attempt on his life. Someone had executed three other people in Kisumu only earlier that night, and they'd done it as casually as killing a chicken. These were all links in a chain, all a part of the escalating pattern. I had to find Tirosh.

"Who *are* you?" Tirosh demanded. They had run out of the villa and the woman had hot-wired a Susita roadster with startling efficiency. Before he knew it they were roaring away at top speed back towards Kisumu. Tirosh was breathing heavily from the adrenaline and the running. Really he wasn't a very fit man at all.

"My name's Nur. We met before, actually. In Berlin."

"In Berlin? But . . ."

"How much do you remember?" she said. She said it almost kindly.

Tirosh gripped his knees. He thought of Isaac on the swing, in the park, the boy's delighted shrieks. "Higher! Higher!" he said. "I like it!"

He was making words, near-sentences, shaping the world to his will as language formed. It was a happy moment, captured in time.

So why did Tirosh feel tears form at the edges of his eyes, why did he feel this overwhelming sadness?

He tried to think of Berlin, but it was hard to get a clear picture of it. It was as though there were two Berlins, one that was still under the German Reich, and one that wasn't; one in which he was from Palestina as he'd always been, and one in which he was from some other, improbable place. The two images were overlaid one on top of another, and he could get no clear sense of the places where they intersected or diverged. Who *was* he? he wondered. Was he even real? He missed Isaac then, missed him terribly, and he wanted to go back right there and then, to scoop his boy up in his arms, to hug him as though he'd never let him go, as though he could keep him safe and protected forever.

Perhaps she could see it on his face. She drove fast, skirting the city, heading away; avoiding pursuit. He didn't know who had tried to kill him, if it was him they were trying to kill at all.

"I remember . . ." he said.

He remembered a cave. Dank air. A tree of skulls. He remembered falling, into icy-cold blackness, falling for so long that he thought he would drown.

He remembered . . .

He remembered not knowing where he was, when he awakened. The fear he felt, and then the search party, and someone shouting "Lior!" and it was—

"We were on holiday in Kenya," he said. "An after-army trip, with a few of the guys. They said I'd gone off from the others, went missing for a few hours. Everyone was looking for me. They were more relieved than angry when they found me. We spent a few more days in Kenya before flying back home, to, to . . . Israel." He said the name wonderingly.

"Israel," he said. "Is that a real place? It feels like a dream I've been having for a long time now, but I don't know which parts of it are real. At first I kept telling them they had it wrong. I didn't want to go there. This is where I was born, where I belonged. I kept looking for Palestina, but they said there was no such place. Everything was gone, like it never existed. And it was so . . . *smudged* in my head. Like a picture with all the colours fading. After a while I stopped asking, and after that I didn't even remember it anymore. I still don't . . ." He shook his head. "Now it's the other side that keeps blurring. Do you know what I mean?" He looked at her then.

"Who *are* you?" he said.

"I told you. My name's Nur."

"You're . . . Are you from there?"

"No," she said. "I'm from another place."

In all of Tirosh's memories there was one black hole, an

emptiness from which he shied away in fear. So instead he tried to reassemble what he knew.

Menhaim's death; Tirosh's missing niece; the theodolite; the bad place Gross spoke about; Mr. Cohen's murder. He told it all to Nur.

He didn't expect her to believe him, but she did, and then she told him another story in return, of where she came from, and what she hoped to prevent.

"We need to get to Elgon," Nur said, when she was done.

Tirosh said, "I must visit my father. He is ill."

"I'm sorry."

"It isn't your fault."

She nodded.

"They'll be looking for me," Tirosh said. "They might be looking for you, too, after the villa. Poor Melody, I must have ruined her party."

"I doubt—" Nur began to say, when the glare of floodlights hit them from farther up the road, momentarily blinding Nur. Another driver would have braked. Nur pressed on the accelerator, driving blind, Tirosh ducking under the dashboard as gunfire opened around them. The car hit at least one person on its way. Its windows exploded in shards of glass. Nur drove them through the ambush. Both were cut by exploding glass, but the gunshots missed them.

What happened later it was harder for me to say.

30.

By the time Barashi and myself arrived at this latest scene I had begun to feel things slipping out of my control. Events were moving too fast, the hidden intelligence behind the sequence of attacks manipulating us all.

It had been a hastily mounted ambush. We found one corpse on the ground, abandoned like the one at the Rosenbergs' villa—this one, too, Barashi identified as a Palestinian mercenary. I suspected at least one other had been hit, but if so his comrades must have dragged him away with them. I saw the signs of the impact, and the blood but no corpse. There were bullet casings on the ground and wheel tracks that peeled off into a dirt road.

"They didn't try to give chase," Barashi said. "It must have caught them by surprise she didn't stop."

"Tell the uniforms to clean this up, will you?" I told him. At this point I wanted to send up helicopters to look for the two fugitives, to put out a call to all police patrols, but I was no longer sure who I could trust.

I could feel it happening already: a sort of *thinning* that was in the air, that was in the ground, and it made the moon look hollow and the cars translucent, and the dead man on the road seemed to me to fade in and out of existence: one moment he was there and the next he wasn't. It was happening, it was *working*, this spell being woven over my beloved country, over this precious night shelter, my Palestina. And I was afraid. I had felt this happen once before.

From here events took a rapid turn. What I know I reconstructed later, and some details are strangely obscured. For instance, I know that you and Tirosh separated for a while, but I don't know why. The whole period from this attack to the events that followed it is obscured to me. For instance, I seem to know that you were wounded, perhaps even hallucinating. You walked in and out of shadows; by which I mean, your passage was not entirely in this world but through adjacent ones, shortcuts into might-have-beens and never-weres, places where you could pass freely.

Tirosh, more prosaically, drove. He chose side roads and dirt tracks, pathways used by farmers and the occasional hunter, and only the moon saw him pass. He knew this land, though his mind was divided.

This land was green and plentiful, the moon shone down on the rolling hills, and it was not long before Mount Elgon appeared in the distance and then grew closer as Tirosh passed along the silent roads that led to his childhood home.

Soon he saw the lonely farmhouse. A solitary light burned on the porch. He eased the car into gear before idling, letting it glide the last few feet before it stopped. He braked and sat there, watching the old homestead. He just sat there. The air smelled so sweet and so thick with memories.

After a while he heard the screen door open and bang closed. Footsteps went along the porch and stopped. Eventually Tirosh got out of the car. He could smell the old man's cigarette. Tirosh felt like a small boy again, coming home.

He opened the gate and stepped in and shut it behind him, like he'd always been told to do.

He heard the old man cough. He took a step, and then another, and the light from the porch fell down on the old man's proud, weathered face. It made him think, irrationally, of a sphinx.

"Hello, Dad," Lior Tirosh said.

PART NINE

EXPLICATIONS

31.

Lior Tirosh studied his father, as though he had never seen him before. He remembered a tall, proud man. Not this stooped figure, body wracked with painful coughs, face lined like a tribal mask. Only the eyes remained the same, the eyes of a bird of prey, and the long, gnarly fingers, nicotine stained, which had once taught Tirosh how to hold a gun, how to plough a field, how to tie a knot and how to hold a pen: he had not seen the old man in years, he realised, and half his memories were false.

"Lior. So you are back."

"Yes."

They studied each other warily. There had been happier times, when he was young, before they moved to Ararat. Then his mother's illness, sudden and inexplicable, and the funeral, and he had to return to the farm. He thought then that his life had been a series of escapes, that in a way he had always searched out that place in the mountain, that black water pool.

He had been desperate to disappear.

And somehow it had worked. He got to forget everything and relive his life . . . elsewhere.

He never expected to be back here again. When he thought of his father it was with a combination of anger and embarrassment, mixed in with what he thought must have been love. He didn't really know. Love wasn't a word the old man used often, unless it was to talk about land, this land.

Tirosh kicked the porch, the way he'd done when he was a child. This *stupid* land.

A memory:

At night on the farm the hyenas come out, hesitant under the full moon. The moon over Palestina is a soft round belly, pregnant with possibilities. When the full moon is high in the sky everything is possible, and the boy, Lior, cannot sleep. He steals outside. The farmhouse is a large wood-and-stone structure; solid, strong. It is of this place. It is here to stay. Father built it, with his own hands and with his own workers he built it. It is almost a small village all its own. Father has stables for the horses and a dairy, where they milk the cows and churn butter, make cheese. There is a village nearby, where many of the workers come from. Father speaks their dialect. Father is well respected, a big, broad man; the papers say he carries Palestina on his shoulders.

On a clear night Lior can smell the woodsmoke from the village, see the lights of cooking fires in the distance, hear a baby cry, a woman laugh, men speaking softly. Their voices are murmurs in the night. The hyenas come out, drawn to the light, their long faces tense, questing. Against Elgon the fever trees provide a postcard contrast. The boy Lior sits on the long veranda with his brother, Gideon. The two square off across a bao board. The night is filled with the clicking of seed pods on wood. Their faces are drawn in concentration. Gideon has learned, already, to use a gun. Father takes him to the hills, teaches him how to hold the rifle, how to load it, how to sight and how to fire. Lior is jealous. He too wants to shoot, to know the power of the gun, but more than that: to know his father's arms protectively around him, the gruff voice instructing him precisely, his father's unshaved cheek pressed against his as he shows him trigger and stock, bolt and safety. His father smells of Matossian cigarettes, unfiltered, and Old Spice. Gideon sweeps up Lior's house and scatters the seeds all across his side of the board. His fingers move deftly, stealing Lior's tokens, until none are left and he slams the final seed into an empty hole with a triumphant cry. Mosquitoes buzz around the lights; the hyenas over the fence grin, lopsided. . . . Then Mum calls them inside.

"So you're sick."

"The land is sick, Lior. My sickness is that of the land."

Tirosh wiped his forehead. The expensive silk shirt stuck to his body. There were glass cuts on his arms. His father's cigarette smoke made him nauseous.

"I've had a long day," he said.

"Writing." It was said with such contempt Tirosh recoiled.

"A book never stopped a bullet, Lior," the old general said.

"That isn't what books are for," Tirosh said.

"This land is sick, Lior. I had hoped . . . I had hoped you, and Gideon, would inherit me. Look after this land. It was fashioned for you. But you both left me. Gideon in the war, you with your fantasies. Now there is no one left."

"Maybe the land is infected with your sickness," Tirosh said. "Not the other way around. This wall—"

"This wall! Do you think I want this wall?"

"I don't know *what* you want."

The old general stabbed his cigarette angrily into the ashtray.

"No walls," he said. "No borders. This should all be ours, Lior. It could still *be* ours! Come inside. I want to show you something."

He turned to go and Tirosh followed. He always followed his father. Inside, the house was sparsely furnished and utilitarian. There were no family photos. Hanging on the wall was a large map.

The old general indicated the map with a nod. Tirosh approached it. He saw Palestina at its centre, ringed with a marker pen. Africa spread outwards from it in all directions. Uganda and Kenya, Tanzania, Malawi were marked in one circle. Beyond them came the Congo, Ethiopia, Namibia. The final circle engulfed Egypt, Nigeria, South Africa and Mali. A dotted line ran from the Cape of Good Hope, making its way through Palestina, up through the continent until it reached Cairo and finally terminated on the Red Sea coast, in Port Said. The old Trans-African Highway.

"All of this," his father said. "Don't you see, Lior? No borders! No walls! A Jewish nation as far as the eye could see, from the Cape to Cairo! And from there . . ." He approached the map and stabbed his finger at the terminus point of the train and ran it along, into the Holy Land.

"All of this, at first," his father said. "But we could do so much more. . . . We are men who live by the sword and by the gun, Lior. And there are other walls, other borders to cross, to conquer. . . ."

Tirosh's eyes were drawn away from the map; horrifyingly; he didn't want to, but it had been there, at the edge of his vision, since he came to the room, a little, old-fashioned trophy cabinet, old stained wood and grimy display glass, a collection of curios sitting forlorn behind the glass; nothing more. And yet . . .

What most of them were he didn't know. A compass, and a stained pocket book with leather covers, and a spear point, broken; a pair of glasses, the frame wire bent; a watch on a chain; and a portable measuring device, rusted with age. A collection of fetishes; and he recognised the last one with a sort of quiet horror: it was—it must have been—a theodolite.

"Deborah," he said. He turned his back on the cabinet of curiosities; turned on his father. "Deborah. Your niece. Gideon's daughter!"

"Lior, please do not take that tone with me," his father said.

"Where *is* she?" Tirosh demanded.

His father said, calmly, "I have no idea."

"It's *you*," Tirosh said. "It was you all this time."

"Lior, please don't be so melodramatic," his father said. "Look. *Look!*"

He pulled down a second map, rolled up on the wall. This one resembled a sort of stunted shrub, or tree, with strange protrusions and excursions, linked spheres each marked in his father's unsteady hand with annotations and lines.

"Look! All of these places, like the godawful one you seem to have spent all your recent time in. Look! There is a place where the Ndebele defeated Cecil Rhodes in the Matobo Hills. There's a place where Shaka survived the assassination attempts on his life and defeated the British in the Battle of Port Elizabeth, and took control of the fledgling Cape Colony. There is a place where Moses became Pharaoh and travelled south with his people. There is a place where—"

Tirosh stared at the map, this child's drawing of impossible worlds, the arrows and diagrams that led from one to another, annotated with numbers of troops, arms shipments, intelligence reports' code numbers. His father's bleating of the never-wheres and haven't-beens washed over him.

He didn't *care.*

He wanted back to his rock-solid reality, to his small apartment overlooking the park, to the clear, impersonal European cold of Germany. To Isaac—

"No," he said. "No. No."

"Lior, it's time for you to stop acting like a child and act like a man," his father said. "Everything is in place, in fact it was thanks to you that I began to understand this destiny, in searching for you, when you disappeared, I learned things. Yes. You have served this land. You will serve it yet, Lior. It is almost ready."

"Deborah," Tirosh said. "What did you do to Deborah!"

"I told you, boy! I don't know where she is. She'll probably turn up, the silly girl always does."

"The men who tried to kill me—"

His father snorted. "Tried," he said. "There is no try in killing, boy. I thought I taught you better than that."

"So who—"

His father nodded. And suddenly there was a gun in the old man's hand. He fired, the blast a painful detonation in the silent room. The air filled with the acrid smell of gunpowder and blood.

"Her," his father said.

Tirosh turned, dumbly. His ears rang with the blast. Behind him stood Nur, a gun in her own hand, unfired. Her face bore pained confusion.

Blood bloomed against her shoulder. Her eyes locked onto Tirosh's, communicating—what? Pain? Bewilderment?

Slowly she collapsed, until Tirosh sprang forward and caught her just before she hit the floor.

32.

Tirosh grabbed the gun from your hand and pointed it, shakily, at his father. Nur groaned softly, trying not to lose consciousness. Something rolled out of her hand and fell under the furniture, but neither man noticed. She'd done it in just such a way.

"Don't shoot,"' Tirosh said.

"She has to die, Lior. She has to die to complete the pattern. We could be in Outremer tomorrow, Lior. In Canaan! In Ursalim! We could win where the Jews should have always won. We'd win at Masada and Qargar and Lachish. Join me, Lior. Be a *man*, for once in your life!"

Did Tirosh want to shoot his father, at that moment? Could he have, even if he'd wanted to? He wasn't the kind of man to hold a gun, let alone use it.

He supported Nur and she stood up, stemming the bleeding as best you could, gaining focus.

"Lior. Don't go."

"I have to."

"You won't get far," the old man warned him. Tirosh ignored him. Still pointing the gun at his father, he edged back, step by step, taking Nur with him.

"Lior—"

"What!"

"You should stay here. It is better."

"Better how, Father?"

"How much do you remember? Of the outside?"

"I remember my *life*! I remember being happy! I wrote books, I had a wife and I had a *child*!"

The word stuck in his throat. Leaning against him, Nur groaned in pain. Tirosh turned his face away. He remembered Isaac. He remembered the boy's smiling, trusting face. The roar of the truck as it came along the road, seemingly out of nowhere. The boy's face in the road. Ada's scream. Tirosh's . . .

"Stay. Here it is different, Lior. We can make it so it didn't happen that way. Here there is still an Isaac, your Isaac, in Berlin. There is a version of you in this world. It doesn't have to be like this—"

Tirosh said, "I saw him die."

"I know about burying one's children," the old general said.

"Do you?" Tirosh said—screamed. "Do you, Father? You know about sending children to die, about training them up, to be soldiers, to hold guns, to fight, always to fight, to die, always to die. For you, for land. What do you know about innocence, about pain? Isaac did no one any harm. He has no part in this. No part."

"Stay."

"*Enough,*" Tirosh said.

He helped Nur out. The old general did nothing. He watched the two of them go. They went outside. They got into the car and Tirosh turned on the ignition. He was crying, stars smudged across the night skies, a child's finger painting. He drove as fast away from there as he could. It didn't matter. The house may have appeared deserted but it wasn't. Men emerged out of the shadows. They had once been children like Tirosh, like Isaac. Now they had grown into trained killers, old General Tirosh's real progeny.

"Get them," he said.

"And your son?"

"He is the last link in the sequence," the old man said, heavily. "Kill him, too. Kill them both."

The men nodded. They slipped into the night and were gone, following their prey.

33.

I watched them go. I had parked the car at the turn in the road and made my way to the farmhouse on foot. I watched them drive away, towards Elgon, and I saw the old general and

I saw his men and I understood it all. I waited awhile. Then I made my way to the house on foot and opened the gate and let myself in.

I think he expected me.

"Bloom," he said, without surprise.

"General."

"Come inside."

He led me to the same room only recently vacated. I saw the fetishes in their display cabinet, these artefacts from a long-ago expedition. I saw the maps on the walls.

"You came from such a place," the old general said.

"Yes."

"You seldom speak of it."

"General, one puts up walls for a reason."

"Oh, Bloom. Don't be naïve. Walls do not keep the enemy out. They keep you locked in. We must break down the walls and take what is ours."

"Sir, with respect—"

"You're either with me or against me, Bloom. There is no middle way."

There was a gun in his hand. It'd been recently fired.

"No," I said, sadly. "There isn't."

I saw the thing Nur had let drop under the furniture. It was nothing remarkable, nothing but a pocket mirror, a vanity. I picked it up and tossed it to him. I don't think he expected me to.

He opened it and stared into the mirror.

I wondered what it showed him.

I turned my back on him and walked away. I wanted to tell him about mimicry, about how organisms can disguise themselves visually in a foreign environment: like weeds pretending to be useful crops so as to avoid destruction.

We must have missed it in customs, I thought. But then, things from the outside always had a way of sneaking in.

The explosion when it came threw me to the ground. When I turned, the farmhouse was on fire.

I stood there watching the blaze, and I saluted. He was a great man and now he was dead.

There was nothing to be said.

I left the place then and followed the car tracks into the darkness.

. . .

Sometimes I still think of the sphinx and wonder why it'd never asked me a riddle.

Perhaps it didn't think I had anything much to say.

. . .

After a time I came on the car abandoned in the foothills of the mountain. It had hit a tree and its chassis was crumpled, but there was no blood and its passengers were no longer inside. I followed on.

. . .

I left two men dead at the entrance to the cave and a third dying, his blood soaking into the earth. . . .

. . .

Another two in a cave with walls decorated with ancient acts of murder.

. . .

My God, that tree! That tree of skulls!

34.

"Not . . . far now," Tirosh said. Nur's weight pressed down on him. They traversed the cave system slowly, Nur's blood trickling down onto the ancient rough-hewn stone floor. Tirosh's eyes stung with sweat. "Not . . . far."

The assassins were behind them and I was behind the assassins. They came to that place in the mountain where time stops.

Black water, a silent pool. Wavelets lapping at the banks. Tirosh sank to his knees. Nur sat there, beside him, holding on to the wound. She was very pale. Her fingers were coated in blood.

"Would you . . . ?" she said to Tirosh.

"What?"

"Would you go? Back?"

He didn't answer you.

The last two men were coming round the tunnel when I killed them with a knife, one each, right through the heart. I helped them down to the ground, gently. I left them there.

The black pool came into view. I slid down to join them.

Tirosh startled, but Nur didn't look surprised. For just a moment, she smiled.

I nodded to her.

It was done.

I helped Tirosh ease her into the water.

The water churned. . . .

She lowered her head, wearily. She sank into the water.

There is a place where the lone and level sands stretch far away. . . .

She was gone.

You were gone.

35.

We had a long talk as we sat there, Tirosh and I, contemplating the black water of the infinite. Nur was gone, and I was hurting more than I realised. I loved this land. I had never thought myself capable of loving another. Person, land: at some point you have to choose one over the other. All history is nothing but a lie we tell ourselves, a story. The land is always there, indifferent to our suffering, our wars, the names we choose to call it. The old general was dead, but Palestina remained, divided by a wall and two different stories.

Tirosh, by my side, grieved for his son.

"So you are an outsider, too?" he said, when we had mostly finished talking. He wasn't that interested, you understand. He was just making noises, it was better than the silence. Perhaps that is all history is, a way for us to ward off the silence of the dead with our fleeting voices.

"Yes."

"What is it like? Your world?" he said.

The old general had asked me that, too. I had never told him.

"It is beautiful," I told Tirosh now. "Altneuland. It sits on the shores of the Mediterranean, with Jerusalem as its eternal capital. Airships glide majestically through the clear blue skies. Children, happy and fat and carefree, run shrieking along the sand beaches of Herzlberg, splashing in the warm water of the sea. The air is scented with the bloom of orange trees. There is no war, no fear. It's paradise."

Tirosh stirred. "And the local people?" he said. A word from his other life, from the outside, came to him then. "The Palestinians?"

I shrugged. "There was no place for them there," I told him. "So they had to go."

He recoiled from me then; as though I were something rotten and slimy. He didn't ask; and I didn't tell him.

"Will you stay?" I asked him.

". . . No," he said, at last.

Then, "You?"

"This is my home, Tirosh."

"Then goodbye, Bloom. I'd like to say it's been a pleasure, but I'd be lying."

"Likewise."

He tried to grin. It didn't suit him, much. He dangled his feet into the water and stared down into the black abyss of its depths. It couldn't have been easy for him, that decision, but I thought I understood it: he'd rejected fantasy, in a way.

He let himself into the water, ungainly, and floated there, shivering.

I don't know what I was thinking. I was thinking of you. I wanted to see you, one more time at least.

. . . I wanted to explain.

He was beginning to sink when I jumped on him.

". . . Let *go*!"

Then we were drowning.

36.

I drowned in a cold, black pool. Stalactites shone, wet with moisture, hanging from the ceiling of the cave. I couldn't breathe. The water was icy-cold and Tirosh was fighting me, trying to push me off, but he couldn't. We were sinking deeper into the water. The pool had no bottom, no end.

I thrashed in the water. I did not want to die. Tirosh fought me off. He was surprisingly strong. Desperation gave him strength. For a moment we were separated and I panicked. Shapes swirled around us in the dark. I reached blindly, caught hold of his wrist, held on tight, fastened myself to him. We were both going to die. We sank. My vision blurred. Why did I follow him? The world was reduced to this one small bubble of air. We were it. Tirosh kicked. I barely felt the pain. The world was agony. My lungs burned. How far had we gone? How much farther could we go? He'd been through once before, I had to believe that. All I had to do was open my mouth and breathe and there would have been an end to it, but still I resisted. A pinprick of light in the distance, impossibly far. I no longer knew which way was up, which way was down. Tirosh had stopped fighting. He dropped like a stone and I held on.

A roar in my ears.

The pool was a black night dotted with stars.

We fell from the edge of the world.

PART TEN

DEPARTURES

37.

. . . and into a raging storm of gunfire.

The night was humid and hot. I was already sweating. They were firing on us from both sides. No, not at us, I realised. At each other. Night, with the stars hanging like cheap decorations overhead. I didn't know where we were. I heard shouts, Arabic, and what sounded like Judean.

". . . Oh, no," Tirosh said. I grabbed him by the lapels, shook him violently.

"Where are we?" I demanded. "What *is* this place!"

He began to laugh. Infuriated, I pushed him to the ground.

"Stay down, damn it!" he said.

I heard a siren in the distance. A dark shape flew overhead, and I heard the whoosh of near-silent missiles, followed a moment later by a huge explosion ahead of us. The shouts in Arabic stopped abruptly. Tirosh grabbed me by the arm.

"Run, you fool! Run!"

Tracer bullets lit up the sky. Ahead of us I could see military jeeps, men in olive-green uniforms firing. Behind them was a huge concrete wall. The wall went on and on forever. It divided up the land. The soldiers were firing on us. Tirosh waved his hands frantically and yelled in some sort of archaic Judean, over and over.

"Don't shoot! Don't shoot! I'm an Israeli!"

It was the first time I'd heard that loathsome word.

I thought we were going to die. Suddenly the gunfire stopped, however. Young men surrounded us, guns drawn. We were tackled and thrown facedown on the ground. In seconds we were in some sort of handcuffs, thin strips of plastic cutting into my skin. Expert hands searched us for weapons. They found my revolver, and I thought I'd be shot right there and then, but Tirosh was keeping up a stream of words all this while, a confused babble about having lost our way, about my being a foreign visitor—

"How did you cross the God damned wall?" one of the soldiers demanded.

"Where are your papers?" another said. Someone kicked me, hard, in the ribs. "Where are your *papers*?"

I closed my eyes.

I thought, at least we weren't dead.

We were taken beyond the wall, and into lockup. Tirosh tried to explain to me, in whispers, where we were. The place was called Israel, or maybe Palestine. We'd been caught somewhere in the Occupied Territories, in the midst of a battle between Palestinian insurgents and an Israeli Defense Force patrol. I let his explanations wash over me. This wasn't where I'd hoped to end up. It was just another fucked up might-have-been.

After a while I managed to tune him out, and slept.

They released Tirosh after a couple of days but kept me in prison for several months while they decided what to do with me.

It wasn't too bad. I kept up with the news and learned to speak their version of Judean, a barbaric mix of Hebrew and Slavic tongues all mixed in liberally with the Arabic of this place. It was the Middle East, the same geographical space as my own, long-lost Altneuland, and yet it couldn't have been further from it.

Tirosh came to visit me during my incarceration, just the once.

"It's my niece," he said.

"Your niece?"

"Deborah. The one who went missing."

"I remember looking into it," I told him. "There was no evidence anything had happened to her, Tirosh."

"Well, I found her," he said, grimly.

"How?"

He told me.

It was on the news, not longer after our . . . arrival. He saw her on the television screen, a youngish woman, a baby strapped to her chest. They were in the midst of a demonstration. A group of left-wing protesters huddled along the Israeli side of the separation wall, carrying placards. Armed police watched them, bored. A short interview, her accent somewhat strange, not quite of this place. Her name was Deborah Glass-Bialik. When he looked, he found her listed in the phone book, and, one autumn day, he drove to see her.

She lived in a small house in the suburbs. There were leaves on the ground, baby toys scattered outside. He hesitated, then knocked on the door, and she answered, holding the baby. She looked at him without much curiosity.

"Yes?"

"Deborah? Deborah Glass?"

"It's Glass-Bialik, now," she said, showing him a wedding ring on her finger. "Do I know you?"

"I . . ." He didn't know what to say.

"Are you a reporter?"

"Oh, no," he said. "It's just, I saw you on the news, demonstrating, and I thought . . ."

"If this is about the next meeting," she said, "hold on." She disappeared inside, returned with a leaflet she thrust into his hand. "All the information's there. I hope you can make it."

She didn't seem bothered by his appearance there. She seemed used to people showing up at her door, and even as Tirosh dawdled, a large bearded man was ambling along towards them, lifting his hand in greeting. He nodded to Tirosh and began to talk to Deborah about the coming Hand-to-Hand Outreach Programme, and the next committee meeting, and after a short while Tirosh made his excuses and left, still clutching the leaflet in his hand like a lifeline. The amateur graphic on the cover showed people on two sides of a wall, tearing it down. Tirosh dumped it in the trash a street later.

"She didn't have any idea who I was," he told me. "And she seemed happy, Bloom. I didn't want to raise old ghosts. I don't know if she even remembers . . . that other place."

"Do you?"

"It does rather seem like a bad dream," he admitted. "Do you believe it, Bloom?"

"I have to," I said. He nodded, slowly, but I don't think he was convinced. He left shortly after, and I never saw him again.

And this is pretty much all of it. After a while I, too, began to fit into that world. My papers were found; I was released with a warning. I often think about you, and wonder where you are.

Tirosh went back to Berlin, for a time at least. He published only one other novel, a sordid little pulp paperback called *Unholy Land*. I saw a copy in a discount bin at the local bookshop once, but neglected to buy it. Last I heard he'd remarried.

As for me, I live in Israel now, in a town called Tel Aviv. It isn't so bad—the beach is nice if often dirty, and it gets too hot in the summer to breathe, but that makes it feel a little like home. I miss the high altitude, though, and the tropical rains. Sometimes I lie awake at night, imagining I hear the call of elephants far away, but it is only a bus going round the corner.

It's out there somewhere, though, I'm sure of that. Last summer I went on a holiday to Kenya, searching for the place it could have been. I found nothing but a peaceful backwater, where the hills I once knew still roll, endlessly, and on a clear day you can see the ocean. In this place, in this time, it was just a footnote to history, a might-have-been, a fantasy. But I am sure it's real, and I think I can find it again. I think I am getting close. Sometimes I turn on the radio, listening to the news of another car bomb or rocket attack, and I add up the tally of the living and the dead.

Sometimes I can't even tell which Palestine it is: their one or ours.

HISTORICAL AFTERWORD

If you go to the city of Haifa today, you may come across Nahum Wilbusch Street down by the harbour. Of the three men who went on that long ago expedition in 1904 he lived the longest, dying of a ripe old age in modern Israel in 1971. An engineer by trade and inclination, he no doubt had little time for the futile exercise of What-If or What-Could-Have-Been.

Zionism's founder, Theodor Herzl, on the other hand, saw the value in imagining impossible futures. In 1902 he published a curious utopian novel: *Altneuland* envisioned a prosperous, idyllic Jewish state in Palestine. In Herzl's vision of the future, an Arab minority exist as full citizens in this land, though even in the novel a politician attempts (yet fails) to take away their rights. The novel was translated into Hebrew as *Tel Aviv*, and subsequently gave its name to the

Jewish suburb of Jaffa established in 1909, now the largest metropolitan area in the State of Israel.

Herzl himself never got to see fiction become reality. He died in 1904, having spent much of his adult life searching for a homeland for the Jews. Other proposed settlements included El-Arish in Egypt; Cyprus; Anatolia and Argentina, though none came to fruition. Herzl's sole surviving daughter, Trude, died in the Theresienstadt concentration camp in 1943. For the Herzl family there hadn't been a happy ending. Perhaps happy endings are harder in reality than in works of fiction.

Israel and Palestine are two lands in one, a single geography divided by competing stories. I myself grew up on a kibbutz in Israel, next to an Arab village whose residents fled in the 1948 War—or the War for Independence, depending on your point of view: their houses had been razed to the ground shortly thereafter, and it remained a curious, empty place for us children to visit. Though I was often told that the residents "fled," it never occurred to me to ask why they didn't simply return.

Many of the Palestinian refugees from that time escaped to the West Bank and Gaza Strip, as well as to Lebanon and Syria, where permanent refugee camps now stand. At the turn of the twenty-first century a massive, seven-hundred-kilometre-long "barrier wall" began to be erected between the West Bank and Israel; it is called a "security fence" in Hebrew, and "the Apartheid Wall" in Arabic. Sporadic peace talks take place every so often, with much fanfare, much as they are briefly mentioned in this novel; as in the novel, they have never amounted to more than a public relations display.

But someone must have made a fortune in construction in the meantime, much like Mr. Gross in this book.

Like Bloom in this novel, no one sees themselves as a villain. And the bumbling, ineffective Tiroshes of this world can do nothing much more than write their little flights of fantasy and get on with life as best they can.

I grew up in Israel and remember much of the euphoric sense of coming peace that characterised the early 1990s. I also grew up in the immediate post-apartheid South Africa, and remember both the white terrorism of the AWB and the sense of excitement of the first democratic elections in that country. I was fortunate enough to travel through and live for a time in East Africa, and to love—much as Tirosh and Bloom do in this novel—that beautiful land.

Like Tirosh, I often think I am merely a pulp writer with delusions of grandeur. Like Tirosh, too, I feel eternally displaced. I, too, would like to escape into fantasy—I would have liked to see the white towers of Kang Diz Huxt rise into the yellow sky under the broken moon, and to have navigated the green gaseous swamps of Samaria where the Awful Ones live . . . whoever they may be.

But there is only one world we live in, as imperfect as it may be, and fantasy provides no escape. That is, perhaps, the harshest lesson we learn as children; though some of us, like Tirosh, keep chafing at the restraints that reality imposes.

—Lavie Tidhar, 2018

AFTERWORD
WARREN ELLIS

Unholy Land is one of those lovely books that starts out presenting itself as one thing, and mutates into another almost without you seeing it.

It begins with a minor pulp detective-fiction writer leaving his home in Berlin to revisit the land of his birth—a Jewish state in Africa. Right away, we're in alternate-history space—this was actually a floated idea around 1900, the British Uganda Program, also referred to as the Uganda Scheme, in the wake of Russian pogroms against the Jewish people. So far, an African take on *The Yiddish Policemen's Union.*

But. The writer's name is Lior Tirosh. Compare that to Lavie Tidhar. Partway through, Tidhar ascribes the authorship of one of his own books to Tirosh. *Osama.* An alternate-history novel featuring a detective and a series of pulp novels. One detects the wake of the grand galleon of Michael Moorcock sailing by on the way to Tanelorn. Tidhar, as most recently evidenced by *Central Station*, is a game-player of a writer who uses the spectrum of science fiction canon for his pieces.

And then the book turns into what it's really about, a grand game of alternate worlds cast like jewels on the sand. The long second act is all dust and blood and madness and glory, and the fast third act comes down on you like a sharpened spade.

Lavie Tidhar is a clever bastard, and this book is a box of little miracles.

—Warren Ellis, 2018

ABOUT THE AUTHOR

Multi-award-winning author Lavie Tidhar was born in Israel. He grew up on a kibbutz and has lived all over the world, including Vanuatu, Laos, and South Africa.

Tidhar won the 2012 World Fantasy Award for his novel *Osama*, a complex tale about the war on terror. That same year, he also won a British Fantasy Award for Best Novella and a British Science Fiction Award for Best Non-Fiction. His next novel, *The Violent Century*, came out in 2013 to rapturous reviews. It was followed by the Jerwood Fiction Uncovered Prize–winning and Premio Roma nominee *A Man Lies Dreaming*, a tour de force parable about the Holocaust. The British newspaper the *Independent* has referred to both novels as masterpieces. Tidhar has, further, been compared to Philip K. Dick by the *Guardian,* and to Kurt Vonnegut by *Locus.*

Tidhar's most recent novel, *Central Station,* received the

John W. Campbell Memorial Award and was shortlisted for the Arthur C. Clarke Award and the Locus Award. It has been published in ten languages.

Lavie Tidhar currently lives in London.